Merry Christmas
2017
Love –
Memaw & Papaw

WAITING FOR BUTTERFLIES

A Novel

by

Karen Sargent

D1571340

Walrus Publishing | St. Louis, MO

Walrus Publishing
Saint Louis, MO 63116

For information, contact:
Walrus Publishing
4168 Hartford Street, Saint Louis, MO 63116
Walrus Publishing is an imprint of Amphorae Publishing Group, LLC
www.amphoraepublishing.com

Manufactured in the United States of America
Cover Design by Kinsley Stocum
Cover photography: Heidi Wharton Photography
Set in Adobe Caslon Pro and Spinoza Pro

Library of Congress Control Number: 2017931447
ISBN: 9781940442204

For Kelli and Randi,
who taught me being their mom
is my most important job of all

WAITING FOR BUTTERFLIES

CHAPTER 1

Maggie heard the key in the front door and looked at the clock on the nightstand: 1:48 a.m. Nearly twenty-four hours had passed since the phone had jarred her awake and Sam out of bed. From his side of the conversation, she gathered an officer had been shot. "An off-duty detective" was Sam's only offering as he got dressed, secured his weapon in his shoulder holster, and clipped his badge to his belt.

"Who?" she had called after him, but he was already out the bedroom door. Throughout the day, news anchors filled in a few details: an officer, who remained unnamed due to a continuing investigation, had been found fatally shot in his parked car near an abandoned boat dock on the Mississippi. The shooting occurred around midnight, and her only communication with Sam all day had been a text saying he would be home late.

Maggie waited up, tucked into her reading chair in the corner of their bedroom, a leather journal open on her lap. The magnitude of the day weighed heavily on her. Her heart was so full of the agony she knew her husband felt that she was surprised there was room for more. But there was. Earlier in the evening a new grief found a vacant place and crowded in. Maggie prayed she could keep it hidden. Sam needed her now, even though she wanted nothing more than to feel safe and protected in his arms. When his footsteps echoed in the hall, she closed her journal and put down her pen.

"Mags, why are you still up?" Sam lumbered through the doorway toward her. He placed a hand on each arm of the chair and leaned forward, his face inches away. Grey eyes, dull from the late hour, found hers.

"I'm so sorry." She placed her hand on his cheek, and he pressed into it, resting a moment. "Do you want to talk?"

A sigh rose from deep inside as he pressed his lips against her forehead. "Right now I just want to take a hot shower and collapse." He straightened with a groan and ran a hand through his tousled hair as he stood. The silver at his temples seemed more distinct, the creases in his forehead more defined.

"You're exhausted." Maggie untucked the front of his shirt, unfastened the bottom button, and started on the next.

He leaned his head back and squeezed the nape of his neck.

"Who was it?"

Hesitating as if saying the name would be physically painful, he loosened his tie, unbuttoned his collar, and turned toward the bathroom. "Ricky Simms. And we don't have a single lead."

"Oh, no," she whispered as the realization seeped in. Sam blames himself. Simms was the new detective Sam had handpicked for his division. He'd groomed the rookie officer, told him to wear the uniform a few years to make himself a viable candidate, joking that Simms reminded him of his younger self when patrolling the streets couldn't provide the challenge he sought. And there were no leads. Was this it? Would this be the cold case that ended up in a box coated with dust and pushed to the back of a dark shelf, haunting her husband the rest of his career? Maybe not. It had only been one day. How many times had Sam voiced his disdain at Hollywood's unrealistic portrayal of police work? This wasn't a one-hour TV drama. But Maggie knew the first twenty-four hours were crucial.

She reached for the journal and squeezed it, measuring the weight of the prayers she had written inside, some with answers and some still waiting. Certain prayers demanded to be written down. The hustle of the day often made it difficult to settle her mind and left her feeling as if her prayers disappeared quicker than visible breath on a frigid day. But when she needed to explore precisely what she was feeling, thinking, questioning, the journal kept her focused. She picked up the pen and rolled it between her fingers. A tinge of guilt bit into her. Sam should have been the center of her prayer tonight. But he wasn't. Nate was.

Maggie could no longer shake the weariness that had enveloped her a few hours earlier. Sam started the shower, and as if on cue, sorrow stung her. She tried to blink away the tears, but it was no use. She opened the journal. The words of her last entry blurred.

Lord, I know children are a gift, not only that You give to us, but a gift we give back to You. You allow us the privilege of experiencing the kind of unconditional, all-consuming love You have for us by giving us these little people to raise for You, to someday return to you with hearts that know You. But not when they are only nine years old, right? Forgive me, but I just can't wrap my heart around it, Lord. What is the purpose?

She placed her pen on the page and continued.

How will Nate's mom get through this? How does a mother watch her little boy slowly lose the battle for his life? How does a mom—

Her hand froze. Did she dare write the words, so visible, so undeniable? Her fingers pushed the pen forward.

—hold on to her faith . . . as she lets go of her child?

The confession weighed on her, crushing her heart, making each beat labored, pounding, painful. To separate herself from her words, she closed the journal and ran her fingers over the smooth brown cover. Her thoughts wandered to morning. She longed to sit on the edge of Olivia's bed and wake her with a kiss, letting her face linger beside her child's, breathing in the warmth of her sleep. She imagined Rachel's morning sounds across the hall, dresser drawers opening and closing, the shower starting, her voice carrying the melody of her latest favorite song above the spray. Then she pictured Nate's mom. What familiar sounds would be replaced by silence in her morning?

Nate's mom, a woman Maggie knew only through pictures and a blog she stumbled upon months ago where she learned about their fight for his life. She followed their struggle, celebrating when the news was good, praying when it wasn't, all the while marveling at the depth of his mother's faith, her lack of anger, her total acceptance of God's will. And each week she fell more in love with the little boy whose smile betrayed the disease that ravaged him.

Last week's post had been a good report: Nate's blood counts were up, and the doctors were encouraged by the initial results of a new experimental treatment. But today, when the latest post appeared, shock and anguish sliced through Maggie as she read the single sentence his mother had written: "Last night we laid Nate in the arms of Jesus."

"What are you writing?"

Sam stood in the doorway to the master bath, toweling his hair. His athletic build from the early years of their marriage was still evident despite the approach of middle age. His bicep flexed at the movement, and Maggie longed for the strength of his arms around her. She clasped the journal once more before tucking it into the side table drawer.

"Oh, just . . . stuff. You know—" She resisted the urge to lighten her burden. Although Sam would want to know about Nate, it wasn't the right time.

"Stuff? I'll never get that, Mags. When something bothers you, you write. When something bothers me, I need to hit golf balls or chop wood, work through it." Sam grabbed her hands and pulled her to him.

"Yes, that's what you always say." Her smile was gentle. "But it's not just writing, remember? It's praying, too."

"Yeah, I don't get that, either. But that's okay. Praying about a problem is your department; doing something about a problem, that's my department."

Sam's arms encircled her waist and her body settled into his. His familiar scent was therapy. Her heartbeat slowed; her tension eased.

"Come on." He pulled back and kissed her forehead. "Let's get some rest."

Maggie slid into bed and tucked herself close to Sam, inviting sleep. But his breathing didn't ease. While she teetered between both worlds, he was still working the case. Resisting the rest that lured her, she skimmed her fingertips up his arm and across his chest. His muscles were rigid, his whole body tense. "Want to talk?"

"No." His chest rose and fell. "Yes. If there was something to talk about."

He was holding back, as he often did, not disclosing information in order to protect the investigation, or maybe to protect her from worry. But he might succumb with a little encouragement. "There has to be something. What's your instinct tell you?"

"My instinct?" He grunted. "It doesn't matter what my instinct tells me. It only matters what the evidence tells me. And there is none."

"Come on, Lieutenant Blake. Trust yourself. You're good at what you do."

He shifted from his side to his back and stared toward the ceiling. The investigation reclaimed her husband. Attempting to keep him with her, she traced a path with her finger from his temple, along his jawline, down his neck. The combination opened the vault.

"It doesn't add up."

His jaw clenched beneath her fingertips.

"Simms was off duty. He'd worked the day shift with me, and had to be back on at 7:00 a.m. So what was he doing parked at the riverfront so late?" He shook his head. "He was a good cop. I know my detectives."

She sensed a question in Sam's statement. "But?"

"But . . . something's off."

He grew quiet again. Maggie brushed her fingers along his temple, imagining thoughts ricocheting inside his head like silver orbs in a pinball machine.

"Ricky was shot at close range, through the driver's window." His voice was a whisper.

"A murdered detective, a mysterious gunman. This is Cape Spring, Sam, not St. Louis or Memphis, not some big city."

"The kind of headline you hear on the evening news somewhere else, right? But it happened. Here. To Ricky Simms." Sam raked his hand through his hair. "No evidence, no witness." He turned back on his side and pulled her close. "Does all this make you nervous, scared?"

"A little," she confessed as she turned her back to him and snuggled closer. "But after all these years of being married to law enforcement, I've learned I can't walk around worried every moment you're at work. It's not in my hands."

Sam kissed the back of her neck. "Good. Don't worry. I can take care of myself. I will take care of myself—so I can take care of you and the girls."

And that's all it took. A sob swelled in her throat. She tried to hold back, but the tears surfaced.

"Hey, what's wrong? Come on, Mags. Don't cry. It'll be okay."

"I know. It's not that. It's just . . . well, I don't want to go into it, but what if something happened to one of the girls? I don't think my heart could survive." She'd presented Sam a mystery, a giant leap from the Simms case to this, but she refused to burden him with the details.

"Why would you say that? Nothing is going to happen to Rachel or Olivia. This doesn't have anything to do with the girls."

"It's just been on my mind tonight, and I can't stop thinking about it." Her throat tightened, restricting her voice to a whisper. "Losing one of the girls is my biggest fear."

Sam lay still beside her. She imagined him visiting that horrific place for a brief second.

"I'm so—" she started.

"No." He shook his head. "We're not talking about this. It's late and we're both exhausted."

His arm tightened around her. "Nothing is going to happen. Our girls are healthy and happy and safe. And we're both here to make sure they stay that way."

"Promise?" Maggie said.

"Promise."

CHAPTER 2

"And that brings us to your assignment."

Rachel stopped doodling on the cover of her notebook and refocused her attention on Mr. Beard.

"This will be a partner project."

In most classes those words signaled doom for Rachel, but not science, the only class she shared with her best friend. Quickly she scanned the faces in the lab until she locked eyes with Kristen, sealing their partnership. Relieved, Rachel turned back to the teacher.

"To explore the impact technology has had upon our society, your assignment is to choose one form of technology to research, and then prepare a visual presentation of how your chosen technology has affected your life." The teacher paused. "You have thirty seconds to find a partner."

Students scrambled. Hand signals were passed and names were called as they claimed one another. Rachel watched the frenzy, grateful this time she wasn't caught in the whirlpool, spinning, reaching for the sound waves passing through the air, hoping to grasp her name spoken by some other invisible student in the room, or if she was lucky, by one of the more popular students whose usual partner was absent.

"Hey" was accompanied by the slap of a notebook dropped on Rachel's lab table. "Any creative ideas in that brain of yours?" Kristen's smirk and raised eyebrow told Rachel everything her friend hadn't said aloud. It wasn't easy being her partner. Rachel, who never thought inside the box, could generate twenty crazy ideas to Kristen's one normal idea, and a ping-pong match would ensue as Kristen served up ordinary and Rachel smashed back spectacular. Inevitably, Rachel would win the match, making Kristen work way harder on the project than she wanted, but she knew Kristen had to admit the final grade was always worth it.

"I'm thinking something about cell phones." Kristen's first serve.

"Yeah, and so is everyone else." Rachel stared into empty air as Mr. Beard passed by, laying a copy of the assignment on their table. In her peripheral vision, Kristen adjusted the low-maintenance ponytail she preferred on and off the soccer field as she appeared to read the guidelines for the project. But more likely, Kristen's mind had wandered to the upcoming game Friday.

"Technology is replacing art."

Kristen looked up from the handout. "Say what?"

"Yeah. Take black and white photography." Rachel's excitement began to build as she envisioned an opportunity to showcase her passion in a class project. "Because of technology, no one develops their own film anymore. Probably no one in this class even knows what a darkroom is." Rachel thought of her own darkroom in the basement at home, the glow of the red light, the smell of the chemicals.

"I don't get it. How does that fit what Mr. Beard said? I think he wants to know how our life is better. I'm okay with doing photography, but let's do digital. That's more like technology." Still playing with her hair, Kristen arched her eyebrows.

"No. You don't get it. It's because of digital that the *art* of photography is disappearing. Anyone can shoot a digital picture, put it on a computer, and click a button to make it black and white." Rachel swept her hair out of her eyes. "Click another button and you have special effects. What about the search for the perfect subject with the right contrast, the right values? What about mastering special effects by experimenting with shutter speeds and F stops and lenses and filters? Digital takes all that away. It takes away the *art.*"

Kristen wrinkled her nose. "You're such a nerd."

Rachel pushed her elbow into her friend. "I know." And she did know; somehow she was different. In the hallway, in the classroom, in the cafeteria, she looked normal, just like everyone else. But there was something intangible, something she couldn't verbalize, that made her peculiar, peculiar in a way Kristen tolerated and some called freaky. Only her mother celebrated her uniqueness, and her words —*creative, brilliant, gifted*—drowned out the snickers that sometimes followed Rachel in the halls.

Kristen's hands dropped from her ponytail to the table. A sign of surrender? "Okay, I don't understand half of what you just said, but what about this? Let me do digital, how it's made photography easier, how anyone can take pictures like a pro. Then you can add your thing about the art."

Rachel manipulated the puzzle pieces in her head to see if they fit. "I like it."

"No way! Really?" Kristen cautiously put a full smile on display. "You like my idea?"

She grinned. "I like *my* idea . . . but yours will work."

As Rachel reached across the table to grab her friend's notebook, Kristen nudged a shoulder into her. She scribbled BFF on the cover, slid the notebook back in place, and then returned the fist bump her best friend offered to seal the deal.

"Mommy!" Olivia leaped from the swing and raced to greet Maggie kneeling on the grass at the edge of the kindergarten playground, ready to catch the hug heading her way. As she wrapped her little girl in her arms, she grieved for Nate's mom, who would never again feel the warmth of her son's embrace.

"You're squishing me, Mommy." The little girl wiggled. Freed from the hug, she bounced with excitement, her blonde curls springing to life. "Guess what! Guess whose turn it is to be student of the week?"

"Hmm, let me guess." Maggie winked. "It must be Samantha."

The dimples in Olivia's cheeks deepened. She shook her head.

"No? Well, it must be Morgan then. Surely it's Morgan's turn to be student of the week."

"It's me! Olivia Alaina Blake! And I get to make a poster about me and then I get to show it to the whole class and tell them about it, and then my teacher will hang it in the hallway for the whole week! Isn't that great, Mom? I have lots of ideas for my poster!"

Maggie kissed the girl on her nose and took her hand. With an apologetic wave to the teacher for being early, she led Olivia to the classroom, all the while listening as the child's plans multiplied and divided and became contagious, lifting the cloud that had followed Maggie all day. Maggie gathered papers out of a cubby, slipped her arm through the straps of a backpack, and steered Olivia toward the car.

"Where are we going, Mommy?" Olivia paused her planning long enough to ask as Maggie turned the car in the opposite direction of their usual route.

"To the store. I have to get a few groceries before we pick up Rachel from school, so I can have dinner ready early tonight. I have some exciting news myself." Maggie decided to give herself permission to share the joy she had suppressed since the phone call she received late morning. "I'm showing the old Hitching house this evening."

Maggie felt as bubbly as Olivia, but she contained it much better. For years she'd wavered between feeling sorry and secretly happy that the 1912 two-story farmhouse that sat just outside city limits had not sold. The few times she'd shown the house, she'd swept potential buyers from room to room, trying to revive the life still left in the old southern belle. But no one seemed able to overlook the flaws and envision the beauty the way Maggie could. She dreamed of holding a contract in her hands, writing her signature on the black line above *buyer* rather than *broker*, and renovating the house into a quaint bed and breakfast.

"Oh, I don't want go to the store." Olivia slumped in her booster seat.

"If we don't go to the store, where will we get supplies to make your fabulous poster?"

The little girl leaned forward and listed the required

items on her dainty fingers. "We need poster board and glue and glitter . . ."

While Olivia inventoried the craft department, Maggie imagined driving past a newly purchased Hitching house every day, admiring each new improvement, witnessing the revival of the magnificent home. Even if she couldn't realize her dream, she hoped someday a new buyer would love the old place as much as she did.

"We're here." A text appeared on Sam's cell. He looked at the time, just after 1500 hours. Reports, interviews, and crime scene photos lay scattered across the table in front of him and two other detectives who were sifting through them, trying to see with new eyes the words they had read over and over, words that led nowhere.

"Hey, I'm gonna take a break. The family's here. Why don't you do the same, and we'll meet back in fifteen."

"Yep. I need to get my head out of this." Donnie Wade tossed a file aside and leaned back in his chair. A young detective, he was sharp, ambitious, and earning the lieutenant's respect.

Nikki Shaw continued to study the interview in her hand. "I'm in my zone. But you go ahead. Family first." Without looking Sam's direction, she tossed a mane of red hair over her shoulder.

Sam flinched. It was her tone, the same tone she'd used when they interviewed Ricky's widow earlier in the day. As much as Sam didn't want to, they'd had to ask her about a single piece of evidence the medical examiner found on Ricky's sleeve. A blonde hair. Ricky's wife, a brunette, had no idea who the hair might belong to, and after a few silent moments, began to cry. "You're not suggesting—" she'd said. That's exactly what Sam was suggesting, though he didn't want to believe it. Was Ricky having an affair? Did a jealous boyfriend or husband find out? But he wouldn't say that to Ricky's widow. Not yet. Detective Shaw, on the other hand, didn't hesitate. "It happens," Shaw had said, in that same tone.

Sam pushed away from the table without comment. He turned down the hall, and beyond the glass doors that led to the police department lobby, his girls waited for him. Olivia, holding Maggie's hand, jumped up and down when she saw him.

"Daddy!"

Sam pushed open the lobby door, bent down, and caught Olivia as she sprang toward him. She threw her arms around his neck as he greeted Maggie with a quick kiss and pulled Rachel to his side for a hug, which she tolerated. At fourteen, public affection from a parent was forbidden, but he planned to pretend he was oblivious to Rachel's discomfort as long as she would allow. "How are my girls?"

"Guess what, Daddy! I'm student of the week!" Olivia proceeded to tell him about her poster and her plans and the three different colors of glitter that would make her poster the best. "Wow, Livi. Sounds like you had a great day." He pecked her nose and turned to Rachel. "And how was your day?"

"Fine."

"Just fine? Not great?" Sam grinned. The teenager before him still resembled the seven-year-old who once announced, "School interrupts my life." Her mantra would make a good bumper sticker for her first car, a car she would get only if she stayed on the honor roll, even if school wasn't her favorite way to spend seven hours every day.

"It's eighth grade, Dad. There's too much drama for any day to be great." She gave him an eye-roll followed by a half smile that mirrored his own.

"And how about Mom? Was Mom's day great?" The glow that had not left her face since he entered the lobby indicated it was.

She poised a finger in the air. "Promising. What about you? Are you getting anywhere with the investigation?"

"Mmm. Maybe. So, what's up?"

She took a deep breath, and Sam sensed her resistance to spill over with excitement.

"I'm showing the Hitching house this evening, and based on my phone conversation with the potential buyers, I think they might be serious."

"That is promising. You haven't shown that property in months." And for good reason, but Sam trapped that thought on the tip of his tongue as always. The house would be a perpetual vacuum on a bank account. He couldn't share her optimism for the potential sale, but he enjoyed seeing his wife distracted from the sadness that enveloped her last night.

"You're showing the house this evening, so—" There must be a connection with the unexpected visit. "Do you need something?" Evidence from the investigation that lay scattered across the table flashed in his mind.

"Well, I'm meeting the buyers at 6:00, which won't leave us much time before dusk, but I thought I could have dinner ready by 5:00. Can you make it home to eat with us, and then stay with the girls while I'm out?"

Sam weighed his options, trying to veil the struggle so Maggie wouldn't see it on his face. Was it really necessary for him to be home with the girls? Couldn't Rachel watch Olivia? He still had so much to do before he wanted to call it a day. He was focused on finding a suspect, or a witness, or at least another piece of evidence. There had to be someone with information to keep this investigation alive. Maybe a blonde.

But he hadn't seen his girls in forty-eight hours, and the weight of Olivia in his arms reminded him of what he was missing. "Sure." He gave Olivia a squeeze. "What's for supper?"

Rachel buttered the garlic bread as Maggie pulled a piece of spaghetti out of boiling water for testing. "So, what do you think, Mom? Can I make a good argument that the art in photography is going extinct because of technology?" She hesitated. "Do you think it's weird?"

"I think it's magnificent." Maggie loved many things about her right-brained, out-of-the-box daughter, but she especially enjoyed their shared passion for photography. Maggie had taken a class in college for fun and found herself immersed in a new hobby. She bought a used Pentax K-1000, an excellent choice for student photographers the shop owner said. She'd spent hours outside of class learning through trial and error, mastering composition, experimenting with depth of field, and just as many hours in the darkroom, watching chemicals wash over blank photo paper to reveal, she hoped, her next masterpiece. The professor recognized Maggie's interest, and as he cleaned out old darkroom supplies, he gave them to her. By the time she graduated, she had acquired nearly everything she needed to start her own darkroom. With her first paycheck after college, she purchased a used enlarger to complete her setup. It was her original camera and enlarger that Rachel learned on and still used.

"Speaking of photography . . ." Maggie stepped aside as her daughter reached for the oven door. "Guess what I saw today?"

Rachel raised her eyebrows as she slid a pan of garlic bread onto the wire rack.

"An old barn on a property I might be listing."

"Cool!" Rachel set the timer and leaned against the counter.

"It has a lot of contrasts that'll make stunning black and whites—boards weathered varying shades of gray, a metal roof covered with large patches of rust, sunrays shining between tired fence posts extending from the barn to enclose a small corral."

Rachel clasped her hands together as if in earnest prayer. "Barns are my favorite, Mom."

Maggie laughed. As if she didn't already know that. She couldn't count the times Rachel had begged to stop when they drove past a dilapidated barn, so she could capture it with her ever present camera.

"There's also an old stone cellar on the property that would make some good shots, too." Maggie answered Rachel's question before she could ask. "Do you want to drive out there with me after school tomorrow? I'm meeting the owners to negotiate the listing. I mentioned that you might enjoy photographing some of the structures on the place."

"S-weet! Mom, that's so awesome! Thank you! Thank you! But . . . I'll be right back." Rachel sprinted out of the kitchen and returned seconds later, camera in hand. "I have a few pictures left on this roll. I need to finish them, so I can reload for tomorrow." She aimed the camera. "Say cheese!"

"Geez, Rachel." Maggie shaded her face with her hand. "I think you can find a better subject than me cooking dinner."

"Aw, come on, Mom. Strike a pose!" Rachel giggled.

Maggie played along, enjoying her daughter's laughter as she focused the lens and finished the last few shots. She rewound the film, popped open the camera, and snatched the canister.

"I'm gonna reload." Rachel disappeared into the hall as the oven timer beeped and Maggie pulled out the garlic bread.

Sam opened the front door. "Something smells good."

"Hey, can you set the table? I lost my helper."

Olivia ran from her bedroom and met Sam as he entered the kitchen. "Daddy, you're home!"

"How about you and me help Mommy with dinner?" Sam ruffled her curls.

After the blessing, the clink of forks on plates mixed with the family chatter. "Olivia, I put a stack of magazines on the coffee table in the family room. You can cut out pictures of a few of your favorite things to put on your poster."

"Like puppies! And ice cream!"

"Or . . ." Rachel hummed a familiar tune and waved her knife in the air like a conductor's baton. Olivia squinted. Rachel hummed louder.

Then the child's face lit up and her mouth fell open.

"Mom, you said 'a few of your favorite things,' like the song!"

Maggie smiled at her inadvertent reference to the song she sang as a lullaby when the girls were babies, and that Olivia still sometimes requested.

"Hey, it's 5:30. You better get going." Sam nodded toward the clock on the wall.

"Yeah, I better." Maggie pushed back her chair. "Olivia, will you help clear the table? Rachel, load the dishwasher, please. I should be home in time to tuck you in. I'll call if I'm going to be late."

She bent down and kissed her girls. Then she placed her hand on Sam's cheek as she passed his chair. "Thanks for coming home for dinner." She paused and gazed into his eyes, acknowledging the work he left behind at the station. A few short years ago, work trumped dinner, her, everything.

"Love you." She glanced back at her family and closed the door behind her.

CHAPTER 3

Once dinner was cleared and the hum of the dishwasher dismissed them, Sam and Olivia retreated to the family room, Sam to lose himself in a sitcom, an old movie, maybe a football game, anything to keep his mind off the investigation. Olivia tackled the stack of magazines.

Rachel didn't join them. Eager to prepare for her photo op the next day, she disappeared to her darkroom. The space was not much larger than a walk-in closet, which her dad converted into a darkroom a couple years ago when her mom decided it was time to revive her old hobby and pass it on to Rachel. But she always suspected there was more behind the plan than her mom revealed, since her mom suggested it about the same time Rachel was cut from the fall soccer league, and Kristen was selected for the all-star traveling team. Rachel wasn't nearly as disappointed as her parents thought she might be. In fact, she was relieved. She only played because Kristen begged her to back in third grade when everybody made the team. She quickly learned Kristen was the athlete, not her. But being on the team allowed them to spend time together, even though

Kristen was on the field most of the time while she yelled from the sidelines. When Kristen was chosen for all-stars, Rachel had no reason to stay on the team without her, so the cut wasn't devastating. Still, she enjoyed her parents' sympathy for a few days, and as far as she was concerned, the resulting darkroom was the best consolation prize a girl could ask for.

Although she wasn't developing film this evening, Rachel turned off the overhead so the darkroom red light could cast its glow. Her eyes adjusted, and a calm washed through her. This was her sanctuary. The roll of film she had finished before dinner was in her hand. Searching for a safe place to keep it until she could develop it, she decided to set it on the counter beside her favorite piece of equipment, the timer. She loved the black square box with the silver toggle switch on top, which controlled the arm that swept by the illuminated numbers and hash marks, counting off the seconds of light exposure needed to develop a photo. Timing was crucial. Too much time or too little would be disastrous.

Rachel proceeded to check her equipment. The bulb on the enlarger worked. The developing trays were in line and ready to process. She had an adequate supply of chemical solution but noted she would need to restock soon. To her right and stretching nearly the length of the room was a clothesline her dad put up, so she could hang her prints to dry. She stepped over to inspect her most recent photos still hanging by clothespins. Her favorite, she decided, was a close-up of Olivia eating a chocolate ice cream cone; the evidence surrounded her mouth. Rachel had taken a series of shots, but the best one showed Olivia rushing to catch drips of chocolate racing down the cone. The photo captured the determination on her face as she squished her brows and stretched her tongue to make the rescue. Maybe Olivia would like to use the picture for her poster. Rachel smiled and unclipped it from the line.

She removed the other photos as well and added them to the album where she stored most of her prints. Her favorites, however, were kept in a special album in her bedroom, and the very best were framed and hung on her wall, surrounded by her other artwork—watercolors, oil pastels, acrylics. Reluctant to leave the darkroom but having no reason to stay, Rachel decided to gather the other three albums she had filled to date and began flipping through the pages, starting with the first and working her way through the last two years of photos. She was amazed how her skills noticeably improved from her early prints to the most recent.

As she closed the last book, a yawn signaled bedtime was near. Surprised at how long she'd been in the darkroom, she returned the albums to their shelf, snatched the photo of Olivia, and started up the stairs, just in time to hear someone open the front door. "Good. Mom's home."

Maggie waited on the front porch of the Hitching house. The buyers were a few minutes late, which gave her time to gather herself after a rushed evening at home and rehearse her dynamic sales pitch. She knew very little about the couple she was soon to meet. They were from Kansas City, newly retired, and searching for a place close to their daughter and grandchildren, Mr. Hill had explained over the phone. He called after seeing the listing on the Internet.

Although it seemed an unlikely match, a retired couple and a large farmhouse, Maggie had a feeling about this. The commission would be nice, but more than that, she looked forward to the property being off the market, so she could squelch the desire to own the house herself.

A blue pick-up slowed as it approached. Its turn signal told Maggie the buyers had arrived. Mr. Hill exited the driver's side, walked around the front of the vehicle, and opened the passenger door for his wife. Maggie liked this couple already. She walked down the steps to meet them on the sidewalk and offered her hand. "Hi, Mr. and Mrs. Hill? I'm Maggie Blake. It's so nice to meet you."

After they exchanged greetings, Maggie gestured toward the house. "I don't mean to rush you, but we better get started. I want you to see everything while we still have daylight." She led the couple to the sweeping porch that wrapped across the front and around both sides of the house.

"This would be perfect for a porch swing and some rocking chairs for a retired couple like us." Mr. Hill grinned and pointed his thumb from himself to his wife.

"Actually the porch extends around the back of the house, too." Maggie let the detail settle before sharing the best feature. "Where it's screened in . . . and it has a hammock."

"Oh, he'll be good for nothing for sure." Mrs. Hill winked at her husband.

Maggie unlocked the front door. "But here's my favorite part." She opened the door to reveal the foyer.

The couple stepped inside, their eyes fixed on the feature Maggie referred to. In front of them, in the center of the entrance, was an oak staircase leading to the second floor where it joined a balcony. The balcony stretched the width of the foyer and extended on both sides back toward the front of the house.

"Isn't this magnificent?" Maggie's voice was reverent.

Mrs. Hill pointed to the oak doors that lined the walls beyond the balcony. "Are those all bedrooms?"

Maggie turned to the right and pointed to two doors above them. "Each side has access to two bedrooms, for a total of six. Two there. Two there. And two there." She directed their gaze in a half circle around the balcony.

Mr. Hill whistled. "That's a lot of rooms."

"Yes, it is." Maggie paused to study the couple. Were they all business? Or would they appreciate the history of the home? She let her intuition lead. "There's a story behind all those doors. Would you like to hear it?"

Mr. Hill shrugged and Maggie debated. The short version or the long version? But Mrs. Hill's face was expectant. She deserved the details.

"Connor Hitching built this house. The railroad boom in the early 1900s made him a wealthy man. When the tracks came through Cape Spring, they say Connor traveled here frequently and fell in love with the land, but that wasn't all he fell in love with. A girl named Anna-Marie, a preacher's daughter, stole his heart."

"Oh, a love story." Mrs. Hill clasped her hands together. Her husband grinned and cut a sideways glance at her.

Maggie held up a finger. "But Connor wasn't ready to settle down. He was still chasing his fortune. He returned every chance he got, to see Anna-Marie, and to purchase more land. But each time he left, he promised it would be the last time. It took Connor Hitching five years to finally keep his word, but when he did, he made Anna-Marie his wife and built her this house, promising to fill every bedroom with Hitching children."

"And did they?" Mrs. Hill's eyes sparkled beneath her raised brow.

"Most definitely. Four girls and four boys, the last of whom passed away a few years ago. His children inherited the property and, well, the house has been on the market ever since."

"If the rest of the house is this beautiful, I can't wait to see it." Mrs. Hill stepped toward the grand staircase.

Maggie accepted the invitation. "Let's look at the first floor, and then we'll go upstairs."

As she led the couple through the home, they visualized each room aloud, and her heart fluttered. They saw the house with her eyes. Rather than examine the flaws one by one like previous clients, they imagined the possibilities.

"You know—" Mr. Hill rubbed his jaw. "This is a lot of house for a retired couple."

Maggie's heart clenched. Of course, it was. The match didn't make sense from the start. She prepared for the letdown.

"So we're thinking about this as a project, a little something to do and a little income after retirement. What are the chances for a B&B to be successful in this area?"

Maggie's mouth opened but no sound followed. She glanced from Mr. Hill to his wife, whose nod confirmed Maggie had heard correctly. The words poured out quickly. "Truthfully, I don't see how a good B&B could fail."

Mr. Hill crossed his arms and cocked his head. Lines deepened between his brows as they pressed together. "Is that so?"

"You're seven miles south of the city limits, so your guests will be a ten-minute drive from restaurants, shopping, the theatre, all the conveniences. Yet they'll enjoy the solitude of this rural setting. And Cape Spring is a river town. With grant funding, the city spent the last few years revitalizing the historic downtown area. They repaired cobblestone streets, developed a river walk, built a gazebo in the park. Your guests can be entertained by live music every weekend evening, and they can even enjoy horse-drawn carriage rides."

Was it too much information too fast? She struggled to remain calm, so her enthusiasm wouldn't overwhelm the Hills. She examined their faces carefully. Was she making the sale?

And there it was. The look, the one buyers get when the house she is showing is not the house they are seeing at all. Instead, they see a home filled with their furniture, their family, their future. It was time to seal the deal, to make the buyers realize what Maggie hoped she already had. "So, Mr. and Mrs. Hill, can you see yourselves welcoming guests to your magnificent bed and breakfast for a romantic getaway or to escape the pace of city life?"

"Possibly." Mr. Hill strolled to a nearby wall and inspected a switch plate.

"I'm sure you read online that the original wiring in the house had been replaced within recent years, and central heat and air were installed as well." Maggie beamed. "Which makes the four fireplaces a luxury, not a necessity." She placed her hand on Mrs. Hill's elbow and motioned toward the front door. "Should we go outside and walk the property? You have ten acres here . . ."

By the time they shook hands for the evening, Maggie

was satisfied she did all she could to make the sale. Now it was up to them.

"We have a lot to discuss." Mr. Hill put his arm around his wife. "We love the property. We like the potential here. But we need some time to decide. It doesn't sound like another buyer is on the horizon."

"True, but in this business you never know." Maggie forced a smile. He was right, of course.

With a promise from the Hills to call soon, Maggie got into her car and checked her cell phone for messages. She tapped a text from Sam. *Made a sale yet?* Though her giddiness had subsided, Maggie still felt some promise. *Cross your fingers. On my way home.* She looked at the clock—8:00 p.m., plenty of time to get home to tell the girls good night.

After mutilating the magazines her mom had left her, Olivia had climbed onto the sofa with her dad and fallen asleep in his lap. It was after 9:00 and he was beginning to wind down himself. He should put Olivia in her PJs and tuck her in, but the sofa had a magnetic force he couldn't resist. Besides, Maggie would be home any minute, surely, and they could put Olivia to bed together. Just as he flipped to another channel, headlights pulled into the driveway.

Maggie decided to stop by the office to drop off the Hitching file. She would be a few minutes late getting home, but the girls wouldn't mind staying up a little past bedtime. As she approached Route 40 and turned north to go into town, the emotion of the last two days rapidly drained energy from her body. From Sam's investigation to the devastation of Nate's death to the elation of having potential buyers, Maggie was ready to soak in a hot bubble bath and collapse into bed.

Her thoughts of relaxation were interrupted by her cell phone, the ringtone identifying it as a business call. She grabbed the phone from its place on the console and glanced at the number on the screen. The Hills. Surely they weren't ready to make an offer already. They probably just had a question. Or maybe they changed their mind. Maybe they weren't interested after all. Quickly, before the call went to voice mail, she pressed the button to answer. But then she fumbled the phone. The rest happened in slow motion: The phone hit the console. It bounced and tumbled to the passenger side floor. Maggie bent forward to reach it. When she looked up, she saw headlights.

With Olivia still asleep in his lap, Sam waited for the sound of the garage door opening and the jingle of Maggie's keys in the kitchen door. The front doorbell rang instead. When the bell rang a second time, Sam gently shifted his sleeping daughter to the sofa. Why was Maggie at the front entrance? And why didn't she use her key? He got up to answer the door.

"Lieutenant." Wade stood in the open doorway with Shaw beside him. For a moment Sam was confused. Then he realized why the detectives must have come to his home at such an unusual hour.

"Did we get a break in the case?" He didn't give them time to respond. "Did you make an arrest?"

"Uh, no." Shaw stammered over her words. "That's not why we're here."

Sam's confusion returned. "Oh. What do you need then?"

Detective Wade looked to Shaw. She looked at him. Sam looked at them both. The pulse at his temple throbbed. "What?"

Wade's hands knotted, and he pressed a fist to his mouth. His voice was hoarse. "It's Maggie."

"What about Maggie?" Sam turned again from Wade to Shaw for an answer, but they both dropped their gaze. Someone stood behind them. In blue jeans and a St. Louis Cardinals pullover rather than his usual Sunday tie and sport coat, Sam almost didn't recognize the pastor from Maggie's church. Why was he here? Clergy only accompanied officers when—

Maggie?

Sam's head spun. As his knees buckled, he leaned against the doorframe to steady himself. His hands went numb. His shoulders sagged as the force of gravity multiplied exponentially, pulling him, pushing him down. He felt himself disconnect from conscious thought, and although his eyes were open, he couldn't focus. Shaw's mouth moved but the words came too quickly and were jumbled and didn't make sense. *Accident . . . crossed the centerline . . . head-on . . . instantly.* His brain scrambled to find logic, but instead closed in on itself, refusing to process.

The pastor's voice drew him back. "Sam, where are the girls?"

The girls. The girls? How could he tell—

Suddenly a sob erupted from the top of the basement steps. He turned to see Rachel trembling, tears racing down her cheeks. Instantly aware that the look on his face betrayed his instinct to protect her, to guard her from the nightmare unfolding before them, he tried to speak, to tell her everything would be okay, but his mouth couldn't form the words. He watched the truth seize her.

"Daddy, no!"

CHAPTER 4

Maggie remembered the blinding lights and then closing her eyes. Her eyes still remained closed as consciousness returned. She wanted to open them, but what would she see? Where was she? She listened. Only stillness surrounded her.

She tried to figure out how long she had been unaware, but all sense of time eluded her. The blinding lights. Now. What happened between? How did she get here, wherever here was? A gentle scent reached Maggie, one she had never experienced before but that demanded to be breathed in. By no will of her own, she inhaled deeply and the sweet fragrance filled her with peace.

She opened her eyes. She stood . . . where? She felt a substance beneath her, but didn't see a ground or a floor. There were no walls or ceiling, and she could see far beyond where she stood, but there was nothing, only empty space. Then, like a morning sun low on the horizon, a lavender glow rose in the distance. It continued until it filled the vast expanse high above, completely surrounding Maggie. She drank in the delicious hue and it quieted all her questions.

A sound reverberated in the distance. Music, yet not music? It seemed to come from above. She looked up to see the lavender sky brilliantly jeweled with diamond-like objects falling toward her like a rain shower. As the diamonds fell closer, they danced into one another, creating a melodic symphony. A light source she could not locate struck the multi-faceted jewels, casting prisms of color all around. She had never seen anything so exquisite.

Anticipating their arrival, she spread her arms wide and marveled how the diamonds disappeared the moment they touched her. Their touch was gentle, the brush of butterfly wings, barely discernable against her skin. As the diamonds rained down, a new sensation moved through Maggie. It started at the top of her head and moved downward across her shoulders, through her outstretched arms, down through her legs. The sensation exited her body through her fingertips and toes, leaving her weightless as if she could simply lie back and float in the purple sea. She laughed out loud.

A movement caught Maggie's attention. Ahead, almost out of view, someone stood as if waiting for her. Instantly her attention shifted from the beauty around her to finding who might be there. Maggie walked effortlessly in the direction the figure appeared. As she drew closer, a definite shape came into view. A few more steps and she could see it was a child. She tried to get closer but now, in spite of each step she took, she could not close the distance between herself and the boy.

The child raised his hand in the air and waved excitedly, as if he were happy to see her. Initially drawn to him out of curiosity, Maggie was now compelled to reach him and frustrated because she couldn't. She smiled and returned his wave. He beamed, his face radiant with expectation. She gazed at the boy, at the blonde messy hair she wanted to push out of his dark eyes. Somehow, he was familiar. Again, he raised his hand, but not in greeting this time. Instead, he motioned her to him, nodding encouragement.

"I can't," she called out, taking another useless step forward, but he didn't seem to hear her. He continued to motion her to him.

Suddenly Maggie froze. Like a camera zooming in on its subject, his face came into focus. It was the face in the photos she had poured over, prayed over, for months. "Nate?" Her whisper carried across the distance between them.

The boy slowly lowered his arm. His smile grew in acknowledgment. How could it be? An urgency to run to him, to pick him up, and swing him around and around, washed over Maggie. "Nate! Look at you! You're okay! You're . . . here—"

But, how?

Heaviness filtered through Maggie's brain. She tried to wade through the thoughts she knew were there, but it took so much effort to push one aside and reach another. "Nate?" she questioned again. And then, another thought broke free, followed by one more.

"Rachel . . . Olivia." As the names crossed her lips, Maggie's heart crumbled. She suddenly knew this place. But she wasn't ready. Not yet.

The boy turned from her and looked behind him as if someone had called his name. He nodded and turned back toward Maggie again. A smile remained on his face, but it was not the same joyful expression that had greeted her. When he raised his hand to wave this time, Maggie knew it was good-bye. Although they both remained still, the distance between them grew rapidly until Nate was once more an unrecognizable figure barely within view.

It began first in her fingertips. The weight returned, crawling through her arms, past her elbows, squeezing her shoulders. It continued on its path, pouring into her chest, down her legs, until it consumed her entirely. She closed her eyes, and from somewhere far away, she recognized the cry of a little girl.

CHAPTER 5

Everyone gathered around the gravesite with heads bowed as the pastor offered the final prayer. Except Sam. His eyes focused ahead. The silver casket taunted him—hateful, unforgiving—adorned with a spray of pink roses and a sash: *Beloved Wife and Mother.* In moments it would be lowered into the ground, taking with it the part of him that had died with Maggie.

He stared ahead, numb, as if he existed under a glass dome, a part of but oddly separate from all the bustle of the last three days. He functioned as his body commanded, putting one foot in front of the other to make funeral arrangements, standing beside the casket during visitation, reaching out to receive sympathetic handshakes or embraces, forming the words "thank you" as friends told him how sorry they were, how much they loved Maggie, to call if he needed anything. And now, as people stirred at the end of the prayer, he wondered if he could remove himself from this place, if he could walk away and leave Maggie behind.

Some people returned to their cars while others

lingered, whispering to Rachel and Olivia or squeezing Sam on the arm. Quiet tears rolled down Olivia's cheeks. He should hold her. But he was certain his heart would implode if he allowed himself to feel. Instead, Rachel reached for the little girl, pulled her close, and whispered in her ear. Soft sobs rippled through the child's chest as she leaned into the embrace. Sam bit his lower lip and turned away.

"Lieutenant. Sam." The chief of police approached, a man with whom Sam shared a deep mutual respect. When Sam was a rookie on patrol, the chief was his lieutenant and mentor. He watched the chief's rise through the ranks, and while Sam had earned his own way up the ladder, he suspected the chief dropped his name a time or two along the way.

"You take all the time you need, son. Give me a call at the end of next week, and we'll decide where to go from there."

Sam nodded. He couldn't begin to think about work, about being a single dad—the long shifts, the unpredictable hours, the danger. He couldn't recall an officer who had raised his kids alone, but he could name several who were divorced because law enforcement and family life were a complicated mix. And, honestly, what did he know about parenting two young girls?

"Yeah, Lieutenant, we've got everything covered." Detective Wade gripped Sam's shoulder.

Standing beside Wade, Nikki Shaw nodded. "Just let us know if there's anything we can do, anything at all."

His mouth moved to form words. "Thank you."

As his fellow officers turned to leave, Sam leaned his head back and inhaled the crisp fall air. Sunlight filtered through the canopy of leaves overhead, bright reds and yellows. Beyond the leaves was a clear blue sky. And beyond that, was there anything?

"Sam."

The interruption brought him back to earth. Laura stood beside him. The grief in her eyes forced Sam to lower his. She had been with Maggie since the beginning of Blake Realty, the only agent beside Maggie for a while, her best agent . . . and her best friend.

"It isn't the right time to bring this up, but it's kind of important." She pulled at the edges of a frayed tissue in her hands.

Sam looked up, granting permission to continue.

"I don't know what your plans are for the office, but we can't sell real estate without a broker." She paused, cleared her throat. "Did Maggie tell you I recently got my broker's license? I'll do whatever I can to help you keep the business going." The real estate office had not even crossed Sam's mind. His mind that was trained to think through complexity, danger, tragedy, was defunct. "I appreciate anything you can do until I can figure things out, Laura. Maggie trusted you. I trust you."

Her tears swelled. "I don't know what I'm going to do without her." She pressed her fingers to her lips and rushed toward her car.

"Me either." The confession was only a whisper, but for the first time since he lost her, he allowed himself an instant to recall the genuine smile Maggie gave away so easily, the tilt of her head as she approached him with a kiss goodnight, the adoration on her face when she admired Rachel's artwork or listened as Olivia made up one of her stories.

"Maggie." Her name sparked something inside him, familiar and painful, but something he could no longer suppress. He searched quickly for the girls. He needed them. He needed to be close to them, to put his arms around them, to instinctively protect them and love them as he hadn't been able to since their nightmare began. He scanned the gravestones surrounding him. Nearly everyone had left. Only Erin, Maggie's sister remained, standing beneath a large oak tree several feet away, hugging the girls and talking to the pastor.

Sam approached and stretched his arms forward, inviting the girls to him. They eagerly entered his embrace. He wrapped his arms around them and squeezed, absorbing the security of holding his girls close. "I'm so sorry. I love you both so much. You know how much I love you, don't you?"

Rachel nodded her head into his chest. Olivia's voice was muffled. "I love you, too, Daddy." He fought back tears.

"Sam, please let me know how I can help. If you need to talk anytime day or night, just call." The pastor offered a business card and locked eyes with Sam. "I'll be praying for you and the girls."

He sensed the pastor studying him like a specimen on a microscope slide, probably for a sign of softness in a weak moment, a chance to reach him when he was most vulnerable. Instead, Sam held his stare and let the card hang in the air between them.

"Yeah? Well, while you're praying, do me a favor. Ask God why."

The pastor rubbed his hand across his chin then turned his head. "Why is a question that often doesn't have an easy answer, if it's ever answered at all." He hesitated before he looked back at Sam. "You could ask Him yourself, you know."

"If I talked to God right now, He wouldn't like what I had to say." Without apology, Sam turned away.

"Girls." Tenderness returned to his voice. "It's time to tell Aunt Erin good-bye. She has a long drive home."

Rachel and Olivia clung to Erin. Sam mouthed "thank you," but this time the words that had been automatic, surface, were genuine and deep. How would they have endured the past few days without her filling the vast void that had invaded their family?

"Call me anytime you want." Erin cupped Rachel's hands in her own then crouched eye-level with Olivia. "I'll be back to see you as soon as I can. I promise."

As the girls released their aunt, Sam put an arm around his daughters. "Let's go home."

Pastor Rob laced his arms across his chest and leaned back into the trunk of the oak tree behind him. As the girls and their father walked toward the funeral director waiting beside a black limousine, he marveled at the mystery that was Sam Blake. Was mystery the right word? Maybe it was challenge, a challenge he seemed destined to lose. Then, perhaps impossibility was the correct term.

He had known Sam ever since he took the church five years ago. In fact, through Maggie, Sam was one of the first people in the congregation Rob and his wife Cindy recognized by name. A deacon introduced them to his daughter, a real estate broker, to help them find a house. They quickly grew fond of Maggie as she proved not only to be a skilled broker but a dedicated member of Bethany Chapel as well, and in time a genuine friend. Rob and Cindy were at the hospital for the birth of Olivia. When Rachel accepted Christ, it was Rob's privilege to baptize her. They grieved for Maggie as Rob buried both of her parents too soon, a year apart, her mother from ovarian cancer, her father from a heart attack. Experiencing life's trials and triumphs with others tends to bring people closer. But not Sam. Sam held Rob at arm's length.

What puzzled Rob more than that, however, was how he felt about Sam. Professionally, he should be concerned about the state of Sam's soul. His head told him he should find ways to push through barriers, to build a relationship with him, to give him spiritual guidance—and possibly to ensure Sam's salvation, which he didn't see much evidence of, though he tried not to judge. It seemed to him, if Sam were concerned about eternity at all, he was intent on getting in by his wife's coat tails.

Maggie had the girls in church nearly every Sunday, yet Sam rarely made an appearance. And for a period of time, two maybe three years ago, he never showed up at all, perhaps on Christmas, if Rob's memory served him right. Maybe he wasn't comfortable worshipping in a group setting. While Rob believed coming together as a body of believers was a vital part of a spiritual life, he wasn't so closed minded to think it was a requirement of salvation. But he couldn't figure Sam out because the man would not let him get closer than an extended handshake. He'd asked Maggie about it a time or two, but she merely made excuses about his work schedule, though her eyes revealed more.

While Rob knew what he was supposed to do with an

estranged congregation member like Sam, what confused him was how he felt about Sam. Or maybe what he didn't feel would be a better way to explain it. Deep in his chest, where the undeniable impression of God's guidance struck him, when it came to Sam Blake, he consistently sensed God telling him no. And to a pastor, that did not make sense. When Rob prayed for guidance, for God to take down the wall and provide an opportunity to connect with Sam, time and again Rob sensed the answer. No.

And the strangest part of all, although Rob prayed the right things, he did so out of duty, not out of conviction. He wanted to pray out of conviction. The most important gift he had been given was compassion for people who needed God—whether for eternal life or for the walk of life. That gift tripled the membership of Bethany to three hundred, a small number in comparison to today's mega-churches, but it was the largest congregation he could minister to in the way he was called to. But any conviction he had for Sam came from his head, not his heart, not the place where God gave him guidance. And Rob could not understand why.

Why? The question Sam wanted answered. The question Rob had been most asked in his years as a pastor. To understand the answer required the deepest of faith, and even then he had seen a person or two shaken whose faith he thought might be stronger than his own. The faithful find it easy to say, "We may never know why, but God has an ultimate plan" or "we live in a broken world, and being a believer doesn't give us an insurance policy to protect us from the storms of life." That is, until one of those storms enters their life—a terminal disease, financial ruin, the loss of a child. So how could Rob begin to answer that question for Sam who, by all evidence, did not have the faith of even a mustard seed? Yet, in a feeble attempt to serve Sam as a pastor, he decided to honor Sam's request, for himself as much as for Sam. "Lord, why? Why Maggie?"

Sam laid on his side, staring at the picture on his night stand. The clock read 9:36. Two more minutes would mark the precise time the doorbell rang three nights ago and shifted his world into this alternate universe. He concentrated on the picture, forcing himself to remember the day it was taken. Last summer, they'd gone to the Smokey Mountains. After hiking all morning, Olivia had grown tired trying to keep up and begged Sam to carry her to the end of the trail. Maggie slowed their pace. "I wish someone could carry me, too." His eyes lit up with mischief. "Your wish is my command." As Sam reached toward her, Maggie protested in a wave of laughter. Olivia bounced and clapped. "Carry her, Daddy! Carry her!" In spite of Maggie's best efforts to hold him off, in one swift motion he reached one arm around her back and the other beneath her legs and scooped her up in hero fashion. That's when Rachel snapped the picture. Once they returned home, she enlarged it to an 8 x 10, framed it, and surprised Sam and Maggie with it for their anniversary. As he studied the picture now, he willed himself to revive the emotion so apparent in the shot . . . his adoring eyes, Maggie's head thrown back in laughter. He could see it. But he could no longer feel it beneath the crushing weight in his chest.

The numbers on the digital clock changed to 9:37. He had barely slept in the last three days. The first night he left Olivia asleep on the couch. Rachel slept beside her while

Sam made phone calls. He listened as his hollow voice betrayed him by speaking words he refused to believe. The first of the calls was the most important. Erin, Maggie's sister, promised to leave Louisville right away. She drove all night, arriving as a ribbon of light broke the horizon. Sam tried to doze in the recliner as he waited for her, but sleep eluded him. When he finally heard her car in the drive, he opened the door, waiting for her to whirl in and take command as he knew she would, and as he needed her to. Erin was the one with the explanation when Olivia awoke and asked for her mommy, the one who cried with Rachel when Sam felt like stone, the one who guided Sam's mechanical decisions for the following days. He wished she could stay longer, but she was pressured to get back to her office to make final preparations for a jury trial scheduled to begin the next morning.

The clock read 9:38. As Sam studied the numbers, he knew they would never again be just numbers. Twice a day the time would appear on his watch. Perhaps a lunch bill would ring up $9.38. He might see the number combination on a car's license plate. And each time, he would remember 9:38 and wish he could turn the numbers back to 8:01, the time on Maggie's last text saved on his phone. *Cross your fingers. On my way home.* How ironic it seemed now. Oh how Sam wished he had texted back. "Come straight home. You said you would be home to put the girls to bed. I need you. Please." What was Maggie doing on Route 40 anyway? She must have decided to stop by the office. What was so important that it couldn't wait until morning?

He had so many questions but no answers, and the weariness of it was unlike any he'd ever experienced, even as a cadet during his first night of police academy. After being physically and verbally stressed until midnight, the cadets were awakened at 3:00 a.m. to watch videos of gruesome crime scenes for two hours, and then struggled through a full day of class and P.T. before they were finally allowed to collapse in their dorms. That exhaustion was nothing compared to what Sam experienced now. That was physical. This was emotional. This was everything.

He had fought and suppressed and denied the pain that threatened to overwhelm him, pain that reached a depth within him he never knew existed. He feared letting it surface, feared letting go. But it was there, rising a little more each moment, a massive, heavy thing, strangling and void of oxygen. It moved into his chest, and he no longer possessed the strength to push it back down. He started to panic. Olivia lay in fitful sleep beside him; Rachel was curled up on Maggie's side of the bed. He choked back a sob, afraid to wake them.

With a final glance at the picture on his night stand, Sam knew the fight was over. He laid the frame face down, unable to bear the agony of remembering, and rushed to the bathroom. He turned on the shower, stepped into the steamy spray and let the sobs rise up, one after another, releasing all the anguish, the tears, the fear, the anger, he had locked inside. Maggie was gone. In an instant it was over. For better, for worse, until death they parted. And Sam had done nothing to stop it. He hadn't protected her. He hadn't saved her. He jerked the shower handle to the left and let the water scald him. "Maggie." He sobbed, pounding his fist on the tiled wall. He raised his face into the steam, the water mixing with his tears until finally no more tears remained, only gasping breaths that rhythmically rocked his body. He leaned back against the shower wall until the hot water ran out and let the coldness numb him.

And then physical exhaustion came. Sam doubted he had the strength to walk from the shower to his bed where all he wanted to do was disappear in a deep sleep. But when he turned off the shower, Olivia cried out. He waited to see if it was isolated, as her nighttime cries sometimes were, or if it would be followed by more, even though she still lie asleep. Sam listened. When the next one came, he grabbed a towel from the rack and wrapped it around his waist, dripping a trail as he hurried to the bedside. As he sat down, Olivia clasped his hand and whispered, "Daddy."

At first he thought she was still asleep, but her eyes were fixed on him. "Are you okay, honey?" Sam pulled her into his lap and brushed her curls away from her face.

Olivia snuggled into his arms. "She heard me cry and she came."

She came? He must not have heard correctly. Or maybe Olivia wasn't really awake after all. He looked at Rachel, sound asleep. "Who came? Rachel?"

"Mommy came. She came and sang to me."

Instantly, the door to Sam's cell clanged shut. He wanted to retreat inside, behind the walls he'd constructed to keep the pain out. He had no idea how to respond. Of course, Olivia had been dreaming, but still, he wanted to yell, he wanted to cry, he wanted to comfort her. But mostly he wanted it to be true.

"Daddy?"

"Um, yeah, okay, honey." He helped her lie back on the pillow and tucked the covers around her. "Try to go back to sleep. It's really late." He pressed his lips to her forehead and lingered a moment.

As he turned to stand, he noticed the picture on his nightstand. "Olivia, did you fix the picture?" He pointed to the upright frame he had lain face down before escaping to the shower.

"Mommy doesn't like the picture down. She wants you to leave it like that."

"Honey, you had a dream." He said it to himself as much as to her.

"No, Daddy," Olivia insisted. "She said that picture is one of her favorite things, you know, like the song she sang me."

Sam was worn thin. He couldn't deal with this now. He would wait until morning, and it was likely Olivia wouldn't even remember it then anyway. "Go to sleep, Olivia." The command came out harsher than he intended.

He returned to the bathroom to finish getting ready for bed. With a final check to make sure both girls slept soundly, Sam grabbed his pillow and headed for the recliner, certain sleep would no longer come as easily as he had hoped.

CHAPTER 6

At the moment Maggie recognized the little girl's cry, she instantly called out. "Olivia!" It wasn't the cry that meant Olivia had awakened and simply wanted tucked in nor the cry of fitful sleep because bedtime had come much too late. It was the cry that could startle Maggie from a coma and propel her ten steps across her bedroom carpet before her eyes were open, acutely aware of her duty. It signaled that Olivia was clutched by terror and would have Maggie calling the little girl's name as she raced to her bedroom, scooping Olivia up, and rocking her back forth to pull her out of a nightmare.

Maggie's heart alternately fluttered and pounded as her attempts to breathe were shallow, suffocating. "Olivia!" She called out again, but she had no direction. "Where are you?"

When she started to her left, the cry seemed to lessen. Yet, when she stepped to her right, the cry seemed stronger from the opposite direction. She turned in a frantic circle, drowning in the lavender sea.

"I'm coming, Olivia!" Desperation filled her, and she panicked as Olivia's cry grew louder. She strained to see beyond the falling diamonds, but it was useless. "I can't find you, Olivia! I can't find you!" Maggie closed her eyes to listen as intently as she could, but still, no direction.

"Please, God. Help me."

And then there was silence.

As Maggie listened in the emptiness, her panic grew stronger. She would never find Olivia now! With urgency she opened her eyes, prepared to search in every direction. But confusion interrupted her mission. She was no longer in that place with Nate.

As her spinning mind began to slow, she realized she was in her own bedroom, and so was Olivia—asleep in her bed. A river of relief rushed through Maggie as her daughter quietly rested in surroundings so familiar, yet not quite the same.

This room was her refuge, her escape after putting the girls to bed at the end of a long day. In the corner was her chair where she had relaxed with a good book, tired feet propped on the ottoman, or her "prayer chair" as she had secretly nicknamed it, her retreat for quiet moments. And one of her favorite escapes was her bed, especially when Sam worked into the evening, and a romantic comedy was in the DVD player.

But now Maggie felt oddly out of place, a visitor, as Olivia tossed fitfully with Rachel asleep next to her, clutching Maggie's pillow. Sam's place was empty, but the way the covers were thrown back suggested he had been lying there, too. She tuned into the sounds around her. Sam was in the shower. A sudden whimper from Olivia put Maggie into motion.

"Olivia, Mommy's here." Maggie sat on the edge of the bed and brushed Olivia's hair away from her face. She rubbed her forehead, trying to relax her eyebrows. "Ssshhh. I'm here. You're safe, baby. Everything's okay. Shh."

Still sleeping, Olivia sighed deeply. Maggie caressed her hair until her breathing settled into a hypnotic pattern, signaling she had once again found peaceful sleep. She studied the little girl's face, the long blonde lashes, the small round nose, the flush of pink on her full cheeks, still the face of a baby.

A sharp longing rose within her. Just as she innately understood the place she had been with Nate, she realized the here and now. This was her home, her family. But they were different. She was different. She did not belong in Nate's world, yet she knew she was no longer a part of her own. Agony, as deep as a fault beneath the earth's crust, shifted viciously, fragmenting her core, forcing its way to the surface. A deep chasm separated Maggie from her children, unnaturally, painfully, too soon. And yet, she was here. Suddenly, her anguish dimmed into a lingering shadow, and a growing sense of purpose consumed her.

She looked from Olivia to Rachel. Her girls. Her children. They still needed her, and she still needed to be their mom. She pulled back the covers and lay down beside Olivia. As she reached across to rest her hand on Rachel's cheek, she cuddled Olivia close and breathed in her little girl smell. She kissed her forehead, her tender cheek, her curls, and rested her lips near her ear. Softly she sang Olivia's favorite lullaby.

Rachel rested beside them. Maggie studied the features of a young woman that had begun to replace those of a little girl. A muscle twitched as Rachel clenched her jaws. Maggie softly stroked her cheek as she continued to sing, trying to help her release the tension. Rachel stirred slightly at the touch then rolled to her side, turning away from Maggie and out of her reach.

When she finished the lullaby, Maggie lay on her back and stared at the ceiling, aware that somehow she had been given a chance to return to her family—grateful beyond words that she had been given this chance, whether it was only moments or for many days. But she was confused. Most of her life she'd anticipated what Heaven would be like. And she'd lived life in the flesh for thirty-eight years. Life she understood. But this. This place between. Maggie had no point of reference. *I am here, Lord.* Maggie prayed. *But I don't understand.*

As she listened for direction in the silence, it was Sam she heard, his voice muffled by the sound of the shower. She turned to rise from the bed, and in doing so, noticed the picture of her and Sam lying face down on the night stand. Instantly her heart gripped. She imagined the moments leading to the picture being placed that way. Had Sam studied it longingly or had he glanced away quickly, unable to bear the memory? Did he lay it down gently out of grief, or violently out of anger? She picked up the picture, cradled it in both hands like a wounded butterfly, and willed herself to be transported back into the moment when her world seemed perfect. It all washed over her, the energy of Olivia's giggles, the strength in Sam's arms, and Rachel's determination as she focused and shot. For an instant, Maggie was weightless. But a sound from the shower drew her attention once again. She returned the photograph to its upright position and whispered to the sleeping girls, "Tell your daddy to leave my favorite picture the way it's supposed to be."

Maggie gripped the doorway to the master bath,

unprepared for the scene before her. The textured shower door framed Sam's silhouette. He stood, his back against the shower wall, with one arm extended and placed against the opposite wall as if to brace himself. One jagged sob after another erupted from the masculine body she associated only with strength and control. Not that she hadn't seen Sam's tears before; she had, at his father's funeral shortly after they were married, at the birth of both girls, when her parents passed away. But she had never seen him like this.

She rushed to the shower and pressed her hands desperately against the hot glass. She cried inside, but she had no tears of her own. "It'll be alright, Sam." Though she insisted, she didn't know how it could be. "Please, Sam." She needed him to stop. The very inside of her twisted unnaturally as she watched her protector lean back against the wall, defeated, silent, though his shoulders still rose and fell as sobs racked his body.

"I can't do this, Maggie."

His words startled her. "Sam!" She pounded the glass. "Sam!"

Hope sliced through her, but then faded. As the shower continued to wash over him, Maggie was only inches away, but Sam was completely unaware. She was helpless.

He spoke again, his words slow, staccato. "I can not do this. I can't raise these girls by myself."

Anguish pressed down on Maggie. She feared Sam was right. What if he couldn't do it? He was a provider, a protector. His identity outside the home had formed the foundation, the structure they lived within. But Maggie's identity was the interior, the life that happened inside their home, inside their family. Olivia, their blossoming child, needed a nurturer, an encourager, someone to protect her self-esteem in the years to come when her innocence would collide with a world that could be so unkind. Did Sam possess the insight that required?

And Rachel, intricate and fragile, needed someone who could hear what she didn't say, who could recognize her needs even when Rachel herself didn't understand them. Maggie feared that was not Sam's nature. And when the girls faltered and made mistakes, would Sam know the difference between grace and discipline, and discern which was called for? Or would he default to his law enforcement mindset, that crime deserved punishment?

Maggie pressed both hands to her chest as if the pressure would keep the shards of her heart from causing more pain. The torment was unbearable. Her family was in crisis. They had no options. Sam would have to learn, and maybe he could. After all, was her intuition as a mother so far removed from Sam's instinct as a detective? It was a wisp of hope, but she longed for something more solid to cling to. Maggie prayed Sam would learn quickly and that the mistakes made in the process would not have devastating consequences for the girls, or for him.

"Maggie."

"I'm here, Sam." Maggie rested her forehead against the glass door. She wanted terribly to pull her husband to her, to let her arms be the strength around him as his had been for her so many times. "I'm here, and I'm going to be here. We promised, remember? Our last night, we promised each other we'd keep our girls safe, happy. Together. I'm here, Sam." As Maggie renewed her vow, she had no idea if she could keep it, or how long she would be allowed to try. But she knew she had to believe she could.

A cry from Olivia summoned her attention. Maggie looked toward the bedroom and then back at Sam, who had raised his head. At the sound of the second cry, he turned off the shower. Maggie stepped back as he swung open the shower door and rushed to Olivia. She was awake, and the tender exchange between father and daughter consoled Maggie. And then, Olivia whispered, "Mommy came."

Sam's back stiffened, but Maggie clutched both hands to her chest, certain her heart would leap out and soar to the clouds. Olivia had heard her! Sam tried to convince Olivia she had been dreaming, but Maggie didn't care. Whether conscious or unconscious of her presence, Olivia knew Maggie had come to her. But what about Rachel? Would she wake and know her mom had tried to comfort her in the night? The wings of hope spread inside her chest, but a sudden thought kept it from taking flight. Sam didn't sense her presence. She had talked to him, but he didn't hear. What if Rachel didn't either?

She both anticipated and feared the morning. What would Sam say to Olivia? Would he convince her she was only dreaming? Would Rachel have an awareness, too? And if Maggie could reach her family, then what? She settled into her chair in the corner. *Please, God, show me what I'm supposed to do.*

CHAPTER 7

Maggie decided to spend the morning experimenting. Based on last night, she was certain Olivia could hear her, but she didn't think Olivia could see her. Sam could do neither. But she was unsure about Rachel. She leaned against the desk as Rachel salvaged a rumpled pair of jeans from her bedroom floor and dug through her dresser for a t-shirt. When she sat on her bed and began to text, it was apparent she intended to go to school.

"Please don't go, Rachel." Maggie waited for a reaction, some indication Rachel heard her, but there was none. "Stay home, just for today." Her plea was selfish. She wanted her family intact, inside their home, together, even if she were the only one who knew it.

Rachel walked to her dressing table and pulled a brush through her hair. Maggie expected her to sit down and use make-up to cover the shadows beneath her eyes or to give her pale complexion some color. But she didn't. Instead, Rachel glared at her reflection in the mirror and ran her fingers into her hair, resting her hands on her head. Then she closed her eyes and gripped her hair tightly. Her jaw clenched and a low moan rumbled in her chest.

Maggie's heart wrenched. Instantly she stood behind Rachel, her face close as she spoke directly into her ear. "Rachel, honey, it's okay. I'm here. I'm right here. Please don't, Rachel. Please." Maggie tried to grasp Rachel's wrists and force her to release her grip. She could feel Rachel, but her touch had no effect on her daughter.

Rachel spun and flung herself face down on her bed. Her whisper was fierce. "I hate it! I hate it, Mom! Why did you have to do this?"

Maggie gasped. "Do this? Rachel, you say that like this was my choice. But it wasn't. I hate it, too, and I'd give anything to change it, to make things the way they are supposed to be. But I can't. I can't."

She imagined how their morning was supposed to be. She was supposed to have a cup of coffee in hand, darting from one girl's room to the next, helping Olivia tie her shoes, telling Rachel to get a move on or she wouldn't have time for breakfast. She was supposed to kiss Sam as he passed her in the hall on his way to the door. She was supposed to be checking the day's schedule in her phone for the time of a closing or an appointment to show a property. That's the way it was supposed to be, but it wasn't. And it never would be again. Maggie let bitterness claim her, but only for a moment. She couldn't waste the precious time she had been given by agonizing over how her family was supposed to be.

She sat beside Rachel and ran her fingers through her daughter's hair, the way she used to when she had trouble falling asleep. "I don't know why it happened any more than I know why I am allowed to be here. But I am here, Rachel. If only you knew."

While her family had slept during the night, Maggie tried to make sense of what she knew.

The accident. Her only memory of it was a fleeting realization when she saw the headlights.

The place. Some point between here and eternity where brief moments had translated into days by the time Maggie found herself back with her family.

The emotions. Though surrounded by the grief of her family, Maggie felt a detached sense of loss, as if she were trying to recall a vivid dream she could only grasp in wisps. The frustration was stronger. Her family was in crisis, yet she was useless. And although she was very grateful for it, why did she seem to have a connection with only Olivia? Love, however, reigned as the principal emotion and fueled her yearning to take care of her family.

Her return. How? Why? For how long? There was nothing about it that she understood. Simply, she was home. For now.

Maggie rested her lips on her daughter's head. Summoning everything within, she willed Rachel to sense her presence. *I'm here, Rachel. Can you feel me? Just be still. Be still and feel me here.*

She was encouraged when Rachel rose and sat on the edge of the bed. She stared ahead. Maggie followed her gaze to an easel in the corner beside the window where Rachel had started a painting, a fall landscape of a pond surrounded by trees, reflecting the colors of the changing leaves. She walked to the easel as if in a trance. *Yes,* Maggie urged. *Use your art, honey. Put your emotion there.*

Her shoulders relaxed as her daughter clutched the palette and dabbed it with paints. But instead of picking up a brush, Rachel pressed her open palm on the palette and smeared the colors together. Maggie watched, horrified, as she then placed her hand in the center of the painting and moved it in circles, leaving behind a mixture of colors that transformed into a trail of dull grey.

"Rachel . . . don't."

But she continued moving her hand over the canvas, covering it entirely. Finally, she stepped away from the easel as if to admire a masterpiece. Her eyes narrowed. She returned to the painting one last time and placed her hand near the top. Her fingers curved into a claw, her nails dug into the canvas, and she dragged them brutally down the center, leaving a trail of scars in the wet paint.

Maggie turned away. Her questions were answered. She could not reach Rachel no matter how hard she tried. Her daughter was fragile and crumbling and needed to be rescued. But Maggie couldn't help her, and she feared Sam wouldn't see it because he didn't know what to look for. She paused at the bedroom door. "Rachel, I'm sorry."

"Dad, wake up."

Voices summoned Sam in the darkness, but he could not climb his way out of the black pit he had fallen into. The smooth stone walls had no crags to grasp or ledges to climb. He tried to answer the voices, but unrecognizable sounds issued from his mouth, which no longer seemed capable of forming words.

"Dad, come on. Wake up."

A hand clasped his shoulder. Turning abruptly to face whatever threatened him, Sam was awakened by his own gasp. He opened his eyes and waited for the scene to come into focus. Rachel stood in front of him, one hand on her hip and head cocked, looking at him like he was something to figure out.

"I'm going to school." Dressed in jeans torn at the knee and a t-shirt with some logo across the front, she stood expectantly, her backpack flung over one shoulder. "Kristen's mom is picking me up."

His heart held the next beat too long, and then he realized the moment was gone, the brief second or two each morning when he woke up not yet realizing that Maggie wasn't there, the instant before he remembered normal no longer existed and he was left lost, searching for his way in an unfamiliar world. He wished he were asleep and back in the nightmare that wasn't real.

"Dad?" Impatience rang in her voice.

"Uh, yeah." He rubbed his hand down his face, trying to think through the fog. "Are you sure, Rach? Are you ready to go back? Don't you want to stay home at least another day?"

"And do what, Dad? Sit around noticing she's not here?" Her shrug punctuated the sarcasm.

The doorbell saved him from a response.

"I gotta go." Rachel already had her hand on the doorknob.

"Did you eat anything?" The door closed and cut off his words.

Sam sat the recliner upright. Should he have stopped her? Isn't the day after the funeral too soon? Besides, school is the last place Rachel would choose to be. She had good attendance and good grades because she had no choice, but she could certainly concoct a good excuse to skip every once in a while. Maybe he should go get her. But she was right, wasn't she? Exactly what was he going to do all day anyway? He tried to put himself in Maggie's place. If she were home today, what would she do? He should make Olivia breakfast. And he could attempt the laundry, since it had been neglected over the weekend. It was only morning, but shouldn't he think about dinner? And how was Rachel getting home from school, did she say? The day hadn't even begun and already he was drained.

His thoughts turned to the open investigation sitting on his desk at the station. He could drop Olivia at school and bury himself in work. While the escape enticed him, he didn't have the intellectual energy to expend on the case. But he wished he could lose himself in something, anything, to get out from under the blanket of sorrow suffocating him.

As Maggie stepped from Rachel's room into the hallway, noise from Olivia's bedroom greeted her. She needed desperately to connect, to see if Olivia would respond to her while awake as she had in her sleep. She found Olivia sitting in her rocking chair, cradling a doll.

"Don't cry, baby. Mommies don't ever stay away." As she rocked she stared through the doorway where Maggie stood. Olivia couldn't see her.

Cautiously, she entered the room. Because Olivia on some level could sense her presence, she wasn't sure how to approach. She leaned against a dresser, quiet, observant.

"No, sweetie. We can't wake up, Daddy." Olivia patted her doll. "He's so tired. But if you are a good girl, Mommy will come home soon."

Maggie couldn't resist. "Olivia?"

"See, baby. Mommy's here. You're a good girl." She hummed softly.

"Livi, can you hear me?"

Olivia continued humming.

"Livi?"

No response.

A moment later, Olivia put down the doll and turned her attention to the unfinished poster lying on the floor. She chose a pink marker and traced the pencil outline of her name, which Rachel must have drawn for her. Maggie smiled as Olivia sat on her knees, bent over her project with the marker clutched tightly in her fingers, and raced her tongue back forth across her lips.

"Does that help you color better?" Maggie teased as she had many times before.

Olivia froze. She closed her mouth then bit her bottom lip. She put down the marker and sorted through the pictures she had cut out for her poster. She set aside one of a grey kitten tangled in a ball of yarn. Cute.

"Mommy likes you." Olivia kissed the picture.

Maggie was puzzled. She halfway expected Olivia to know she was there, even to communicate openly maybe. But the best she could tell, Olivia had no idea Maggie was beside her, and her attempts to talk with her were unsuccessful. Yet, somehow, Maggie's words, and maybe even her thoughts, seemed to influence the child.

As Olivia sorted pictures, Maggie moved through the room. A few books on a shelf had fallen, and Maggie instinctively thought to straighten them. She reached for the first book. She could feel it as her hand passed over, just like she could feel Rachel's hair as she brushed her fingers through, but her contact had no effect on either. After a night alone, exploring her home while her family slept, Maggie knew her touch was futile. With one exception. The picture on Sam's nightstand.

Olivia held up a cut-out of fluffy white clouds. "Mommy went there."

Maggie, concentrating on her daughter, was startled when Sam appeared in the doorway. A tingle raced through her.

Olivia glanced up. "Hey, Daddy. See my poster? I put my name on it, and I'm gonna glue my favorite things on it, like Mommy said."

Sam cringed and closed his eyes for a brief moment. Maggie was certain the word *Mommy*, not the poster, prompted his reaction. He cleared his throat. "It's great, honey. How about some breakfast?"

"Okay."

"What would you like?"

"Um . . ." She shuffled through pictures and placed the grey kitten next to her name.

"Livi, what do you want to eat?" His fingers found his temples and pressed as Olivia rubbed a glue stick on the back of the kitten and secured it in place.

"Just make her some oatmeal." Maggie muttered. "Peaches and cream."

Their daughter tilted her head and froze in position. Then Olivia shocked her. "Mommy says oatmeal, the peaches and cream kind."

But she wasn't nearly as shocked as Sam seemed. He filled his lungs and then exhaled slowly. It took him a few seconds to find words.

"Mommy says?"

"Yeah." She gripped a chunky marker and drew a heart on the poster board.

Maggie ached for husband as she realized once again the task she had left him with, guiding two young girls through the loss of their mother while trying to find his way through grief himself. As he stood there in his flannel pajama pants and grey T-shirt, hair tousled and face puffy from sleep, Maggie wanted to protect him. He looked like a little boy.

Olivia giggled. "Mommy's funny."

Rachel sat in her usual place at the lunch table across from Kristen, surrounded by the soccer team. The noise escalated as each girl talked over the others, fighting for the spotlight. Coming to school had been the right decision, Rachel concluded, as the scene unfolded before her the same as it did every lunch period. This was normal, though she wasn't so certain of her decision when she first arrived at school.

She did not expect the reaction, and lack thereof, she received when she walked into the building. Some kids she knew huddled around her with various versions of "OMG, I'm so sorry . . . I can't believe it . . . If there's *anything* you need," and in the next breath asked who did the algebra homework and if anyone had heard that Megan Willis broke up with Jayson Jones. Other kids looked at her as they passed, some with sympathy, some with curiosity, some glancing at her like a regular kid passing another because they didn't know her or her tragic story, which she preferred. The teachers were not much different. A few spoke to her a moment before or after class; others seemed as if they didn't know what to say, so they substituted compassionate smiles for words. Some acted as if they knew nothing at all, and Rachel hoped they didn't. She just wanted every day to go on like every day before. Just like now.

She half listened to Lacey, the team goalie, broadcast a play-by-play of a fight she had with her mother last night. Something about a sophomore boy with a car who Lacey had been meeting up with, which her mom discovered by reading her texts.

"You know, really, in a way you're lucky, Rachel," Lacey said.

The sound of her name brought Rachel's attention back to the table. "What?"

"My mom makes me so mad. Sometimes I wish *she* were dead."

Stone silence. Nobody moved. All eyes focused on Rachel. Heat rose up her neck and settled in her cheeks. Her heartbeat pounded out Morse code in her ears. SOS. SOS. Kristen received the message.

"You are *so* stupid, Lacey! Even if you think it, how can you say that to Rachel? You idiot." Kristen reached across the table and flipped Lacey's tray of spaghetti into her lap. "You suck."

The girls sat in shock, speechless, Rachel included. She had never seen Kristen so angry, ever. She wasn't sure if she felt rescued or mortified. Either way, she needed to escape.

"I'm sorry," she apologized to Kristen, though she wasn't sure why. Then she scrambled from the table and ran toward the hall. Kristen called after her, but she didn't stop running.

With no direction, Rachel ran down one hallway and then the next. She passed the lab. Science was her next class, but there was no way she could go in there. She couldn't imagine going to any class for that matter. She reached the end of the hallway and raced up the staircase to the second floor, unknown territory where ninth grade classes were held. At the top of the staircase she hesitated, unfamiliar with the halls, not sure where to go. She heard the voice of the principal approaching. Afraid to be found on the wrong floor, she pushed open a classroom door and ducked inside.

Her heart pounded as footsteps advanced. Pressed against the door, Rachel peaked through a narrow window into the hallway. The principal scolded a student as he escorted him to the office. When they had safely passed, Rachel surveyed the empty classroom for the first time. She drew in a sharp breath. Easels lined the room, holding canvases of chalk portraits. Ceramics, sculptures, and drawings were displayed on shelves and bulletin boards. A pottery wheel and kiln were in one corner. In the opposite corner was a sink with paint brushes soaking. Instantly the past five minutes were erased, and Rachel walked through the art room as if she were in a fairytale.

"Do you have permission to be in here?"

She spun around. A teacher stood in the doorway, hands tucked into the pockets of her paint-stained smock. Rachel didn't trust her voice, but she had to ask. "Is this your art room?"

"Has been for thirty years, teaching eighth and ninth grade art. If you don't mind my asking, what are you doing here?"

Rachel searched for an answer but everything she could think of sounded pathetic. A girl at lunch said something really cruel. My best friend saved me, or embarrassed me, I'm not sure which. My mom died. Instead, she shrugged her shoulders.

"Hmm." The art teacher's gaze rested on her. "What's your name, hon?"

She glanced at the door and lowered her head. Was she in trouble? Should she apologize and escape and hope the teacher wouldn't remember what she looked like? As the teacher waited for an answer, Rachel forced herself to look up. Soft lines around the teacher's mouth and eyes deepened as she smiled. She was probably somebody's grandma.

"Rachel."

She peered over her glasses as if she expected more.

"Rachel Blake."

"Nice to meet you, Rachel Blake. I'm Mrs. Swane."

Mrs. Swane pressed a finger to her lips and seemed lost in thought for a moment. Then she removed a newspaper from under her arm. "Rachel Blake." As if meditating on the name, she repeated it softly as she turned pages. When she found the page she was searching for, she laid the paper on a table in front of her. "This Rachel Blake?" Her finger underlined the name in print.

The top of the page read "Obituaries." A few lines above the teacher's finger was her mom's name in bold black print. Rachel's vision blurred as she read the words: ". . . survived by her husband Lt. Samuel Blake and two daughters, Rachel and Olivia."

Mrs. Swane's teacher voice found its grandmotherly tone. "Are you an artist, honey?"

As Rachel nodded the tears that filled her eyes broke free and rolled down her face, plump and wet, one after another.

"I could tell." She reached for Rachel's hands and inspected her fingers, which were stained with the paint from earlier that morning. She squeezed tenderly before letting go. "Well, Rachel. You didn't find my room by accident." After a thoughtful pause, Mrs. Swane said, "Why aren't you in my art class?"

Rachel couldn't find her voice to explain that she was bored in art last year because it was too easy and that she didn't make room for art in her schedule this year and that suddenly she regretted it.

The teacher put an arm around Rachel's shoulders, and without acknowledging her tears or discussing the death of her mother, she gave Rachel a tour of her classroom. She discussed her favorite artists, showed off student work, and asked Rachel about her preferred medium. When the bell rang to end the lunch hour, art students filtered into the classroom. Rachel wished she were one of them.

"Maybe you should head to class, so you won't be tardy." Soft lines deepened in the teacher's face again.

Rachel was reluctant to leave, but somehow the idea of going to science was now tolerable.

"You'll come back to see me, won't you?" Mrs. Swane walked her toward the door.

Rachel hesitated then decided she must ask before she lost the chance. "Can I come back tomorrow?"

"I'd love that." She scrawled Rachel's name on a hall pass, left the date blank, and handed it to her. "This will keep you out of trouble if you get caught on the second floor during lunch. Keep it in your backpack. And, Rachel, bring some of your work."

Rachel had spoken hardly ten words the entire conversation, but already she was planning everything she would say tomorrow.

CHAPTER 8

By the end of the week, Sam was beyond exhaustion, although he hadn't done much of anything. His mornings began with taking the girls to school. Then he'd come home and meander from room to room, or settle in his recliner to channel surf or doze to make up for nights of sporadic sleep. He avoided thinking and didn't answer most phone calls. He found he wasn't good at small talk when friends or people from Maggie's church called to check on the family. Conversation was stilted, even with Erin. People wanted to hear he was okay, the girls were okay, everything was okay, but not the truth, which he feared would spill over if he allowed himself to really talk. *I can't do this*, he might confess. Until now, Sam had relied on his strength, his instinct. He'd never questioned his ability. But his steely exterior had never been put into a blazing furnace and liquefied. *It should have been me*, he wanted to tell someone. *Maggie and the girls would have been better off. She would have known what to do.* And then there was the confession he feared most, which he would never allow to surface. When his mind betrayed him and tried to give it life, he crushed it like a wrecking ball at a demolition site.

The clock revealed he had survived another day alone, and soon it would be time to pick up the girls. His biggest decision of each day was still before him. Which casserole would he thaw from the many delivered by the neighbors and church ladies? He was incapable of making decisions more important than that, although several loomed overhead like a cement cloud. The real estate office was a big one. What did he know about running the business? And what about his own career? He'd worked so hard to make a place for himself in the department, and though he never spoke it aloud, he was still determined to be chief some day. Or was he? Was that even a possibility now? How could he put in the time it would take to work his way up, or face the dangers of the job, and still be the father the girls needed? And mother.

In spite of fourteen years of parenting, he felt grossly under qualified. He could interrogate a murder suspect, but he couldn't force Rachel to talk. "Fine" was her new word of choice. How are you doing? Fine. How's homework? Fine. Will you help with the dishes? Fine. And she was fine, secluded in her bedroom. But Sam worried she wasn't fine at all. She was just like him, disappearing within herself. Yet, that was how he preferred to cope, so shouldn't he let Rachel do the same? And Olivia—he could call out a lying witness, but he couldn't make himself deal with Olivia's fictional world that still included her mother. For one thing, Olivia seemed to cope better than any of them. She slept at night, she played, she laughed. Part of Sam didn't want to disturb that. The other part was very disturbed by it. But right now, it was easier to leave it alone.

Sam walked into the kitchen and stared at everything, at nothing. Body and mind, he was bound in a straightjacket, each movement, each thought constrained. Wherever he looked, Maggie remained—her favorite mug beside the coffee maker, her handwriting on the grocery list stuck on the refrigerator. No matter what room he entered, it was the same. The faint scent of her perfume lingered in the master bath. And her chair. When Sam walked into their bedroom, he half expected Maggie to be there, curled up with a book. Sometimes he imagined her laying a finger on the page to keep her place as she raised her chin to invite a kiss and ask him about his day. The little reminders pulled pain to the surface, forcing him into an endless battle to push it back down. Enough already. How long was he going to go on like this? Maggie was gone and he couldn't do anything about it. But he had to do something, something besides sulk away every minute of every hour of every day.

He opened the freezer, grabbed a foil-wrapped package, and set it on the counter to thaw. He turned and followed his feet to the bedroom as they commanded. He snatched his cell phone from the nightstand, exhaled through his mouth, and punched in a number. After four rings, voicemail answered.

"Hey, Wade. It's Sam Blake. Just wondering what's going on with the Simms case. Think I might come by the office in a few minutes. If you're not involved, maybe I'll see you there. If not, I'll talk to you later."

He thrust his shoulders back and attempted to ignore the knot in his stomach. Was he ready for this, ready to step back into the world? Part of him insisted, eager to escape everything that made him think of Maggie. Yet another part feared being away from all that kept her close. But as each day passed, he was drawn deeper into a darkness inside himself. How far would it go until he wouldn't be able to pull himself out? His fists tensed. "I've got to do this."

Sam pulled on jeans and a sweatshirt.

"You're doing the right thing, Sam." During the week of her new existence, Maggie had grown accustomed to one-sided conversations. "You need to get back to the office, to your investigation, think about something else for a while. I'll be here when you get back." Of that Maggie was certain, although she still had questions without answers. Especially one. How could she help Sam, or Rachel, when they didn't even know she was there? Sam was so closed up, he would never know. Only when she lay beside him at night did he seem to have the slightest response. He rested more soundly, but only for short periods at a time.

Rachel, however, responded much differently. Maggie's presence agitated her. When Rachel was home, she seldom left her bedroom. If she was working on homework when Maggie entered the room, Rachel would shove her book off the desk or pound the computer keyboard before slamming the lid. She could be sketching, focused and intentional, but as soon as Maggie approached, Rachel would scribble vigorously and tear through the paper. But nights bothered Maggie most. When she sat beside Rachel, she would fight in her sleep, kicking, tossing, tearing at the covers.

One night Maggie thought she finally broke through. Rachel lay still as Maggie sat beside her, enjoying the peaceful moments she was finally able to share with her daughter. But when she leaned over to kiss Rachel's cheek, she discovered a path left by tears that had rolled down and puddled into a wet stain on the pillow. Maggie wiped a new tear as it fell, whispered "I love you," and reluctantly left the room. So, she began most nights with Olivia, cuddled beside her to sing her to sleep or sitting in the rocking chair near her bed, guarding against bad dreams or waiting for the smile that occasionally appeared while her little girl dreamed. Once Olivia was asleep, Maggie would slip into bed next to Sam.

Sam grabbed his car keys off the dresser and stopped. He gripped them in one hand and pushed the other through his hair.

"Go." The thought of him leaving left Maggie empty, but it was necessary. "I miss you already."

Sam turned and she followed him from the bedroom to the kitchen to the garage. She remained after he closed the door, waiting for the car engine to start and Sam to back into the driveway. As the sounds moved farther away, an unwelcome sensation overwhelmed her. Faintness washed through her, leaving her hazy, listless. She panicked. Was this it? Was her time up? Olivia's giggles, Rachel's anger, Sam's emptiness. It was too soon. She wasn't ready. She desperately clung to her promise to Sam, a promise she couldn't break twice.

As quickly as it started, the sensation faded, and heaviness settled in so deeply she labored to move. She searched for an explanation. She hadn't yet been in the house alone, without Sam or the girls. In her death, did they give her some semblance of life? Was she sustained by their presence? Without them, she was weak, and for the first time since she returned home, Maggie needed to rest. She gripped the edge of the island for support as she started through the kitchen toward her bedroom.

She stopped. As she passed a dish towel near the sink, her hand had brushed against it. Was it her imagination, or did the dish towel move? She touched the edge of the towel and pushed her hand forward. The dish towel moved. She pulled her hand back. The towel moved again. Sam's coffee cup was in the sink. She nudged it. The spoon inside rattled. But what did that mean? Last night she had tried to cover Olivia, but she couldn't grab the blanket. And when Sam had fallen asleep watching TV, she couldn't use the remote control. The picture frame beside Sam's bed remained the only object she could hold, but even then only while everyone slept. Maggie picked up the dish towel, folded it, and placed in neatly on the island. New questions surfaced, and maybe, she hoped, so did new possibilities. Rachel.

Maggie summoned the faint wisps of energy she sensed in her body and channeled them so she could begin her task. As she walked to her daughter's bedroom, her movements were leaden. She dropped into the desk chair, relieved, and stared at the dark computer screen in front of her. This was a good idea. How couldn't it be? As unwanted answers to that question threatened to bombard her, Maggie suppressed them, determined to succeed. She rubbed the mousepad to wake the laptop from sleep mode. When the screen appeared, she opened a new document and prayed she was doing the right thing. She placed her fingertips on the keyboard and gingerly pressed down.

My sweet Rachel,

Olivia is right. I'm here. I don't know how, and I don't know for how long, but I am here. I haven't abandoned you, and you have to believe I would have never chosen to go. As much as you

still need me, I still need you, too—and Olivia
and Dad. My family. And as broken as we are, at
least we are together, and now you know. I may
not be able to love you in the same ways, but I
love you just as much as I always have . . . and
always will.

Love, Mom

Maggie sat back in the chair to review the message.
Did she say enough? Too much? The few lines on the
screen looked nominal compared to everything she could
say, everything she wanted to say. But after she read her
words again, she was satisfied she had written what Rachel
needed to hear most.

Her heart eased. Tension drained from her shoulders
as she rested in the quiet of her daughter's room, absorbing
the serenity that would dissipate with Rachel's return. Her
art easel in the corner, her camera waiting on the dresser,
the sketchpad beside her computer—neglected mementos
of the life Maggie longed for her daughter to revive.

And then, movement on the screen captured her
attention. One by one, starting with *My sweet Rachel*,
the letters Maggie typed began to fade. She hit the enter
key to stop it, the backspace, the escape key, then any key
her fingers contacted. She pounded on the keyboard, but
it didn't matter. She clicked the save icon, the print icon,
before it was too late. Frantically she retyped the letters
as they disappeared. But within moments, only a black
cursor blinked in the middle of a blank, white page. Maggie
lowered her head and her shoulders drooped, crushed in
defeat. She fought to suppress a sob caught in her chest.

Then she saw paper in Rachel's trashcan, a wadded

piece of notebook paper. Would it work? She salvaged it, rustled through the clutter in the desk drawer for a pen, and began her message again. As the ink flowed freely on the page, Maggie tensed as if walking a tightrope, knowing each letter, each word, inched her closer to the end. But just as the letters on the computer screen began to fade, so did the ink on the paper. Each word Maggie wrote erased the word that came before, leaving only a blank trail behind her pen. She had barely written Rachel's name when her attempt to reach her daughter was once again sabotaged. She slammed the pen on the desk, crumbled the paper, and threw it back in the trash.

She was livid. Why was she here if she couldn't communicate with her family? She had so many questions, so much she didn't understand. She glared at the empty computer screen, the mocking cursor, the empty page. And then, a new idea surfaced. Maybe there were answers to be found. Once again she manipulated the mousepad, but this time she navigated to the Internet. She moved the cursor to the search box. Where to begin? She drummed her fingers on the desk. Life after death? She typed the phrase and scrolled through a list of results—secular explanations of eternity, religious explanations of eternity, a review of a rapper's album. One result lured her: *Are Ghosts Real?* She smirked. "Am I a ghost?" The notion hadn't occurred to her. The girls' mother? Yes. Sam's wife? Yes. But a ghost? She snickered but clicked the link anyway.

A website appeared, surprising Maggie with its professional appearance and lack of animated phantoms floating across the page. The photo of a man she assumed was the author roused suspicion though. She didn't want to stereotype, but if he didn't live in his mother's basement, he surely lived in somebody's basement. Yet, she couldn't resist scanning the topics listed in a column on the left side of the screen.

"Trapped Spirit. Hmm. I don't feel trapped. Haunting Spirit?" Maggie decided to test that one. "Boo!" She snickered, shaking her head at the crazy idea. "Possessed Spirit. Well, I don't feel entirely like myself, but I'm pretty sure what's here is all me."

But the next topic caused her to pause. Her voice softened. "Lingering Spirit." She let the cursor hover while she glanced at the final topic in the list, Angelic Spirit. "This is ridiculous." She scoffed, yet she couldn't resist. She clicked the word *lingering*.

"A spirit may linger for a number of reasons." Maggie mumbled as she skimmed. "It may have an urgent message or an unfinished task. It may be a young spirit unwilling to leave an unfulfilled life or a spirit in need of atonement before it can move into the next world. Sometimes, a spirit simply does not know that it has died. A spirit is usually confined to the area of its demise, yet it is believed some spirits return to a location of importance."

Maggie closed her eyes and recalled the fragrant lavender place, the diamonds showering down on her weightless body, the little boy beckoning her. Even now, something inside her yearned to return. Then she remembered Olivia's cry and the immediacy she had to go to her child. Olivia. Rachel. Sam. Her unfinished task? Her home—her location of importance? Maggie opened her eyes and continued.

"A lingering spirit is usually nonmaterial. That is, it cannot be seen and it cannot interact with the physical world or make itself known in the presence of the living.

In rare cases, some lingering spirits develop an ability to interact with the physical world. As such, these cases appear to share one commonality: the spirit's reason to linger is an unfinished task and the interaction is directly linked to that task."

Develop an ability to interact . . . Did that suggest she could gain more control over her existence? If so, how? Was it a matter of determination, will power? Or would her spirit simply grow stronger over time? She chided herself for considering all this mumbo-jumbo, and then chided herself again. After all, she was here, wasn't she? She looked at the pen she had used, the paper she wadded. She considered the dish towel on the island, Sam's coffee cup in the sink. Was her ability developing now? Then she remembered another phrase on screen: *in the presence of the living.* Maybe this wasn't something new. After all, someone had always been home with her which, apparently, prevented her from interacting with anything. Except for the picture on the nightstand. Could the picture be directly linked to her unfinished task? Did that explain why she could hold the frame in her hands? Maggie contemplated. Then she shook her head to bring herself back to reality. "This is ridiculous. How would anyone even know this stuff?" Still, she couldn't resist scanning the remaining information.

"The nonmaterial nature of a spirit, and its ability to interact with the physical, also explains a spirit's ability to pass through solid forms unimpaired, such as a wall or an unopened door."

Maggie laughed. "And who would write this stuff?" The name beneath the picture of the website author read Paulie Milton. "So, if I'm a ghost, Paulie—"

She raised her hand and reached forward. "I can put

my hand through that wall." She shifted a doubtful smile to one side, and slowly extended her arm until her fingers touched the surface. She pushed. She laid her palm flat and pushed harder. She couldn't pass through the solid form. Maggie raised an eyebrow. "Well, it's a good thing I tested your theory before I tried walking through a closed door, don't you think, Paulie?"

Still, Maggie considered the information and weighed it against what she knew. She couldn't deny the similarities. She clicked the back arrow to return to the homepage, and the list of topics reappeared. "Angelic Spirits. Angel." She repeated the word, curious how an angel differed from a lingering spirit.

She clicked again and the page appeared on the screen. "An angelic spirit . . ." Maggie glanced at the author's picture. "So you say, 'materializes into human form and moves about freely for the purpose of assisting those in need. Although the recipient of such assistance can be a person once known by the spirit, more often the recipient is a stranger unaware he is interacting with an angel. Thus, the existence of stories such as a fireman pulling a person from a burning building even though the firefighters had not yet arrived. Unlike the lingering spirit who is attached to its world by emotion, the angelic spirit is attached by purpose, who it can help, and how much it can accomplish during its existence.'"

Maggie clicked the red "x" at the top of the screen to close the browser. "That settles it. I'm not an angel." She leaned back in the chair, hollow. She didn't want to be an angel or a ghost or a spirit. She wanted to be a mother, a wife. She wanted to wrap her arms around her daughters, to feel Sam's arms wrapped around her.

The reserves she had gathered were depleted. She looked at the time on the computer screen and estimated how long until her family would return. So what if she could move a dish towel or use the laptop when the house was empty? It didn't bring her any closer to the people she loved. And she didn't like being alone and feeling lifeless. Only when someone was here did her house feel like a home—albeit a broken one. Slowly Maggie rose and walked to her bedroom. She laid her head on Sam's pillow and breathed him in. Turned on her side, she studied the picture on the nightstand and let herself get lost in the memory.

CHAPTER 9

It was lunch time and Rachel shoved her way through the hall with Kristen immediately behind her.

"Rachel, just stop and listen to me!"

The plea in Kristen's voice had no effect. Rachel marched forward, determined to get to the art room before another second was lost. On the day she showed Mrs. Swane her artwork, Rachel was perturbed to find another girl in the classroom. She was eager to share that part of herself with the teacher who so quickly gained her trust. As soon as she stepped through the door, Rachel spotted the stranger and closed up. But Mrs. Swane wouldn't allow it. One piece after another, she celebrated Rachel's talent and invited the intruder into the circle. Rachel learned the girl was Cricket, and every Tuesday and Friday the art room was Cricket's escape, from peers, Rachel supposed, or family, or maybe even from Cricket herself, which she judged by the pink hair, thick eyeliner, and many silver hoops piercing her eyebrow and lip. But all judgments were denied when Rachel glanced at the piece Cricket was working on—a pastel portrait of a man and a little girl looking into each other's eyes, the little girl's dimpled hands pressed against both his cheeks. The scene lived and breathed on the easel. When the bell rang to end lunch, Mrs. Swane invited Rachel to join them on Friday. And now it was Friday, and waiting for this moment was the only thing that kept Rachel going all week.

"Our science presentation is due today, Rachel! I know your life stinks right now, but you said all week you'd have your part done and we'd practice the presentation at lunch! You can't do this to me!" Kristen's voice competed with the boisterous hallway.

"It'll be fine, Kristen." Long strides increased the distance between Rachel and her friend. "Just do the stuff on digital photography. You did your part." She reached the flight of stairs and glanced back. Kristen stopped chasing and threw her hands in the air. "But what about you?"

Without response she raced to the second floor, two steps at a time. What was Kristen's problem? Her grade wasn't at risk. And Rachel didn't care about the science project, at least not enough to revisit her old hobby. Nope, she was done with that. She didn't want to think about her darkroom. She didn't want to think about photography. She didn't want to think about her mom. That story was over, and she refused to rewrite it for anyone.

Rachel slowed her pace as she approached the art room door, which was open just a crack. She peered in. Cricket stood with her back to the door, working at an easel. There was no sign of Mrs. Swane. Rachel stepped inside and waited. After a few seconds, Cricket turned around.

"You standing there watching me? That's kind of creepy."

"Sorry."

"Don't be. Just stop watching me."

"I . . . uh . . . wasn't watch—"

"There's all Mrs. Swane's extra supplies." Cricket pointed to an open cabinet in the corner hidden behind the kiln. "You can see what's there."

Rachel wanted to run to the cabinet like a little girl after the ice cream truck, excited to see all the flavors she had to choose from, wondering which she would end up with. Instead she forced herself to walk slowly, not to seem too enthused. She pulled open a cabinet door and peered inside, eager to discover the unthinkable treasures within. Oils, acrylics, chalks, plaster, mosaic tiles, and that was just at first glance. Paper and brushes and looms and colored pencils crowded in there, too. What might she find if she dug to the back of the deep shelves?

Where to begin? She moved some art supplies aside and uncovered a piece of scratch board. She picked it up and held it in both hands, staring into the blackness for the image waiting to be revealed, waiting for her to give it life. She found a blade among a cupful of old paint brushes and dull pencils. With supplies in hand, she chose a seat at the table closest to the door and sat with her back to Cricket.

Rachel opened her backpack to find paper and a pencil so she could experiment with a sketch before committing to the scratch board. Cricket's voice made her jump.

"Just because I don't want you watching me, it doesn't mean you have to sit all the way over there."

Rachel peered over her shoulder. Cricket was looking at her.

"Oh. Well, I didn't want to bother you."

"Sitting by me doesn't bother me." Cricket's mouth cocked to the side. "But standing behind me in an empty room when I don't know you're there, well, that'd bother anyone, don't you think?" Her eyebrows arched to punctuate the question.

Rachel offered a half grin as an apology and moved to the table next to Cricket's easel.

"That's magnificent." Rachel pointed to the portrait.

"Thanks."

"I don't think I've ever done anything that good."

"I don't know." Cricket argued. "The stuff 1 saw the other day was pretty cool."

"Really? Thanks." Rachel savored the compliment, although none of her artwork ever captured life— emotion—the way Cricket's portrait did. "Who is that?"

Cricket was quiet. Rachel glanced at her, wondering if she heard the question. When she opened her mouth to repeat it, Cricket spoke.

"That's my dad. And me. I was three." She handed Rachel the photo she was working from.

The image was grainy, probably taken with a disposable camera, but the angle of the shot was good, and the composition—

Rachel handed the photo back. She wasn't going there. No more photography.

The girls worked quietly. Rachel attempted her third sketch but scribbled it out as she had the others before it. Instead of holding a pencil in her hand, she felt as if she were gripping a jumbo marker in a mitten. She wiggled her fingers. What was wrong with them? Why wouldn't they work right?

"So, your mom died."

Rachel froze. The words rushed her like an avalanche. Her mind screamed run, but her body was too heavy to move. Her chest collapsed on her lungs, making it impossible to breathe. Only her heart survived, thudding violently against her ribcage.

"Mrs. Swane told me."

Instant fury ignited and heat rose up Rachel's neck, into her cheeks. Mrs. Swane? How could she? Although she barely knew the woman, Rachel was convinced if anyone understood her, the art teacher did. She didn't press her the first day they met or ooze sympathy when she realized who Rachel was, daughter of the deceased Maggie Blake. Instead, Mrs. Swane removed her from a situation, pulled her into her own world, and talked about art. She had rescued Rachel. Hadn't she?

Cricket looked at her, but Rachel couldn't stop the hot tears from forming. She jerked away sharply and stared toward the second story window, imagining how it would feel, how it would sound, if she could crash through the glass.

"It's okay. It happened to me, too."

It happened? Rachel shifted her gaze from the window to Cricket.

Cricket pointed a thumb at her masterpiece on the easel and looked into Rachel's eyes.

"You mean, your dad?" Rachel's whisper pushed passed her rage and ushered in a new feeling.

"Yeah, and it really sucks." She pulled out the chair next to Rachel and plopped down.

For the first time in a week, Rachel felt something for someone beside herself. She had been drowning, choking on the grief that swelled inside her that she thought only she experienced. Her dad couldn't feel what she did. He was an adult. And Olivia? Olivia infuriated her, living in her make-believe world. Mixed with empathy, Rachel felt something else. Was it relief? Gently, the slightest bit of heaviness lifted from her chest. She wasn't the only one.

"My dad died last year, cancer." Cricket crossed her arms on the table and rested her chin on top. "I had Mrs. Swane's class before lunch. After … you know … I hated going to the cafeteria, sitting at the table, listening to all the meaningless drama stupid teenagers think is so important. One day I couldn't resist telling them how stupid they were." She grinned. "Needless to say, it didn't take long for me to lose friends. But I didn't care. They didn't get it. Even my best friend didn't know how to be a friend when I needed her most. So, one day I asked Mrs. Swane if I could stay in here during lunch. And now I guess she figures you might need a place, too."

Maybe Mrs. Swane hadn't betrayed her after all. Rachel had so many questions, but she wasn't sure if she should ask, especially since the last thing she wanted was for anyone to ask her anything. But she had to know.

"Can I ask you something?"

Cricket raised an eyebrow.

"Was it hard, your dad dying of cancer? I mean, were you there?"

"Every day. And it was awful. He was in a so much pain and watching it, being there, was . . ."

Rachel's chest fluttered as sobs threatened to surface. Tears spilled over her lashes, but she wiped them away.

"But I wouldn't give that up." Cricket's voice quivered. "We cried a lot as time got closer, but we talked a lot, too, said things we probably never would have said."

"But you—" Rachel's voice sounded far away but the words were right there, waiting to escape. "You got to say good-bye?" She held back no longer. A sob stole her breath and shuddered through her chest.

Cricket's eyes filled as she covered Rachel's hand with her own. A clock above the teacher's desk ticked off each second. Birds, perched on a branch outside the window, chirped in the autumn sunshine.

Cricket exhaled. "It gets easier, I promise." She turned Rachel's palm up, pressed something in it, and closed her hand over it. "But until it does, this will help."

But it would never get easier. Because there was one thing Cricket didn't understand. Her dad had cancer. She wasn't the reason he died. Rachel winced and forced her secret deeper into the black pit in her heart where she kept it hidden.

The bell rang. Cricket grabbed her backpack and hesitated at the door. "See you Tuesday?"

Rachel nodded. As Cricket disappeared into the hallway, Rachel opened her hand to see what she had placed inside. It was a small white pill.

CHAPTER 10

Sam walked into the police station, surprised how comfortable it was, like lying down in his own bed after sleeping a week in a cheap hotel.

"Hey, L-T." The desk sergeant greeted Sam as he passed the lobby window and punched his code into a keypad on the wall. Without looking at the officer, he raised a hand in acknowledgement and opened the door leading to the interior offices, hoping to avoid all questions or expressions of sympathy.

The familiar scent of the department welcomed him as he walked down the hallway. When his office door came into view, he felt as if he were breaking free from a cocoon. Voices chattered inside.

"Lieutenant!" Detective Wade, seated behind Sam's desk, offered an outstretched hand.

Sam accepted the handshake then jerked his thumb upward at Wade. The detective sprang out of the lieutenant's chair

"Are you back?" Shaw rifled through paperwork strewn on the table in front of her.

"Maybe." Sam took the chair behind his desk and leaned back, hands locked behind his head. His pulse quickened. His brain rewired itself. This was familiar. "So what's going on?"

"Still waiting on DNA from the hair sample for the Simms case. The regional crime lab is backlogged, as always." Wade leaned against the doorframe. "So we've spent the last few days trying to bust an arson and burglary ring. Three vacant buildings have been burned, and on the same nights about the time fire and police were dispatched to the scenes, businesses on the opposite side of town were broken into. We were suspicious after the second one. With the third, we figured it was a definite pattern."

Nikki Shaw held up a crime scene photo for Wade to relay to Sam.

"It never amazes me how smart stupid people can be sometimes." Sam shook his head and took the photo.

"We've been making progress on the arson investigation while waiting for the crime lab." Shaw glanced from her paperwork to Sam, opened her mouth as if to say more, but stopped.

"So, how are you doing?" Wade placed a hand on Sam's shoulder.

Determined to keep his armor intact, Sam ignored the hole Wade punctured. "You need to call the crime lab and get the DNA expedited. Remind them the homicide victim was an off-duty officer." He shuffled through a pile stacked on his desk to see what required his attention. He needed to sign time records, schedule his detectives for the shooting range to qualify their weapons, build the work schedule for next quarter. At the bottom of the pile was a subpoena for him to give an affidavit in a hit and run. He needed to get back to work, to get back to himself. "Is the chief in today?"

"I don't think so. I heard him say something about a budget meeting with the mayor." Wade looked at Shaw to affirm.

She nodded, so Sam directed his attention to the mundane paperwork in front of him. Mundane or not, it had to get done. While he struggled to focus, he sensed Nikki Shaw watching him.

"Here." She pushed a file across Sam's desk. "You can go over what we have on the arson-burglary."

Sam grabbed the file without looking at her. He flipped through the pages, absorbing each detail as it pulled him further from his desk and deeper into the crime scene. Something was about to click. He could feel it as his brain sifted through fact after fact. His eyes narrowed to study a particular report, and then he snapped his fingers.

"What is it?" Wade stepped behind him and read over his shoulder.

Sam lifted the phone from the base and punched numbers.

"What you got, L-T?" Wade shrugged at his partner. She shrugged back.

Still, Sam gave no response.

Wade huffed. "I hate when he does that." His smile spoke otherwise.

"Detective Wilson. This is Lt. Sam Blake from Cape Spring P.D. We're investigating an apparent arson-burglary ring. You had a rash of arson and burglaries not too long ago, if I remember correctly. Did you make any arrests? No? I see. Well, I'm checking over our investigation now, and the fire marshal made some unusual remarks about the accelerant. Yours, too, huh?" Sam clenched his jaw and thrust a thumbs-up at his detectives.

"I hate when he does that, too." Wade grinned, crossing his arms in front of him.

"It sounds like we need to get together on this for a joint investigation. Detectives Wade and Shaw will be in touch. You're welcome, Detective Wilson. And thank you."

Sam leaned back in his chair and snickered. "I get more accomplished in twenty minutes than you jokers do in a week."

"Yeah, thanks to our grunt work." Wade pointed from himself to Shaw.

She remained silent.

"Hey, I'm only kidding, Shaw." Sam leaned forward to rest his arms on the desk.

She attempted a laugh. "Yeah, I know."

He waited for more, but the silence lasted a moment too long for his comfort. "Well, detectives, I'm going to pick up my girls from school. I'll be in Monday morning to talk to the chief."

Wade grinned like he had driven in the game-winning run. "Good to have you back."

Shaw cleared her throat and retrieved the file from Sam's desk. And Lieutenant Sam Blake walked out the door, feeling less like himself with every step he took away from the office.

"Daddy, I like the way Mommy makes mac and cheese better." Olivia pushed the pasta around on her plate with her fork.

Rage, like a river of molten lava, poured through Rachel's head. She hated when Olivia talked about their mom, and she did it all the time. *Mommy sang to me . . . Mommy doesn't want you to do that . . . Mommy says . . .*

"Olivia, just eat it. It's the kind out of the box, the cheesiest. It's good." With an exaggerated scooping motion, her dad filled his fork and put it in his mouth to demonstrate how delicious it was.

"By the way, Rachel, you left your computer on again." He waited for her response, but she scowled instead. "You need to shut it down when you're not using it."

"Mommy doesn't make it out of a box." Olivia's whine intensified.

Rachel's insides rumbled. The red-hot lava bubbled up, reaching the crucial point of eruption. "Shut up, Olivia! Stop talking about Mom all the time like she's still here!"

Her dad's head snapped in her direction. "Rachel, stop—"

"I can't take it!" She screamed at her dad then turned toward her sister and leaned in, face-to-face, nose-to-nose. "She's dead. Dead! And she's not coming back to play with you, and she doesn't sing to you, and she doesn't talk to you—"

"She does too talk to me!"

"Hey! Hey!" Her dad tried to intervene but Rachel refused to allow it.

"I'm sick of it. She lives in some fantasy land—and you—you just sit there and let her! You have to make her stop this!"

Her sister's chin quivered. Rachel shook with fury. And her dad, all he did was look from her to Olivia and back at her again. Useless.

"Being a detective is so much easier than parenting." He inhaled and held it. "Livi, Rachel is right."

Finally.

Betrayal covered Olivia's face. "No, she's not, Daddy! She doesn't know!"

Tears spilled from her little sister's eyes, and Rachel didn't care, but her dad apparently did. He pushed back his chair and held out his arms. He'd melted, of course.

"Come here, Sissy."

Olivia climbed on his lap and wrapped her arms around his neck. As she buried her face into his shoulder, hiccups shook her body. Rachel wanted to vomit.

"Okay, honey. It's okay."

She erupted again. "No, it's not, Dad. It's not okay. I don't believe you! You're as bad as she is, living in your own little world, ignoring everything around you, so you don't have to deal with it. At least she has an excuse—she's five!"

"Hey—" Her dad issued a warning she chose to ignore.

"Mommy is too here." Sobs choked Olivia's weak attempt at one final argument.

Rachel shoved back her chair and stood up, glaring at her sister. "Oh yeah?" Her voice cracked. Suddenly, she didn't have enough oxygen. Her ears pounded; her eyes blurred. But she couldn't retreat now. "If Mom is really here, then why does she only talk to you? Why—"

She was crumbling. The eruption had weakened her stony exterior and the walls were caving in. It was her turn to fight back tears.

"Why . . . doesn't she talk to me?" She threw her napkin on her plate and raced to her bedroom.

From the empty seat at the dining room table, Maggie watched her family unravel.

Sam paused at Rachel's bedroom on his way to tuck in Olivia, surprised the door was closed and the lights were out already. After the dinner theatrics, he spent the rest of the evening rehearsing the conversation he knew he must have with Rachel, though he wasn't sure how. Such an outburst from her was a rarity, but she was right on all accounts. Olivia needed to stop pretending, he needed to make her, and it was driving them both crazy. But there was one thing Rachel said that he didn't want to think about, that he couldn't shake because at some level he wondered it as well. What if Maggie really were there? And if she were, why couldn't he know it, too? He shook his head. It was official. He was losing it.

He turned the doorknob and opened Rachel's door enough to cast a sliver of light from the hallway into her room. He peeked in, trying to detect if she were faking sleep. He wasn't sure. "Rachel?" He approached her bed. She didn't move but her breathing quickened. "Honey, I'm sorry. You're right. I want you to know I know that. I promise I'll try to deal with Olivia and this pretending thing, okay?" He waited in case she responded. When she didn't, he leaned over and kissed her cheek. "I love you, Rach."

"Love you, too."

Her whisper was salve to his wounded heart. He brushed his hand over her hair, hoping she would open her eyes, say more, but she didn't. He rested his lips on her forehead and absorbed the moment before leaving to tuck in Olivia.

Sam found Olivia arranging the stuffed animals on her bed.

"Okay, Lambie, you get to sleep up here by my pillow next to Horsey." She put her mouth against Lambie's ear, and her voice lowered to a raspy whisper. "Because you're my favorite." Then she picked up a bear and placed him on the other side of her pillow. "Teddy, you go right here. And Baby, I'll hold you." She wrapped her arm around a stuffed doll wearing a diaper and a blue bonnet. Then she patted the edge of her bed and addressed them all. "We'll save this place for Mommy. She can lay with us when she gets tired."

The pulse at Sam's temple throbbed. He hadn't planned to follow through on his promise to Rachel so soon. Besides, his motive for ignoring Olivia's obvious state of denial was somewhat selfish. Yes, he would feel more comfortable interrogating a treacherous criminal. And yes, he enjoyed Olivia sleeping in her own bed once she believed Maggie was with her. But forcing his little girl to admit her mommy really was gone felt cruel. For three days he'd watched Olivia wrestle with understanding that her mom could die and would never come back. She'd grieved from a place so deep he couldn't bear to face it himself. Then, after the funeral, Olivia had changed. How could he force her back there, back to that despair?

"Olivia, honey, are you ready to be tucked in?"

She hopped onto her bed. "Say bedtime prayers with me."

The muscles across Sam's shoulders tensed. He did good night kisses and tucking in. Maggie did bedtime stories and prayers. "Why don't you say your prayers after I turn out the light?"

"Pray, Daddy." She pouted.

Sam cleared his throat and looked away. "I'm not very good at praying, Livi." He pulled up the covers and tucked them in all around her.

"It's just talking to God. That's what Mommy says. Just talk to God like he's your friend sitting right in front of you."

He had no escape. "Well, how about you show me, and I'll listen."

Her cheeks blossomed as he kneeled at the edge of her bed. She clasped her hands together, fingers interlocked, and squeezed her eyes closed.

Despite stretching his already-thin patience even thinner, Olivia's long list of blessings touched a tender place in his heart. "Amen," Sam echoed when she finished.

"Butterfly kisses." Olivia presented her cheek.

He leaned in close and blinked several times, brushing his eyelashes against her face.

"Eskimo." She ordered and he obeyed.

"Puppy love."

Sam rubbed his cheek against hers.

"I love you, Daddy."

Olivia looked up with trusting eyes, and every part of Sam wanted to hold her, to protect her from everything bad in the world. But he couldn't.

"Love you, too." He hesitated, trying to decide how to begin. "Livi?"

"Hmm?" She snuggled into the blankets.

"Is, uh—" He cleared his throat again. "Is . . . Mommy here?"

"No."

"Oh." That was not the answer he had anticipated. Now what? He fought the temptation to abandon the conversation and retreat while he had the chance. He forced himself to try again. "Where is she?"

Olivia shrugged and rolled onto her side to face him. "Maybe she's in Rachel's room. Or in your room."

"Is that where Mommy goes sometimes?"

"Mommy goes there all the time. She goes everywhere in the house, so she can be with us."

"Hm." His ears grew warm. "So, do you think she'll be coming in here soon?"

"She always helps me go to sleep. She rocks and tells me stories. Sometimes she sings to me." Olivia shifted to her back and hugged her doll to her chest. "If I wake up at night, she lays with me."

Her answers were specific, disturbing, but Sam's curiosity was peaked. "Do you, uh, see her?"

Olivia pursed her lips and shook her head. "I hear her, in my head not my ears. She tells me when she's in the rocker. And she asks if she can lay by me."

"Does she ever say anything? I mean, besides stories or singing? Does she say anything important?" His words sounded foreign to him. Who was asking these questions?

Olivia yawned. "She wants me to keep my room clean. To help you."

Sam surveyed the bedroom. Books were tucked into the bookcase. Markers were stored in their plastic container on the desk. Even the toy box closed all the way with no doll clothes or plastic animals bulging from underneath the lid. Olivia moved her stuffed lamb closer on her pillow. "She said maybe she saw Heaven, but she isn't sure." She turned to face Sam. "Mommy said it's gonna be beautiful."

Hairs tingled on the back of his neck. Olivia's imagination was remarkable, tempting even him to get caught up in her make-believe. But this had to end. "Honey, you know, people who believe in Heaven think that's where they go when they die."

"I know."

"And, your mom, well, if she were to see Heaven, it would mean she would have to die."

"She did die, Daddy." Her blue eyes were wide and honest.

What was going on in Olivia's little mind? How could he help her sort this out? "Well, if you know Mommy died, why do you keep pretending she's still here?" It was a gentle question, but he couldn't mask the accusation in his voice.

"I'm not pretending. She *is* here." Olivia squeezed her fists as she hugged her doll tighter. "She died. She just didn't go away. She doesn't know why." Her voice grew softer. She was tired of the debate.

Sam let her win. "Well, maybe we'll talk some more another day." He leaned in to kiss her a final time. "Good night, sissy."

"Daddy, Mommy wishes you and Rachel weren't so sad."

Sam let the words linger. He caressed his little girl's hair, twirled a blonde curl around his finger. So innocent. "Me, too. We just miss her. A lot."

"I miss her, too, Daddy." Her whisper twisted his heart. "I know she's here, but it's not the same. But I try not to be sad because I don't want to make her sad."

"Oh, she understands." His hand curved around her delicate cheek. "She knows how much we miss her. And I bet she misses us, too."

What was he saying? His mixed message would add to Olivia's confusion. He clarified. "If there is a Heaven, Mommy is there, looking down. So even if we can't see her, maybe she can see us."

Olivia narrowed her stare. "There is a Heaven, but Mommy's not there." She rolled to her side. Her back faced him. "She said she's standing behind you."

Sam sprang up and cursed under his breath. "Olivia, it's time for sleep." He turned off the lamp beside her bed and hurried out of the room.

CHAPTER 11

It was Saturday and Maggie was happy. The weekdays had been lonely with Rachel and Olivia at school. She anticipated a day of family activity bringing her home to life, even though she was only a spectator watching from the sidelines. The sun shone through the living room windows, and noise from the girls' bedrooms told Maggie they were awake. Sam, on the other hand, was still sleeping soundly, Maggie guessed. She spent most of the night in their bedroom, watching him lie awake until the early hours. She recognized the deep concentration on his face and wondered what thoughts were churning inside his head, keeping him from the rest he needed.

She reflected on the events of the last evening, and though it was painful to watch the personal battles each of them fought, she hoped it was the beginning of her family coming together. Sam had admitted to Rachel, and to himself, that he needed to stop avoiding tough conversations. And he seemed a little more willing to listen to Olivia. Maybe there was hope for healing.

Her plans for the day focused on Rachel. She was

determined to reach her. Rachel admitted she was hurt because only Olivia had a connection with Maggie. Surely that would give Maggie some kind of opening, a way in.

She approached the bedroom doorway. Rachel was awake, lying on her back with both arms at her sides, music escaping her earphones as she stared at the ceiling, oddly calm. She held something in her fingers, rolling it back and forth. As Maggie moved closer, Rachel raised her hand and studied the object pinched between her thumb and finger. Maggie went numb. It was a pill she did not recognize. Instinct took over.

"What is that, Rachel?" She demanded to know, even though Rachel couldn't hear her. "What are you doing? I'm here, Rachel! I'm here!"

No matter how much Maggie yelled, the only indication Rachel showed that she was aware of Maggie's presence was the usual increase of agitation. She gripped the pill in her fist and violently punched the mattress in sync with the bass booming through the earphones. Maggie grabbed Rachel's fist to force her fingers open, so she could take the pill away from her. But her daughter's hand passed through her grip. No matter how hard she tried, she could not make physical contact with her. Rachel pounded more fiercely.

"Stop it, Rachel! This is not who you are!"

As if to rebel against her mother's commands, Rachel whispered, coarse and fierce. "Cricket, I hope you're right." She opened her hand, and without looking at its contents, quickly popped the pill into her mouth. Her eyes widened. Her movements stopped as the bass thumped on without her. Maggie tried to read her expression. Shock? Disbelief? Whatever it was didn't last. Resolve took its place as she clenched her jaw and held her breath.

Maggie sank to the floor in surrender and hid her face in her hands. "Please, God, help me! I don't know what to do!"

A sudden movement pulled Maggie from her desperate plea. Rachel stood beside her desk; she spit the pill into the trashcan. As pieces of the dissolved pill fell, relief seeped through Maggie's body, leaving a trail of weakness in its wake.

Her daughter placed both hands on the edge of her desk. Leaning forward, she whispered just loudly enough for Maggie to hear. "This is not who I am."

Warm tears trailed down Maggie's face. Had Rachel heard her? She stood to walk closer to her daughter, to hold her, protect her. But as she reached out, Rachel's body tightened, her fists clenched. Maggie stepped back. Rachel took a deep, cleansing breath. Not yet.

While she could not describe the depth of her relief, Maggie could hardly count it a victory. Confusion and terror ran through her. What was the pill? Where did she get it? Who was Cricket? Although Maggie believed Rachel needed her now more than ever, she helplessly moved toward the door, giving her daughter space.

Although she left Rachel's room, Maggie knew she couldn't ignore what she had just witnessed. She ran to her own bedroom where Sam was still sound asleep.

"Sam!" Maggie yelled from the doorway. "Wake up! You have to wake up!"

She hurried to the bed, leaned over and yelled directly into his ear. "You have to go to Rachel! Wake up!"

Still, there was no sign her words impacted him. Her frustration multiplied as she gripped his shoulder to shake him, but again, she was unable to make physical contact.

She looked around, desperate for a solution. The picture frame. Could she slam it down loudly enough to wake him? She reached for it, but her grip had no effect. She remembered: the family was present, the girls wide awake.

"Please, Sam." Her voice weakened. "Don't fail Rachel."

But the truth was Maggie was the failure. She had failed Sam. Her promise was nothing but emptiness because no matter how hard she tried, she couldn't help Rachel. And she couldn't help him. He was on his own. "Please," she whispered one last time.

Accepting defeat, she retreated to the chair in the corner. A myriad of emotions washed over her, but anger left the deepest mark. What was happening to her family? Rachel was not the kid who took pills as a desperate escape. And Sam wasn't a father unaware of danger that threatened his home. Yet if he remained oblivious to Rachel's needs, how could he stop what Maggie had just witnessed? But her sharpest anger was aimed at herself, at her inability to help her children, her husband, the very people at the center of her existence.

She leaned her head back, tilted her face upward. *Why am I here if I can do nothing but watch my family fall apart? Are you punishing me, God? Is that what this is? For the times I wasn't the mother or wife I should have been?*

She buried her face in her hands and let guilt wash over her as she recalled the crimes that may have led to this punishment. The time when Olivia was three and Maggie left her in the bathtub to go answer the phone. She could still hear the crash as Olivia slipped trying to get out of the tub, and her screams in the ER as they stitched her chin. And all the times Rachel begged for Maggie's undivided attention to play a game or to watch a movie when Maggie had been consumed by buyer-seller negotiations. How many times had she put work before her girls? Before her husband? How often had she denied Sam the physical connection he desired, knowing it had been too long, but needing sleep more than she needed him?

"That's it, isn't it, God?" Maggie lifted her chin and raised her voice, certain this time her words were heard. "You're punishing me."

Her hands trembled with fury. What did God expect? Hadn't she done her best most of the time? She'd lived her life exhausted, always trying to meet the demands placed on her. She wasn't perfect, but didn't she try her hardest to be a loving mom, a supportive wife, and to build a successful business so her girls could grow up secure? Isn't that what a parent is supposed to do? And hadn't she been committed to raising the girls in church, without Sam most of the time? Her fingernails bit into her palms.

"Okay, so this is it? My punishment is to watch my family suffer and think about all the opportunities I missed? To agonize over the damage that now I can't do anything about?" Rage pulsed in her temples.

She leaned back, drained, and closed her eyes. She had one last question. "Is this my eternity?" Her heart ached at the thought. She did not want to leave her family, but if she could do nothing to help them, what was the point?

A tingle in Maggie's chest startled her. She opened her eyes and sat upright. She recognized it, almost physical, the same sensation she had in the place where she'd seen Nate. As it grew stronger, heaviness radiated from her torso, through her arms, and exited her body through her fingertips. Until that moment, she had not realized how heavy the burden for her family had grown throughout the past week. She tried to access the anger that had consumed her only moments ago. It was gone. While she could still detect a sense of sadness, it was once again dull and distant. Peace slowly replaced the turmoil. Love once again became her principal emotion.

Then somehow she knew. This wasn't punishment. This wasn't her eternity. And though she still felt helpless, she was confident a time would come when she would understand.

"Forgive me." She rose from the chair, grateful for the renewed strength.

Sam rolled over and opened his eyes. If he could see Maggie, he would have been staring right at her.

"Good morning, honey." Maggie smiled.

Sam reached for the frame on the night stand and pulled it closer. "Morning, Mags," he said to the picture.

Sam crawled out of bed feeling like he had gone three rounds in a cage fight. But one glance at the clock told him it was past time to be up and moving.

Olivia, he saw, had migrated to the family room to watch cartoons.

"Hey, Livi."

"Morning, Daddy." She waved her hand without breaking her trance from the screen.

"How do chocolate chip pancakes sound?"

"Yummy!"

"Okay then. Chocolate chip pancakes coming right up. But first, let me wake Rachel."

Sam found Rachel lying on her bed with her cell phone in her hand, fingers frantically dancing across the keys.

"Good morning." He was curious if she'd acknowledge their exchange last night.

"Hmm." She stayed focused on the screen.

"Who you texting?"

"A friend."

"Kristen?"

"Mmm."

Rachel's terse responses drained Sam's tolerance. He'd hoped they had taken a step forward.

"Rachel Nicole, put that down and talk to me."

She lowered the phone to her stomach and glared at him with raised eyebrows. A challenge?

His temperature escalated. "Listen, young lady, I understand you're going through a lot right now—we all are. But that is no excuse for your disrespect. I've tried to understand your frustration with Olivia, and to give you space when you disappear into your bedroom, but this attitude has to stop. Now, I am going to ask you one more time. Who are you texting?" Her expression didn't change. Was it still attitude? A bluff? Finally she spoke.

"Kristen."

"Kristen, huh?" He had an idea. "Why don't you ask her to come over, maybe spend the night? A girls' night— that would be good, wouldn't it?" It might not be so good for him, but he was willing to sacrifice a peaceful afternoon if it meant hearing Rachel giggle and be a silly girl for a few hours.

"Uh, no." The answer was too quick.

"No? Why not?"

"Just no. It's complicated, Dad." She rolled her eyes.

"Okay. Wanna talk about it?"

As if weighing the option, Rachel looked at her father.

Sam shrugged and held up his palms, acknowledging his lack of expertise in girl drama, but hoping she would accept his invitation.

"It's just—" Rachel shook her head. "She doesn't understand. She doesn't know what it feels like right now, you know? And I don't want to talk about who she has a crush on, or what new movie is coming out."

It was an opening. He had to take it. He walked over to her bed and sat down next to her. "What *do* you want to talk about?" Silence hung between them for several moments before he persisted. "You know, you can talk to me, Rach."

She turned her face away from him, but he saw her chin quiver and her teeth press into her bottom lip.

"Rachel?"

"I can't."

Her whisper punctured his heart. His own tears swelled as he watched his daughter wrestle with her grief. He wanted to reach out, to comfort his little girl, but he wasn't sure how, or if he should. She was such a mystery in so many ways. To compromise, he gently stroked her hair as he waited for his voice to return, uncertain what to say when it did. He decided not to push. Their conversation, though brief, was the most meaningful exchange they had shared since their nightmare began. For now, it was enough.

"Well, if you feel like breakfast, I'm making chocolate chip pancakes."

Rachel nodded then turned on her side to face the wall.

Before her dad came into her room, Rachel had texted Kristen to see if she was still mad about the project. She was willing to admit Kristen was right; she had dumped the project on her. If Rachel didn't want to think about black and white photography, she could have at least come up with another way to contribute.

Rachel did not get a response to her first text. But after the second text, when Kristen did respond, Rachel wished she hadn't. Yes, Kristen was still mad. It was too late for sorry. No, she didn't want to do something today. Then Rachel got angry. And the more she thought about it, the angrier she became. Kristen was so selfish. She didn't know what it was like to lose her mom. She would never understand. Suddenly, Kristen's friendship seemed unnecessary. Rachel didn't have to explain things to Cricket. Cricket understood. Mostly.

Then came her dad's interrogation. And he wanted her to talk, seriously? What would she tell him? Did he expect her to describe the pain that pulsed throughout her body each time her heart beat? Or how every nerve ending burned with anger? Or maybe . . . maybe he was waiting for her to confess.

Did he know about the text? The one she'd sent her mom? The thought made every muscle in her body quake. Did he know the accident was her fault? That her mom was dead, his wife was dead, and everything was falling apart because of her? The night that Detective Wade described the accident, she heard him say it. Surely, her dad had to hear it, too. From the witness's description of how sharply her mom veered into the other lane, she must have been distracted, that maybe she had reached for something, her purse, her cell phone.

Every time Rachel thought she was strong enough to suppress the guilt, something forced it to the surface. This morning it was her dad. Maybe she couldn't do this by herself. Maybe Cricket was right. Maybe she should have taken the pill. Would it make all the feelings go away? She texted Cricket.

> *Hey*
> *Sup*
> *What was that u gave me*
> *Take it?*

She didn't want to admit she chickened out.

> *Sorta.*
> *It help*
> *Dunno yet what was it*
> *Oxy pain med*
> *K cu*
> *K*

Pain medicine? Her dad took pain medicine after his wisdom teeth were removed. She tiptoed from her bedroom and peeked from the hall into the kitchen. Her sister stood on a chair beside her dad in front of a griddle, placing chocolate chips on a pancake, making a smiley face no doubt. Her dad flipped the pancake and Olivia started on the next one. Rachel ducked back before they saw her, and then snuck into her parents' bathroom. Cautious not to make noise, she pulled open the medicine cabinet and scanned the shelves. There it was. A prescription bottle with her dad's name on it. She skimmed the label. *Take for pain. Oxycodone.* Oxy. That must be the same thing. She pressed down firmly on the cap and turned it until it opened. Several pills were inside. She should take only a few, so her dad wouldn't know they were missing. She replaced the cap and closed the medicine cabinet.

"What are you doing?"

Her dad's voice triggered a rush of adrenaline. She squeezed the pills tightly in her fist and froze. Her heart pounded so loudly she could barely hear her response. "I have a headache."

"You know you're not supposed to take anything without asking first. Besides, the ibuprofen is in the kitchen."

"Oh yeah. I forgot."

"Well, come eat some pancakes. See if a little food takes care of your headache before you take anything."

Relieved he hadn't noticed the pills in her hand, Rachel hoped her weak knees could carry her to the kitchen without collapsing.

The phone rang as Sam put pancakes on the table. He checked the caller ID. Pastor Rob. He should ignore it, but if he did, the guy would probably keep calling. He answered, annoyed, hoping the pastor could hear it.

"Hey, Sam. I hope this isn't a bad time. I wanted to call to see how you're doing."

The edge in the pastor's voice suggested he'd picked up on Sam's tone. Unsure why, a hint of guilt nipped at him. He eased his grip on the phone and summoned a dose of patience.

"Well, we're making it, I guess. Trying to find our way back to normal."

"Things are different now, you know. You might need to adjust your expectations, find a new normal."

"A new normal?" Sam hated to admit it, but the pastor was right. He had spent the days since Maggie's death wondering how long until life would feel like it had before the accident.

"It seems impossible now, but one day you'll wake up and things will feel normal, just different normal. It's a strange transition, but it will happen in time." The pastor's voice relaxed. "How are the girls?"

Sam thought about it. "Better. We kind of had a meltdown last night, but I think that was a good thing."

"Is it anything I can help with? Your family has endured a lot. Have you considered counseling?"

Counseling? The very thought of a practical stranger manipulating his emotions like a game of Jenga set Sam on edge. He didn't respond.

The pastor broke the silence. "Well, I had another reason for calling. If you like, we can pick up the girls in the morning. We drive right past your neighborhood."

"In the morning?" Sam was confused. "Oh, tomorrow, Sunday. Yeah, uh, I'm not sure."

"Unless you're planning to bring them?" The edge returned to Rob's voice.

"Don't think so." It would take more than a phone call to get him in a church pew, but Maggie would want the girls to go. "If it's not too much trouble to stop by on your way through, the girls will be ready."

Sam hung up the phone, not anticipating the battle that would ensue.

"Who was that?" Olivia stuffed a forkful of pancake into her mouth.

"Pastor Rob. His family is going to pick you up on their way to church tomorrow."

Rachel pushed her breakfast away. "I'm not going."

"What do you mean you're not going?" She rarely missed church or youth group before the accident. He thought she'd be happy to go back.

"I mean I'm not going."

Tension emanated from Rachel. He forged ahead carefully, uncertain what might set her off. "Why not?"

"Why?"

Sam didn't expect that question. He fumbled for an answer. "Because your mom would want you to go to church."

Rachel raised her eyebrows. There it was again—the challenge. "So? She wanted you to go, but you didn't."

"That's different. I'm an adult. That's my decision to make." His argument was full of holes, but it was the best he had.

"It's not different. You know church doesn't do any good. That's why you don't go. Now I know it, too. And I'm not going. Not to church and not to youth group." Rachel locked her arms in front of her.

Olivia dropped her fork on her plate. "But I want to go to church, Daddy."

Rachel directed her rebuttal toward her little sister. "Don't be dumb, Olivia. It's a waste of time."

"Daddy!"

Olivia's eyes searched him for answers, answers he did not have. Should he force Rachel to go to church? Somehow he felt that was the right thing to do, but how could he with the precedent he'd set? And he certainly wasn't in an emotional place to step through the doors himself for the sake of setting an example for his daughters. Shouldn't he, of all people, understand where Rachel was coming from?

"It's okay, Livi. You can go to church."

Olivia smiled and took bite of bacon.

"And me?" Rachel lifted her chin.

Sam inhaled deeply, sensing he was about to make a big mistake, but unable to justify any other answer. He shrugged and shook his head.

Rachel pulled her plate back toward her and picked up her fork.

CHAPTER 12

Sam opened the pantry. The calendar hanging inside the door was still turned to September even though the chill of the October air had settled in days ago. He lifted the page and found today's date. He counted back . . . three, four, five weeks since Maggie's green eyes last looked into his and locked briefly above the chatter of the girls and the noisy dinner activity, stealing a moment for the two of them before she rushed off to meet her clients. The familiar emptiness settled in, like a part of him had been hollowed out. How could five weeks have passed so quickly when each day was such a struggle?

He and the girls had settled into a semblance of routine he supposed. He returned to work part-time. The chief generously accommodated his needs as a single dad, allowing him to take the girls to school on his way to work and leave early to pick them up in the afternoon. Although it was unspoken, his lenient schedule was temporary, but a suitable solution eluded him. He considered allowing the girls to ride the school bus, but Olivia's bus arrived home nearly a half hour earlier than Rachel's, and leaving

Olivia home by herself was unthinkable. Sam's job kept his protective instinct in overdrive. It would be too easy for a predator to pick up on the routine, and he refused to put Olivia at risk. And even if the school bus were an option, investigations didn't take place only during banker's hours. At times the girls could be alone until late into the night. That wasn't acceptable either.

And parenting didn't take place only after work hours, Sam learned. A meeting with the school counselor ended his day early because she insisted they discuss Olivia's inability to accept her mother's death. Phone calls from Rachel's teachers prompted a conference with the principal to discuss her dropping grades. And more than once, Sam had to apologize to an agitated kindergarten teacher in a nearly empty parking lot as she consoled his crying little girl because he was late. He quickly developed a new appreciation for Maggie.

Sam grabbed a bag of chips before he closed the pantry door. The girls were asleep, and it was past time for him to be in bed, too. But he chose the recliner and an old WWII movie instead. Staring mindlessly at the television, he contemplated what the pastor said about finding a new normal. He thought about it, desired it. He could hardly remember what normal felt like five weeks ago, and he couldn't imagine what normal might feel like in the future. But whatever it was he felt now, he didn't want normal to be that.

The doorbell rang. Sam froze. His heart thudded wildly as the sound transported him back to the night of Maggie's accident. His muscles turned to liquid as he relived the moments after answering the door. The doorbell rang again, followed by several sharp knocks. Sam took a deep breath to regain control and stood. He glanced at the clock, almost 11:00, and hurried to the door before the bell rang again and woke the girls. Through the peephole he saw his detectives waiting. He opened the door.

"The DNA report came in earlier this evening." Nikki Shaw shifted from one foot to the other and turned toward the steps. "Officers picked up a prostitute. They're holding her at the station for questioning."

"The P.A.'s there waiting on you—" Wade's voice trailed after Sam, who had already crossed the living room and headed to his bedroom. He retrieved his coat, his weapon, and his badge. When he grabbed his cell phone from the nightstand, the screen lit up with several missed calls.

Sam approached the detectives. "So what do we know?" He stepped through the doorway, pulled the door closed behind him, and turned to insert his key into the dead bolt.

He stopped. What was he thinking? He couldn't go to the station at this time of night and leave the girls. The detectives charged down the steps, relaying details. They were beside the car before they realized Sam was not with them.

"You coming, Lieutenant?" Shaw opened the driver's door.

Was he? His instincts battled. The girls would be alone, sleeping. But the break in the Simms case could be sitting at the station right now. He looked at the time on his phone, at the patrol car, at his hand gripping the key in the deadbolt. Two hours. If he couldn't get the information they needed in two hours, he would turn the interrogation over to someone else and return home without the girls ever knowing he had left.

Sam turned the key and tested the door. Certain the house was secure, he bounded down the steps and slid into the passenger seat. "What've we got?"

Shaw shoved the car into reverse and backed into the street. "A white female, early twenties, alias Crystal Starr. Apparently her boss runs a big operation in Memphis and has been trying to expand his territory. He moved Crystal and a few other girls into an apartment here at the beginning of the summer. As for the homicide, she claims to know nothing."

"What do we know about her boss?"

"Not much. His name is Emmanuel 'Manny' Jackson, white male, 36." Detective Wade handed Sam a file from the backseat. "We ran him, but he came back clean. I talked to narcotics. They've been working with Memphis P.D., watching him when he's in town. He drives a blacked-out BMW. Our guys stopped him twice for minor traffic violations. He consented to a search but came up clean both times. He's slick. Everybody knows what he's doing, but nobody can catch him at it."

"He hasn't made the right mistake yet." Sam opened the file and studied a surveillance photo of Jackson. "But he will."

The rest of the ride was silent. Sam sifted through the details, calculating as he added them up, but the bottom line did not compute. He refused to believe Ricky Simms would solicit services from a prostitute. Yet, they had to follow the evidence.

When they arrived at the station, the prosecutor greeted Sam in the lobby. "Lieutenant, it's shaky but this is our best shot, so I need you in charge of questioning. By the book."

Sam matched strides with him as they rushed toward the interrogation room. The men stood on the opposite side of a two-way mirror. On the other side sat a blonde girl with a tiny frame. She barely looked older than Rachel— his daughter, he reminded himself, who he'd left sleeping at home alone at this hour. "By the book," Sam repeated as he reached for the doorknob.

An hour later he exited the interrogation room with a written statement, a witness for the prosecution, and a renewed assurance that Ricky Simms was indeed the man Sam believed he was. As the witness talked, somewhere in Sam's brain a discarded conversation surfaced. Late in the summer, Simms had approached him about undercover work to get girls off the street and to a safe house Simms's church supported in the northern part of the state. Girls could get medical treatment, rehab, counseling—a new life. Simms had been persuasive, but Sam said no. Their unit didn't have the resources for an undercover operation— or for a religious mission, he'd added sarcastically. Ricky insisted, said he would do it on his own time if the lieutenant approved. But Sam didn't approve—and he'd forgotten about it. Now it all made sense. Ricky did it anyway. And Manny Jackson must have figured him out.

Sam looked at the clock and then at his detectives. "You got it from here?"

"Got it. Nice work, Lieutenant." Shaw tossed Sam her keys to the patrol car. "Wade can drop me at my apartment."

During the drive home, the adrenaline surge that had fueled Sam drained from his body. By the time he turned into his neighborhood, he had been hypnotized by the street lights. Suddenly, bright headlights flashed on, jerking him from his trance, blinding him. He raised his hand to shield his eyes, pulled into the drive, and parked. His side mirror reflected a solitary car parked across the street from his home. It was blacked out, a BMW. A streetlight shining through the passenger window faintly outlined the silhouette of the driver.

Sam took a sharp breath, put his hand on his holster, and unsnapped it with his thumb. An engine revved, then the car slowly pulled away.

When Sam's key turned in the lock, Maggie sank to her knees. She had never felt so powerless. Two hours ago she watched him transform seamlessly from a father into a detective without a moment's consideration for the sleeping daughters he would abandon. She had trailed him into the bedroom, scolding as he grabbed his gear, and followed him back through the living room, determined to stop him. But it was she who was stopped. As Sam reached the door and crossed the threshold, Maggie followed. But as she stepped into the darkness, faintness surged through her, depleting the essence of her existence. At first, she didn't understand. Then instinctively she grasped she was losing herself. With the energy that remained, she lunged into the house just as Sam closed the door. He secured the lock, and her strength was restored. She raced through her mind for an explanation, desperate to comprehend what had occurred. Then she remembered the website, what she'd read about the lingering spirit. This, her home, was her "location of importance." Inside was her unfinished task. So did that mean beyond her home she didn't exist? It must.

Maggie spent the first hour pacing like a sentry from the living room to the hallway that joined the girls' bedrooms. After that, she stationed herself in front of the living room window and didn't move. Finally headlights approached. She released a deep sigh, believing Sam had returned. She watched though the sheers as an unfamiliar car pulled up across the street. An unmarked police car dropping Sam off? Maybe. She grew suspicious when the engine stopped, but no one got out. It was difficult to see through the car's tinted glass, but Maggie was certain the driver was staring at her house. And that Sam wasn't in the car.

After several minutes, the driver got out, gently pushed his door closed, and walked in her direction. As he climbed the front steps, fear seized her. She glanced at the door and watched the doorknob slowly turn. She imagined stepping in front of the door and pushing against it with all her force. But she was paralyzed. She stood alone, her husband at the station, her girls in their beds sleeping. She was incapable of protecting them. The force of a shoulder pushed against the door, stopped by the deadbolt. Then silence. Maggie waited for the driver to descend the steps, but he didn't. She stepped closer to the window and peered to the side toward the door. Suddenly, she gasped and jerked back. A face appeared, separated from Maggie's by a slim pane of glass. She froze as he looked through her and examined the inside of her home. She closed her eyes and prayed from a depth she'd never known. A final rattle of the doorknob startled her, and she watched the long strides that carried the driver back to his car, where he waited. For what?

Finally, the car Sam had left in turned onto their street. Relief washed through her but only momentarily. If the driver had malicious intent, and she was certain he did, Sam would be caught unaware. Bright headlights blared from the parked car, and suddenly Maggie felt as if she were living a movie.

So when she heard Sam's keys in the door, she sank to her knees where she stayed while Sam rushed down the hallway and opened each girl's bedroom door. She didn't have the strength, nor the words she needed to go after him. But what would it matter anyway? He didn't even know she was there.

CHAPTER 13

The Sunday morning alarm rang too soon. The last Sam remembered, 3:00 a.m. lit up the clock. Then, barely two hours into a fitful sleep, he woke to a ringing phone. It was Wade. Crystal Starr had been found in an alley beside her apartment building, an apparent heroin O.D. Sam recalled the sleeveless dress the girl had worn to the station. Her arms were clean. No track marks. His instinct told him this was no coincidence.

"He got to her."

Wade agreed. And they found themselves in a familiar predicament, with a homicide to solve and no evidence. Sam was certain he hadn't slept after the phone call, but the jolt of the alarm told him otherwise.

Sam willed himself out of bed to wake Olivia. On his way down the hall, he heard noises from Rachel's room. The door was cracked so he peered in. Rachel, consumed by her laptop, didn't notice him.

"Morning."

She jumped and quickly pushed down her computer screen. "Oh, morning."

"What're you doing?" he proceeded casually, pointing to the laptop.

"Messaging . . . Cricket."

"What's that?"

Rachel snickered. "Messaging, you know, direct messaging. It's a social media thing."

"And cricket? Is that a social media thing, too?"

"No—" Rachel bit her lip, but couldn't hold back a grin. "I told you about Cricket, remember? The art teacher introduced us."

"Oh yeah, weeks ago. But you haven't talked about her. I didn't realize you're friends now." Sam interrogated cautiously.

"Yeah."

Rachel seemed uncomfortable, trying to divert his attention with conversation, so he decided to take advantage of the free-flowing information.

"So, what about Kristen? I guess you two are still friends?"

"Sorta, I guess. It's just that . . . well . . . Cricket knows what it's like. Her dad died last year. It's easier being friends with her right now."

"Really? Hmm. So when am I going to meet this Cricket? I'd like to know who you're friends with."

Rachel shrugged. "Uh, soon, I guess."

"Humor me." He smiled, acting as casual as possible. "Mom knew all your friends."

She looked away. "Yeah."

"So . . . what's she like? What about her family?"

"Well, she has a brother in high school. And a mom."

"What else?"

Rachel shrugged again.

"For being friends, it doesn't seem like you know much about her."

"It's not like that. We just talk at school, at lunch mostly. She's in ninth grade so I don't see her most of the day, and we don't have a lot of time to talk about other stuff."

"Uh-huh." Something didn't quite settle with Sam. He walked closer to Rachel. "So you're messaging her now? Can I see?" He sat on the bed beside her.

"Dad," she protested. "Really?"

"Yeah. Really." Sam lifted the laptop lid. His eyebrows furrowed as he moved from one line to the next. "This is like reading a foreign language."

Rachel grinned. "That's how we message. Guess you're too old to understand it."

"Guess so." Sam turned the laptop back toward Rachel, relieved he hadn't seen anything concerning. He decided to change the topic. "So, it's Sunday. Church today?"

"Nope." Rachel's answer, as it had been every Sunday morning, was sharp.

Sam was too tired for his weekly hypocritical cajoling to convince her she needed to go back to church. Besides, connecting with that Cricket girl might be better for her than going to church anyway. But he had one last request before he left her alone.

"I need you to write down your login and password for me."

"You mean for my laptop?"

"Yeah, that and any accounts you have, social media, e-mail, whatever."

She groaned. "So, what, are you going to like start spying on me or something?"

Sam stopped at the door and looked directly at her. "If I have to. I'm your parent. It's my job. Put them on the kitchen counter sometime this morning."

Sam walked toward the church entrance and gave a quick wave to the pastor's wife as Olivia ran to her. He decided a few weeks ago that he would drive Olivia to church and then spend a couple hours in his office until it was time to pick her up. As he walked back to his car, he thought about the Simms case. Less than twelve hours earlier, he got the break he needed to bring to justice a fellow detective's killer and to possibly gain recognition for himself. Accolades from the chief and the mayor, local TV interviews, could all add up to good promotion material, preparing the way for a future behind the chief's desk someday. But now Sam feared his vision of the future was evaporating. Not only because one homicide investigation now had two victims, but also because of the black BMW parked outside his house, taunting him when he returned home from the station. And the girls. Once Sam had rushed down the hall and checked on each one to make sure they were unharmed, he'd leaned against the wall beside Rachel's bedroom door and fought back the nausea rushing through him.

Sam neared the church parking lot exit, prepared to turn toward the office. But, he didn't want to go in this morning. Technically, he had worked most of the night, and he needed a break. So, he pulled out and turned in the opposite direction, uncertain where to go for the next couple of hours. He continued driving south, all the while fighting an unsettling feeling that loomed.

As Sam drove, the city limits fell behind him, and rolling hills lay in front him, their vibrant fall colors nearing the end of their reign. He cracked the window to let in the fresh air and let himself sink into the driver's seat, heading nowhere in particular, leaving everything behind. He turned on a soft rock radio station and quietly sang along, mindlessly following the yellow lines where they led. For a few moments, his life was undisturbed, his mind at peace, suspended in a world in which only he, the music, and the countryside existed. Then he saw it. He pressed hard on the brake pedal and pulled to the shoulder of the road. After a quick check for traffic, he made a U-turn and pulled into the driveway. He stared at the sign in the yard. White with blue lettering, it read: FOR SALE *Another Excellent Property by Blake Real Estate, Maggie Blake, Broker.*

The Hitching house.

He read Maggie's name on the sign and looked at the house that was her dream, a dream Sam had not shared. A boulder crashed down on his chest. Breathing was nearly impossible, and grief threatened to strangle him. Maggie had seen potential and beauty, the vision of a real estate broker as well as a certified interior designer. Sam had only seen stress and money, his experience from working summers with his dad, and the lessons drilled into him from the time since he was old enough to hit a nail straight until he finished college: It's always easier to build new than to fix old.

Sam had walked the property a few times with Maggie, the first time to appease her as she tried to infect him with her desire to renovate the abandoned house. She'd gushed when she talked about turning the house into a B&B. Sam listened but offered little response. As Maggie neared the end of her long list of plans, her enthusiasm waned, and Sam almost felt guilty. It was a good dream, but it wasn't a practical dream. They didn't have the money or the time it would take to revive the old house, and Sam didn't have the desire. The second time he was on the property was a few months later when Maggie packed a lunch and the family picnicked on the back porch. The girls played in the yard while Sam and Maggie relaxed under a shade tree. And the last time was nearly a year ago. Maggie asked Sam to fix the broken lock box that held the key to the house. Her final ploy to convert him, he suspected. Soon after, Maggie's dream of turning the Hitching house into a B&B transformed into a dream of selling it to someone else who would, and she sought the dream with renewed vigor each time a buyer showed interest in the property, which wasn't often.

He got out of the car and faced the old house, its peeling paint, its sagging shutters, the last place that saw Maggie alive. He walked up the sidewalk, up the porch steps. He stood with his back to the front door, peering across the road, past the fields, and into the distant hills. If Olivia was right, if Maggie did come back, this is where she'd be. Sam sat on the top step and leaned forward, resting his forearms on his knees. Sorrow tightened around his throat.

"Mags." Her name sounded comfortable in the air around him. "I miss you so much." He lowered his head as he allowed his emotions to surface. He pushed past the grief of missing her, the anger of losing her in such a senseless way, and focused instead on the love he shared with his wife. "I don't know what to do without you. I need to know what you want me to do."

Sam studied the sign in the yard. "What about Blake Real Estate? How would you feel if I turned it over to Laura? And what do I do about the girls? I'm trying, but I'm not doing a very good job helping them through this. Olivia copes by escaping reality, and Rachel escapes by keeping herself distant." He lowered his head. "I don't know how I'm going to get myself through this."

Sam tried to imagine a time beyond this tragedy, a morning when he would wake up to sunshine streaming through the window, and his first action would be to breathe in the morning air rather than roll over to feel the empty place beside him. He wondered how it would be if the first thought on his mind were, *What am I going to do today?* Not, *How am I going to get through the day?* He doubted the possibility of a new normal.

"And what about my job?" Sam shook his head as he prepared for his confession. "I did something really stupid, Mags. Really stupid." His fists were clenched, and a vein bulged at his temple. He fought his imagination as he visualized scenarios of everything that could have gone wrong because he left the girls alone. "I feel like I'm two separate people—a father, and a detective—and without you, the two don't mix," Sam confessed. "But what choice do I have?"

He twisted the wedding ring on his finger. "I need you to tell me what to do."

He waited quietly for the burden to rise from his chest, but it didn't. This was the place life had led him to, and he was going to have to find the way out on his own. Resigned to accept there were no easy answers, Sam stood and walked to the front door. He tried the door knob, even though he knew it was locked. He pressed his forehead against the glass and peered into the foyer. He spotted the staircase Maggie loved and followed the steps to the landing at the top. He had never been upstairs. Maggie had tried to lure him up, to show him the possibilities, but he'd held back, pretending to be oblivious to her disappointment and how she tried to gloss over it. A sharp pain flicked through him. He shaded his eyes and counted doors, five maybe six bedrooms. Then he focused on the main floor, which he had toured with Maggie the first time she'd brought him to the Hitching house. He could see the formal living room on the right, and the entrance to the dining room beyond. His attention shifted to the hallway that ran along the left side of the staircase, straining to see into the galley kitchen that spanned the back of the house, but the dim light made it difficult. The house had potential, Sam admitted with a pang of guilt. He couldn't recall admitting that to Maggie, though. Every time she mentioned the Hitching house, he felt he had to maintain his guard, or risk giving her false hope.

He pushed away the shame and glanced at his watch. It was nearly time to pick up Olivia. He gave the doorknob one more twist then turned to go. He paused at the bottom step of the porch and looked at the house one final time.

"Bye, Mags," he whispered.

"Rachel!" Sam's voice echoed as he marched through the house. He opened the door to the basement and called her name into the darkness. When no answer came, he returned to her bedroom to search for a note, then to the kitchen. Surely she wouldn't leave without telling him where she was going. He checked his cell phone once more for a text he knew didn't exist. "Rachel!" he yelled again, releasing anger more than expecting an answer at this point. Olivia's voice mimicked Sam's throughout the house as she called for her sister.

He punched numbers into his cell phone and reached Rachel's voice mail. "Rachel, call me as soon as you get this." He hung up and typed a text with the same message. He dialed another number.

"Kristen, this is Sam Blake. Is Rachel with you?"

"No. . . ?" Kristen answered with a question in her voice.

"Do you have any idea where she might be? I just got home and she's not here, and she's not answering her cell phone."

"I don't know, Mr. Blake. I haven't talked to Rachel in weeks."

Sam recalled his conversation with Rachel that morning. She didn't indicate that she and Kristen weren't talking at all.

"Kristen, is everything okay?"

"Well, yeah, I guess so. It's just that we kind of had a fight, about school stuff, and I know Rachel's going through a lot right now, but I kind of got mad at her. And we haven't really talked."

"I'm sorry to hear that, Kristen, but can you think of anyone who might know where she is?"

"There's this one girl. Maybe Rachel's with her. They've been hanging out at school. Her name's Cricket."

"Yeah, Rachel mentioned her. Do you know how to get a hold of her?"

"No. I don't know her really."

"Do you know her last name, where she lives, anything?"

"No, I'm really sorry. I never knew her till I saw Rachel eating lunch with her, but maybe that's where she is. I'm sorry I'm not much help. Mr. Blake, is everything okay?"

"Um, yeah, sure. Thanks, Kristen." Sam hung up and went to Rachel's room. He pushed a key to wake up her laptop. Maybe she made plans with Cricket while they were messaging. He didn't see anything. Her backpack rested against her desk. He pulled out notebooks and binders and flipped through pages, searching for anything about Cricket that Rachel may have written down, her last name, address, cell number, anything. The only items of interest were an algebra paper with red ink all over it and an 'F' at the top, and a scoring guide with a zero and a note in a teacher's writing: *Rachel, please see me for an extension on the science project.* Sam made a mental note to talk to Rachel about her schoolwork—again. He understood the last several weeks had been difficult, nearly impossible, but this was unacceptable.

He continued his search. The bulletin board above her desk? The top of her dresser? Her nightstand? Nothing. Sam pulled out his cell phone and dialed again. Voicemail. "Rachel, if I don't hear from you in the next five minutes, the next time you walk out of this house will be for your high school graduation."

He hung up and ran a mental scan of conversations they had. Did Rachel mention anything about Cricket he may have missed? Was there something in the direct messaging he read, but didn't understand? Nothing came to him.

Suddenly the unsettling feeling Sam fought all morning fashioned into an arrow and pierced his brain. He cursed and left Rachel's room. When he reached the front door, he stepped outside and closed the door behind him. As he punched Wade's number into his cell, he inspected the lock, the door frame, the area around the porch. He tried to steady his hand as he waited for Wade to answer.

"Hey, L-T, what's—"

"Rachel's not here. I picked up Olivia from church, and when we got home, Rachel was gone. No note, no text, nothing. And she's not answering her phone." Sam couldn't control the panic in his voice.

"Hey, calm down, Lieutenant. She's probably with a friend. Did you call around?"

"Of course I did." Sam clenched his jaw.

"Well, Rachel's getting to that age, wanting her independence and all. Try not to over react—"

"I'm not overreacting!" His anger at Wade was unwarranted, but it grew from fear. "Last night when I got home, a black BMW was parked in front of my house. What if—" Sam didn't finish, but he didn't have to.

"I'm on it. We'll be there in ten minutes."

We? Sam realized he must have meant Shaw.

"No, come alone, and don't tell anyone." Sam was mortified. How stupid was he to leave Rachel alone after the incident last night? The possible consequences of his interrogation of Crystal Starr terrified him. At the moment, until he knew what they were facing, the fewer people who knew about it, the better.

Sam hung up. He was frantic. How could he let the investigation become more important than protecting his family? Was it so important to him that he may have sacrificed his own daughter? For what? An arrest that would be legendary in the department, remembered when promotions rolled around? His body tremored from the inside out as he paced the length of the porch. Then the door opened. Sam spun around, somehow hoping Rachel would be standing there.

"Daddy?"

"Livi, honey." Sam struggled for control. "Go back inside. I'm just getting some fresh air."

"Can I get some fresh air, too?" Olivia reached for his hand.

At the innocence in her voice, another wave of guilt rushed over him. He picked her up and held her close, protecting her, kissing her cheek, feeling her arms squeeze his neck. "Just for a bit." He spoke into her hair. "Detective Wade is going to be here in a few minutes. We have to talk about work." He held her tight a moment longer, then set her back down on the porch. "Why don't you watch TV for a while? I'll be in as soon as I can."

"Okay."

When Olivia closed the door, Sam watched down the street for Wade's vehicle. Within moments, he saw it take a right at the four-way. Sam bounded down the porch steps and stood in the drive to meet him as he got out of the car.

"Okay, Lieutenant, I've been thinking." Before Wade could continue, a silver SUV pulled in and parked behind his car. The logo on the driver's door read KFTS Channel 12 News. Instantly, a reporter Sam recognized from the evening broadcast approached him. A cameraman followed with the camera already rolling.

"Lieutenant Sam Blake? I'm Anna Austin with KFTS news. Would you care to answer a few questions about the death of Crystal Starr? Was she involved in the Simms murder? Was the overdose accidental, or is it being investigated as a homicide? Do you have a suspect?" She shoved a microphone toward Sam.

Sam stared at the reporter, at the microphone, at the camera. This was his stage, and he knew how to perform, how to caress his words and look into the camera with authority, as he had with previous cases that drew public attention. This was the kind of thing the department and city council would notice when promotions came around. Sam was speechless.

"Lieutenant, we'll only take a few minutes of your time," the reporter persisted.

He looked at Wade who was waiting for him to answer the reporter's questions. Sam shook his head, an almost imperceptible movement, and Wade stepped in.

"I'm Detective Donnie Wade." At the introduction Anna Austin and the cameraman turned toward him.

"I can tell you we are investigating an apparent over-dose, but details will not be released at this time."

"Detective, can you tell us if this is connected to the Simms investigation?"

"I have no further comment." Wade repeated the phrase three more times before the reporter was satisfied she had all the information she was going to get.

As the news crew backed down the driveway, Sam exhaled and lowered his shoulders. "Thanks."

"No problem. Now, I was thinking on the way over here. I know you are worried sick, and I would be, too, sick out of my mind. But, this can't be connected to last night. There's a logical answer."

"She left, first, without asking. Rachel knows better. Second, she didn't leave a note. Third, she's not answering her cell phone. That's the logic I've got to work with." Sam held up his hands. "Rachel doesn't do this. She doesn't just leave or not answer her cell. Something is wrong."

"Okay." Wade conceded. "Is there anyone you haven't called?"

"Yeah, a girl named Cricket, a new friend Rachel made at school. But I don't know how to get a hold of her. I don't even know her last name."

At that instant, a black car screeched to a sudden stop at the four-way. Sam and Wade jerked their heads in that direction. Instinctively, they moved behind Wade's car, prepared to take cover. Sam's heart rate tripled. He reached for his holster. It wasn't there. A loud bass pounded through the open windows, but as the car drove closer, Sam realized it wasn't the car that had been parked outside last night. It was a Mustang, and as it neared the house, it rolled to a stop. The passenger door opened, and Rachel emerged from the back seat.

Sam's knees buckled beneath him. He placed both hands on Wade's car to brace himself as he watched Rachel say something and laugh into the passenger window. Then she turned and saw Sam and Detective Wade. For an instant, her facial expression changed. Surprise? Fear? Sam couldn't be sure. It was too brief. Rachel pulled back her shoulders and tossed her head to the side, clearing her bangs from her face. With her jaw set, she looked at her father.

Sam glared at his daughter as he spoke to Detective Wade. "Thanks for coming. Seems you were right. Sorry for wasting your time."

"No problem, Lieutenant. I'm glad she's safe." Wade opened his car door.

Sam marched toward the Mustang, his pulse

pounding against his skull. Rachel stepped away from the car as it took off, tires squealing, leaving a black mark on the pavement in its wake. Wade flipped on the emergency lights inside his unmarked car, backed out of the driveway, and raced after the car.

"Oh, great. Just what I need. Cricket's brother getting a ticket!" Disapproval was thick in Rachel's voice as she attempted to walk past Sam.

Sam stepped into her path and clenched his teeth. "Where have you been?" Rachel met his glare. He stared at a stranger.

"I got bored and decided to hang out with some friends." She sounded as nonchalant as confessing she ate a cookie before dinner.

Rage swelled inside him. He grabbed her by the arm and escorted her to the house, shouting a stream of accusations. "You're riding in a car with a driver I don't know, and a kid at that. You didn't tell me where you were going, or even that you were going, or who you were going with. You didn't leave a note. And why didn't you answer your cell phone? What do you think you're doing, Rachel?"

Rachel took a step back and looked up at him. "Why are you making such a big deal out of this, Dad? I was with Cricket and her brother. We'd been texting, and the next thing I knew she was at the door. I was bored and decided to go for a ride. And I couldn't answer my cell—it's dead." She held the phone in the air, and waved it mockingly back and forth.

Sam released her arm and faced her. "Rachel, you don't leave this house without permission. I have to know where you are. That's the rule. It's always been the rule."

"Well, you weren't here for me to ask."

"At the very least, you could have left a note."

"Dad, I didn't plan this. It just happened." She rolled her eyes. "Geez, I just wanted to go have some fun for once. I wasn't even gone long, like less than an hour."

"If I ever catch you in that car again, so help me—" He couldn't finish. He ran his hand through his hair as if to clear his thinking. "Give me your phone. You broke the rules, and you knew what you were doing when you did. You're grounded from your phone, and you are not to leave this house except to go to school." Sam couldn't believe the words as he heard them come out of his mouth. Rachel had never been grounded. Sometimes, Maggie had to practically force her to accept invitations to birthday parties or sleepovers. It wasn't Rachel being social that bothered him; it was all the rules she broke in the process, her dismissive attitude, their conversation that morning. None of this was familiar. And neither was his daughter as he looked into her face masked in defiance. She wrapped her arms around herself and stood with her weight on one foot.

Sam held out his hand. "Cell phone."

"Uh!" Rachel huffed as she slammed it into his palm. "This is so unfair!" She turned on her heel.

"You better stop right there, young lady."

Rachel halted, but kept her back to Sam.

"Don't you ever forget who you're talking to. Let me remind you that you're only fourteen years old, and I am your father. You will respect the rules of this house, and you better lose the tone because it's not working for you."

Rachel stood still. Sam sensed a showdown. He waited for her next move, uncertain what his counter move would be. Finally, she dropped her arms to her side and glanced over her shoulder. "Sorry." She stood for a moment as if she had something more to say, but she remained silent. Then she raised both hands in mock surrender, went inside, and closed the door behind her.

Sam stood in disbelief. What had he just witnessed? He wanted to believe he heard sincerity in the apology. Had Rachel ever challenged Maggie like that, with that tone? Maggie never talked about it if she did, but surely this change in their daughter couldn't have taken place over the course of the last several weeks, could it?

Sam went inside and found Olivia, wide-eyed, sitting in his recliner. He sat down, shifting Olivia to his lap.

"Is Rachel in trouble?"

Sam considered his answer, sorry Olivia had witnessed the confrontation. "Yes, she is."

Olivia settled in and leaned back against him.

"Livi, did Mom ever yell at Rachel like that?"

"Um, maybe. Like if she had to keep telling her to clean her room."

"Did Rachel talk to Mom like she just talked to me?"

Olivia wrinkled her nose and shook her head.

Sam wasn't sure if the answer made him feel better or worse. If only this were about the pile of clothes on her bedroom floor. If only it were about her leaving without telling him. But somehow it had escalated into something bigger. Although Wade was right and Rachel was home safe, Sam still could not forgive himself. He had compromised his family again. Even though the ending to this day's saga could have been much worse, he couldn't forgive himself.

Maggie couldn't decide who she was angrier with, Sam or Rachel. She watched strangers living in her home. She stood between Sam's recliner and the TV, trying to penetrate his thoughts with her glare.

"Get your head out of the sand, Sam! Talk to your daughter for crying out loud! Can't you see she needs you? Discipline her all you want, but that's not the answer here. She's sinking fast, and you better get her to talk!"

Part of Maggie could admit being angry with Sam was unfair. He didn't know the things she knew. He wasn't able to watch Rachel like she was. He didn't see her sneak into the medicine cabinet and steal the painkillers. He couldn't stand over her shoulder and read the messages she texted, or her online chats with Cricket, or see some of Cricket's friends Rachel followed on social media. He asked for her passwords, but would he actually monitor Rachel's online activity? Was it fair to hold him accountable as he was still learning to step in and fill her role?

And Rachel. Maggie was heartbroken by the choices she made. The worst thing she could remember punishing Rachel for was lying when she thought she lost her cell phone while they were shopping. Rachel had lain it down on a display and walked away. Maggie picked it up, and when she questioned her, Rachel insisted the phone was in her purse, although her voice betrayed her. Now she's taking pills? And sneaking around to hang out with older kids they didn't know? And she refused to go to church? Maggie began to realize the extent of Rachel's pain and her desperation to escape it. She wondered if Rachel were more like Sam than she had realized, lacking faith when life didn't offer easy answers. She stood in the middle of the living room, utterly useless.

Sam continued to stare through her, focused on the sports highlights, with Olivia snuggled beside him, so precious, innocent. But Maggie was beginning to worry about her, too. Her presence interrupted Olivia's ability to accept and grieve the loss of her mother. Although Maggie needed her connection with her daughter, she feared how it might be affecting Olivia. As upset as she was with Sam and Rachel, at least their anger and grief were part of a natural process.

"Sam." Maggie tried one final plea. "Hear me. Please. Take care of the girls."

Sam picked up the remote control and muted the TV.

"What's wrong, Daddy?" Olivia turned her head to look up at him

"Sshhh." Sam listened.

"What do you hear?" Olivia whispered.

"Nothing, I guess. I thought I heard someone."

"Maybe you heard Mommy."

"Mommy?" Sam raised an eyebrow.

"Yeah, she said to take care of me and Rachel."

Stone faced, Sam turned up the volume on the TV. "I'm trying."

CHAPTER 14

"That's epic!" Cricket laughed as Rachel relayed the details of her standoff with her dad. She pushed the remains of her lunch aside, and gave Rachel a high five.

"Yeah, epic." Rachel smiled, but behind her bravado, she swam in confusion. She didn't expect Cricket to applaud her. She expected some advice, maybe a little sympathy. Instead, Cricket treated her like a hero, and the confusing part was Rachel kind of liked it. She had her first major face-off with her dad, and although she didn't win, she didn't lose, either. She was surprised at how well she handled herself. On the inside, she crumbled, yet, she didn't let it show. But once she was safe in her bedroom, she went numb as she replayed the confrontation in her head, amazed at the power that had rushed through her, and a little scared at the brief glimpse of helplessness that surfaced on her dad's face.

She didn't know what it was about Cricket, how she could be such a source of courage. Rachel enjoyed it, and feared it. She liked making decisions for herself, having some control. She welcomed the changes she could feel happening within herself, but they were happening so quickly. And though she didn't want to be the Rachel she used to be, she somehow feared losing touch with that part of herself. But that part did everything right, obeyed her parents, worked hard in school, went to church. And what did that get her? Pain, that's what. Her whole life turned upside down. Life isn't fair. How many times had she heard that? Now she believed it, so she'd better toughen up so she could face it.

"So, he took your cell phone but not your laptop?"

"Yeah, I guess he thought I'd need it for school or something."

"No, he just didn't think about it. You'll see, he's so wrapped up in his own grief, he can't really think about you. My mom did the same thing. When she was taking care of my dad, I kind of understood it. She was so tired all the time, and sad, but she kept trying to be strong. I felt sorry for her. But after Dad died, well, I guess I thought I'd get my mom back. But it didn't take long for me to realize I'd lost her, too. She kind of caved in. That's when I realized I would have to take care of myself." Cricket looked Rachel in the eyes. "Just like you're going to have to take care of yourself."

Rachel didn't want that last statement to be true. Her dad hadn't caved in, had he? He was making an effort, right? He just wasn't Mom. He didn't know how to be. A pang of regret moved sharply through Rachel as she admitted that. She wanted to get into a time machine and beg her mom not to go to the Hutching house, or lie and say the clients had called and cancelled. Or—not send that text. Then her mom would still be here to take care of everything, just like she always had. And her dad could go back to being the dad he knew how to be. But there was no time machine. No going back. Cricket was right.

The bell rang to end lunch.

"See ya after school?" Cricket started up the steps to the freshmen floor.

"Yeah, see ya." Rachel walked toward the science lab, the class she dreaded most. Partly because her grade was in the toilet, but mostly because Kristen would be there, trying to make eye contact, looking for an opening, a chance to fix things. But Rachel didn't want to fix things, and how was she supposed to say that to Kristen? Kristen the soccer star, the straight-A student, the girl with a dad and a mom. What would she say? *You live a charmed life, Kristen. You don't know what I'm going through. Cricket does. You wouldn't understand.* In particular, she wouldn't understand the pills, and Rachel didn't want to worry about hiding them from her, too. Too much pressure. What was the big deal anyway? She never took them during school. Concentrating was hard enough without the haze. But at home, the haze had become her mode of survival. And it wasn't like she was smoking weed or something illegal. They were pills from her dad's medicine cabinet, prescribed by a doctor for crying out loud. Medicine. Something to help her get through the rough stuff. Until it gets easier, like Cricket said.

It was noon and Sam was in his recliner, not behind the desk in his office buried in paperwork, as he should be. Instead, he sat in silence, unable to will himself into action. He had never been a man of indecision. He identified a situation, studied all the options, and put solutions into motion. Why was this any different? He had a situation. His job. The girls. But what were his options? Oh, how he wished he could talk to Maggie.

Or touch her. Or tell her one more time how much he loved her. Did he even know how much until now? Had he ever realized how much Maggie had helped him be the man he wanted to be? Husband, father, detective. She made him better. The last night they lay in bed together, how she listened—again—to his frustration with an investigation. He never realized how much he relied on her to allow him to process, logically, and even emotionally. He longed to be able to share his burden with her again.

The longing consumed him and drew him to their bedroom. He reached for the photo beside his bed and walked to the chair in the corner. Maggie's chair. Sam let himself sink into the cushions and feel the chair envelop him. He rubbed his hands along the armrests, leaned his head back. He pictured Maggie sitting in this very place and imagined the warmth he felt between the chair and his body transferring into him any part of her that remained.

He placed the photograph on the table beside the chair. Would he ever feel that happy again? He stared at the picture, then drifted to the other items on the table. Near the edge lay a book Maggie hadn't finished reading, her place marked with a scrap of paper covered with artistic doodles. Rachel's no doubt. He imagined her salvaging the scrap from Rachel's trashcan or maybe from her backpack. Sam quickly passed over Maggie's Bible, now covered with a light coat of dust. Beside it were her reading glasses and a pen. He picked up the pen and rolled it between his fingers. How many of Maggie's words flowed through the pen, its ink carrying her deepest thoughts from her heart to the page? His eyes found the drawer that kept the journal. Her journal. Sam's heart raced. Inside those pages he could find her. It was all he had left of her, honest and uncensored. He pulled open the drawer and lifted the journal, gently, reverently. Sam had never considered reading it before, and now he wondered if he was trespassing.

He studied the distressed leather cover as if waiting for its permission to read the pages it protected. His fingers brushed across the smooth finish, then rested on a quote embossed at the bottom: *If nothing ever changed, there'd be no butterflies.* Sam preferred that nothing ever changed, that his family was complete, that Maggie was the one sitting in the chair with the journal in her hands. His fingers moved from the quote to the upper corner of the cover and across an imprint of a butterfly. Carefully, he opened the journal to reveal the first page.

Maggie's delicate handwriting filled a brief paragraph:

As life presents each new day and each new day presents its challenges, this journal is my reminder that challenges change me, and change is necessary. This journal speaks to the part of me that prefers predictability, that fears the unknown. When I open its pages to pray my way through life's trials, the butterfly is my visual reminder that good things, beauty, can result from change. I find solace in the reminder, in the butterfly, and ultimately, in its Creator.

Sam read the words with a mixture of anger and jealousy. Maggie didn't know anything about change. She wasn't here to see the debris that resulted from the change thrust upon her family. There was nothing beautiful in it, no solace to be found. Yet, he envied her, knowing somehow she would have found peace in the crisis. Is that what she would call faith? It should have been him, he thought for the thousandth time. She would have known how to cope.

Sam turned to the back of the journal. Several pages were blank. He flipped through them until he saw Maggie's writing again and stopped. He wondered what her final entry, her last prayer, had been. When he read the date, he recalled the night she had waited up for him, how she had listened to his frustration about the Simms case. Had she prayed about the case? Had she prayed for him? As he began to read, Sam realized Maggie had her own concerns that night. Nate, the little boy she had mentioned from time to time. Genuine compassion touched him. Why didn't Maggie tell him? Then he remembered. Her fear of losing one of the girls. It made sense now. The case hadn't ignited her anxiety. Nate's death had. What had he promised Maggie that night? That the girls were safe and happy, and together they would make sure they stayed that way? How quickly that promise was broken.

Sam began to doubt his decision to read Maggie's entries. He wanted to find comfort in her words, to find a hiding place inside her heart. Instead, he felt exposed. But he couldn't force himself to stop reading. Instead, he turned to the front to find the first dated entry and estimated the journal covered nearly five years. He flipped through to find the date Maggie's father passed away. Yes, there was an entry. He turned a few pages and found an entry about the ribbon cutting ceremony for Blake Real Estate. Near the back again, he searched the dates in September. There it was, an entry about Olivia starting kindergarten. Sam leafed through more pages, skimming some, stopping to read others, feeling there was a part of Maggie he hadn't really known. But what married couple communicated on such an intimate level as Maggie shared in her journal?

Finally, he decided he'd read enough for now. He'd heard Maggie's voice in her words, touched her heart even if for a moment. It was Maggie, comforting . . . and painful. As Sam closed the journal, the pages fluttered. A name caught his attention, then disappeared within the journal. A gasp caught in his throat. Why would Maggie have written that? It must have been something else, a combination of letters that at quick glance looked familiar. Did he dare open the journal to see if he could find it? What if he did?

Sam opened the cover once more, convinced he would not find the name he thought he saw. There's no way. Yet a long suppressed guilt began its revival. He turned to the section where he guessed it might be. The dates, they would help. Two years back. There were a handful of entries in April, some in May. Sam took a deep breath and held it. He slowly turned the pages for June, his eyes scanning the words, searching, searching, searching. They stopped. There it was. The single name that held the power to drop Sam to his knees. Shaw. In Maggie's handwriting. Nikki Shaw. Sam forced himself to read the words surrounding the name. Maggie knew.

"Oh, Maggie. I am so sorry." Agony filled Sam's broken voice. "I never wanted you to know."

Maggie sat on the leather ottoman, facing him, listening to a confession she didn't want to hear. She hadn't been certain her husband had been unfaithful, so she chose to bury her suspicion, forced herself to forget it. But now her means of surviving that painful period betrayed her as the truth forced her denial to the surface. Rage pierced her, bringing into perfect focus all the clues that had once seemed so blurred. She thought it strange when a new detective joined the division, yet Sam rarely mentioned it. The topic usually consumed his conversation for weeks as he talked about training, the new guy's potential, rookie mistakes. And the few times she asked about the new guy, Sam referred only to "Shaw," and his comments were always brief.

Then, a couple months later, Maggie stopped by the department unannounced and found Sam reclined in his chair behind the desk, an attractive young female facing him, leaning against his desk, too close. Her caramel hair, swept over her left shoulder, led Maggie's eyes to the opening in her blouse that begged for one more button to be fastened. Guilt surfaced on Sam's face when he saw Maggie. She recalled their heated discussion that evening, and finally, Sam convincing her she was acting like a jealous teenager. In hindsight, Maggie was sure he told a version of the truth. Nothing had happened between Sam and Nikki Shaw—yet. But now she was certain she knew when it did, a month later when Sam flew to Atlanta for a conference. Maggie suspected he wasn't going alone. She journaled about her fears and that she wouldn't force Sam to choose. Was she being noble, or was she a coward? Should she fight for a man who desired another woman?

But Maggie thought she didn't have to fight, because two days later Sam returned from Atlanta a different man. Being a father became important to him, and he adored Maggie like he hadn't in years. She was convinced that if a rendezvous had been planned, he didn't go through with it. She also convinced herself that if he had, she was partly to blame. On her own list of commitments, her marriage had fallen to the bottom. Her growing business required nurturing, as did the girls. Maggie had a house to manage and commitments at church. She had no time for herself and less time for her marriage, which had settled into an exhausting routine that Maggie accepted as normal. So, when she pictured the striking Nikki Shaw leaning against her husband's desk, sending signals that Maggie no longer sent, how could she blame him for being tempted? She couldn't.

But now she could blame him for acting on the temptation. As Maggie exhumed the past, it didn't lessen the shock of sitting in front of Sam, listening to his confession. The betrayal she once feared, that she had exiled to a desolate place in her heart, threatened to rise from the darkness. Until Maggie shifted her focus to her husband's face. His eyes were closed and tears formed a continuous, silent stream down his cheeks.

Maggie sighed as she watched guilt devour any part of Sam that managed to survive the past weeks. Suddenly, her anger, which she knew was justified, dissipated as if it had exceeded its expiration date.

"Oh, Sam. What does it matter now?" Maggie moved from the ottoman and kneeled in front of him. She pressed her hands on his thighs, trying to communicate the intensity of what she was saying. "Besides, the last two years of our marriage were the *best*. We found each other again. And if it took an affair to do that, well, then shame on both of us." Maggie wished her words could reach Sam, but as she watched him suffer, she knew they were wasted in the empty air.

Suddenly, resolve came over his face. Maggie sat back as he stood and walked to the chest of drawers. From on top, he took a leather shoulder holster and fastened it around his shoulders. He reached for the sport coat hanging from the doorknob. Then he unlocked the top drawer of the chest and removed two items. The pistol he secured in the holster. The badge he shoved into the inside front coat pocket.

As Maggie heard Sam back out of the garage, she was certain of two things. She had forgiven Sam. But he would never forgive himself.

Detective Shaw was like an oscillating fan, alternating her gaze from the clock to the office door as each minute passed. The lieutenant—Sam—should have been in hours ago. She suffered through the weekend as one hour wearily dragged into the next until finally Monday morning arrived. She woke up early, showered, and dressed in the outfit she had laid out the evening before—grey slacks that sat low on her hips and a jewel green blouse, close-fitting and tucked in to reveal her trim waistline. The blouse, long hidden away in her closet, was specifically chosen for the occasion. It had been Sam's favorite. The color, he once said, made her eyes sultry. Would he remember?

Nikki tried to concentrate on the case in front of her, an identity theft, typically tough to solve, but this case looked promising. Recent activity on the victim's credit card put the suspect at the Cape Spring Mall Saturday afternoon. Nikki made calls to store managers who agreed to let her view security video, which is what she should be doing now, instead of sitting at her desk, waiting.

Waiting for a man whose wife's name was recently engraved on a tombstone. Was this the woman she had become? What happened to the girl who sang in the church choir? The girl who scorned the teenagers who partied all weekend and dozed through her grandpa's sermons on Sunday? Who would have guessed that Miss Goody-Two-Shoes would become The Girl Most Likely? Certainly not Nikki. But she never knew she would meet a man like Samuel Blake. The place in life she found herself was so far from the life she had planned, but she didn't know how to find her way back. And now that Sam was alone, she wasn't sure she wanted to find her way back.

She heard him before she saw him. As Sam's voice drew closer, her heartbeat echoed in her head. She fought for control, which she gained in mere seconds. She had become an expert at suppressing her emotions. Detachment had become her most important survival skill, personally and professionally. With no uncertainty, Sam had made sure she knew they were over. But she had fallen in love with him. And working beside him every day was a privilege she kept only through circumstance. Sam threatened to transfer her out of the detective division, but the one night they'd spent together in Atlanta had given her power. Sam's career goals ranked higher than lieutenant stripes, but sleeping with a subordinate and walking out on her the next morning could have professional ramifications. Not that Nikki planned to play her wild card. After all, she had aspirations to make rank herself, and the secret she shared with Sam might someday play in her favor.

Sam passed the office door, walking in step with the chief.

"You aren't thinking clearly, Sam."

Nikki detected frustration in the chief's voice.

"Yes, I am." Sam was insistent.

Nikki moved to the filing cabinet near the door. As she pretended to search for a file, her eyes followed the two men as they approached the chief's office. The chief stepped inside, but Sam stopped in the doorway. He reached inside his sport coat and pulled out his service weapon. Then he reached into his coat pocket and withdrew his silver badge. Nikki's hand covered her mouth too late to stifle her gasp. She watched as Sam handed over the two items that identified him as an officer of the law.

"I'm going to HR to get the paperwork started." Sam turned away from the chief.

Nikki watched until he disappeared through the double doors leading to the administrative offices. Fearing she could no longer resist the urge to go after him, she grabbed the keys off her desk and walked in the opposite direction. She had security videos to watch.

CHAPTER 15

Sam pulled into the parking lot and turned off the engine. Letters painted on the window read Joe Friendly's. This wasn't Sam's first trip to this bar. He broke up a bar fight or two during his day on patrol, and investigations brought him here on occasion, looking for information or a suspect. But what brought him here now? After sitting a few minutes, he pushed open the car door.

Sam surveyed his surroundings as he walked in. A couple of men were shooting pool in the back. Another drank alone in a booth near the entrance. The place was nearly empty, not surprising for a Monday afternoon. He walked to the bar and chose a stool facing the entrance, obeying a rule of law enforcement, to never sit with his back to the door. The bartender was at the far end, stacking clean glasses on the shelves below the bar.

"Be right with you, my friend."

As the bartender approached, Sam sensed he was being studied. He raised his chin and met the face of a woman, who, by appearance, had lived life hard. Grey pushed through a faded dye job. Deep creases circled her mouth and defined her brow. But her smile was easy and inviting. "What can I get you?"

Sam gave a half grin and shrugged. "I don't know."

As the bartender's blue eyes stared into his, Sam felt like she was reading his soul. "You don't know? Well, sometimes the drink depends on the occasion. What brings you here on a Monday afternoon? Forgetting or celebrating?"

Sam contemplated. "Celebrating."

"Yeah? What are we celebrating, friend? I might have a drink with you."

"Retirement." The word sounded foreign as it rolled off Sam's lips. "Twenty-two years with the police department. Time to hang it up." *I think*, Sam added silently, certain no option could possibly surface, allowing him to be both the detective he wanted to be and the father he needed to be.

"Is that right? Well, that definitely calls for a celebration. A drink for us both." She arched her eyebrows, waiting for him to name his drink.

He shrugged. "I'll have whatever you're having."

The bartender smiled. "Good choice. My name's Roxy, by the way."

"Sam."

"Okay, Sam. Let's get this party started." Roxy pulled two tall glasses from beneath the counter, filled them with ice, a beverage from a decanter, and finished it with a shot. She pushed the drink toward Sam and took a sip of her own.

Sam put both hands around his glass, letting the coolness soak into his palms. He breathed in deeply and looked up to find Roxy still watching him.

"Somehow this doesn't seem like much of a celebra-tion."

He didn't answer. Instead he looked back at the bartender, trying to detect the face hidden beneath the mask that life had painted on her. He bet she had been an attractive girl once.

"Five bucks says you got a story, Sam. Everybody's got a story. Been tending this bar twenty-five years. I've heard them all."

"Everybody's got one, huh? Well, what's yours?" Sam deferred, and leaned forward to rest his arms on the bar.

"Hmm." Roxy puckered. "Now that's a question nobody ever asks a bartender."

"Well, I'm asking." Sam watched as Roxy's eyes transported her somewhere, some time ago.

"My story. Let's see . . . married too young. He was a jerk, of course. Left me with two young boys and no income. Got a job checking groceries, but it wasn't enough to feed the kids. Then a friend got me a job waiting these tables here on the weekends. Tips were good. Before long, I went full time, Monday through Saturday. Worked every hour I could get. Except Sunday. Sunday was for my boys, Taylor, Brandon, and Jesus."

Sam cocked his head, wondering if he misunderstood.

"Didn't take me for a holy roller, did you?" A grin deepened the lines in her face.

He tried to picture the woman now standing behind the bar instead sitting in a pew, singing hymns or reciting the Lord's prayer. "But you're a bartender, no offense."

Roxy laughed. "None taken. Not by me anyway. But plenty of church people have taken offense over the years, that's for sure." She placed her arms on the bar and leaned in, mirroring Sam. "But you know what? I don't answer to them. I answer to my Lord God Almighty. And they'll have to answer to Him someday, too."

Sam grunted disapproval. "See, that's what I don't get. There you were, a good Christian girl, doing your best to raise your boys alone, and you end up—" Sam turned his palms up, swept the bar with his eyes, and shrugged. "What I'd like to know is where's God in all that?"

"Oh, He's in it plenty." Roxy nodded, her lips pressed in a tight line. "But I used to ask the same thing. I prayed for a better job. Prayed and prayed. The offers I got didn't pay. The jobs that paid weren't offered. Actually, I got pretty angry with God for a while. I thought He was punishing me for working here, but He sure wasn't opening any other doors for me." Roxy took a long sip of her drink and pointed to Sam's. "You gonna drink that?" He rotated the full glass in front of him.

"It's my specialty." She held up her glass, toasted the air, and continued. "Anyway, one day the owner, Joe, says he wants to teach me to tend bar. Before long, I got a raise and better tips. And that's when it hit me. God just gave me a better job with better pay. He obviously wasn't going to get me out of the bar, so I realized then that He must have me here for a reason."

"What reason would that be?" Skepticism was clear in Sam's voice.

"Well, here's how I see it. If Jesus came back to live in this world today, I don't see Him hanging out in the churches." Roxy laughed and shook her head. "Although there are certainly some people there who wouldn't recognize Him if he sang in the choir. No, I imagine Jesus would be visiting this bar, and He'd be down at the shelter on Broadway, places like that, searching for people who don't know Him, people who are hurting. But He's not here in this bar walking around in the flesh. I am. And I think there's a reason for that."

"Really?" Sam challenged. "Such as?"

Roxy studied him again. "You, for one, maybe. Why are you here? In the middle of a Monday afternoon, celebrating retirement, alone?"

Sam looked at his hands. "Well, if you think I came in here by some divine providence so you could save my soul, I'm sorry to disappoint you, Roxy. God and I have an understanding."

"Oh?"

"Yeah. I leave Him alone, and He leaves me alone." As Sam heard the words escape his mouth, for a brief moment he felt dark, detached. He diverted the feeling by tossing judgment at Roxy. "So, how do you account for all the alcohol you serve? Do you know how many fatalities and assaults and domestics I've worked because of alcohol?"

"Good point, my friend. But, you know, if someone wants to drink, they're going to find a bar, whether I'm the one tending it or not. When they come here, I keep track of how much they drink and tell them when they've had enough. If I need to, I take car keys and call cabs. And you know what? Customers come back and tips are still good."

He wasn't convinced, but Roxy had given him a perspective he hadn't considered.

"Besides, I'm only fifty percent bartender. The other half the time I'm a counselor. Hurting people come in here every day, needing someone to listen. And sometimes I get the chance to speak a little truth into their lives." Roxy emptied her glass and wiped away the wet ring it left on the bar. "So, that's my story, friend. And yours?"

Sam turned the cool glass in his hands while Roxy waited. What was his story? He didn't know where to begin, or how much to tell, or why he was enticed to share anything with this bartender he'd just met. He decided on the basics, no details. "My wife died. I've got two girls to raise. Can't do it being a detective. Have my twenty years in, so I'm retiring." As his eyes met hers, he sensed a confession rising. He stared into his glass and spoke more to himself than to Roxy. "This job made me a good detective . . . but it broke my marriage, broke me as a father. I need to fix that."

Roxy placed her hand over his and stared hard into him. "You'll do what you have to do. I did. And I know you don't want to hear this now, but God is at work. We can't see it because we don't know what to look for. But one day you'll look back, just like I do, and you'll wonder how you missed it." She straightened up and laughed. "Yep, someday you're gonna walk back in here, my friend, and tell me all about it, about how you see God."

Sam shook his head and gestured toward her empty glass. "I think that went to your head."

"What? A little raspberry iced tea? No, I can handle my caffeine pretty well." She winked.

"Ice tea, huh?" One corner of his mouth curved as he raised his glass to take a drink. "Roxy, you're a complex woman."

"No. I'm pretty simple really. I just try to do the next right thing."

The next right thing? That was the mystery that plagued Sam, but suddenly the picture started to come into focus. Maybe. Was it time for him to accept that he knew what the right thing was? But it just seemed so . . . not him. So then, what was it? Sam pushed back from the bar and took out his wallet. "Roxy, it's been a pleasure, but I've got some business to take care of."

"The pleasure's been mine, my friend. Put your money away. The drink's on the house." Roxy picked up his empty glass and wiped the bar.

"Thanks, Roxy." Sam patted the bar and hesitated. "I mean, thanks, really."

She smiled, and as Sam walked out of the bar into the glare of the afternoon sun, he chuckled at the absurdity of God using a bartender. He wasn't close to being convinced, but he was willing to admit Roxy was one-of-a-kind.

What a horrible day. Rachel's teachers must have had a secret meeting in the teachers' lounge to coordinate their efforts and pounce on her all at once. During pre-algebra Mrs. Brunk placed a note on Rachel's desk, *Please see me after class.* The teacher was distracted with helping a student when the bell rang, so Rachel took the opportunity to sneak out unnoticed. Besides, Mrs. Brunk wasn't going to tell her anything she didn't already know. She didn't get so lucky in English. After Ms. Campbell gave a reading assignment, she called Rachel to her desk. Although she whispered her concerns about Rachel's inattentiveness, missed assignments, and plummeting grade, Rachel was certain the entire class could hear. She glanced at the other students only to find their eyes glued on the pages they were reading, but she still felt publicly humiliated. Ms. Campbell put her hand on Rachel's shoulder to call her attention back to the conversation and assured her she knew this was a difficult time for her, and that Rachel must let her know how she could help. And then there was Mr. Beard. He had tried to give Rachel a chance to salvage her grade and redo the science project, but she didn't take it. He was monitoring the hall and stopped her before she entered the classroom. She had given him no choice but to flunk her for the quarter. Rachel kept her head down as she walked to her lab table.

She didn't like it. She didn't like being confronted by her teachers. She didn't like that her grades were dropping. But mostly she didn't like the sympathetic disappointment in the teachers' voices. Behind the words they spoke, she could hear, "We know your mom is dead. We are so sorry about that. But here are the assignments you didn't turn in and the tests you bombed and you don't pay attention in class and. . . ."

Rachel wanted to scream. "What does it matter? Why should anything matter? Do you really think solving linear equations or finding symbolism in a poem matters to me? And you want to know how technology changed my life? Well, let me tell you. I sent a text, and now my mom is dead! Is that enough change for you?" Maybe saying that out loud would be easier than listening silently as teachers tried to pressure her into thinking whatever they had to teach her was more important than having a mother.

Then there was Kristen. Why couldn't she let things be? She caught Rachel after science, trying to make small talk, hanging at her elbow as Rachel pushed past students in the hall, squeezing through the congestion to force Kristen back. By the time she reached her locker, Kristen was several steps behind, maneuvering her way through the crowd. Rachel opened her locker and traded her science book for American history. When she closed her locker door, Kristen was waiting, fury in her eyes. Rachel was surprised when it didn't come out in her voice.

"I don't know what to do, Rachel, how to make things all right. You don't return my texts. You won't talk to me. You avoid me at school. You won't even give me a chance to say I'm sorry." Kristen pulled at her ponytail and adjusted her backpack. "I just want to be friends again."

How was she supposed to respond to that? Perhaps honestly would be best. "Kristen, you can't help me. No one can help me. And you just think you want to be friends. You don't know me anymore." Rachel looked down.

Kristen held back no longer. "Oh, but this Cricket girl somehow knows you? We've been friends since like forever, but all of a sudden you go through a really bad time in life and some pierced freak with pink hair is the friend you turn to?"

"You don't understand—"

"No! I don't understand! You're right, Rachel, I don't know you. And I'm finished trying." Kristen slammed her fist into Rachel's locker. "Finished!"

Hollow and bruised, Rachel whispered as she watched her former best friend blend into the stream of students moving to sixth hour. "I don't even know me anymore."

And now the text from her dad: *Picking up Olivia; ride bus.* Was he kidding? Her mom never made her ride the school bus. It was a social feeding frenzy, and Rachel found herself at the bottom of the food chain more than once, begging for a seat, picking spit wads out of her hair, listening to the filth pour from the mouths of the sharks who dominated the back of the bus. Her mom always kept her schedule open so she could pick her up from school, and on the rare occasion when she couldn't, Rachel would catch a ride with Kristen's mom. But that wasn't an option. Instead, she grabbed her phone and texted: *can i get a ride?* Within seconds her phone buzzed with a reply, and she walked to the front entrance of the school.

"Hey." Cricket, perched on the back of a bench, tugged on the cords to her earphones and shoved them in her backpack.

Before Rachel could reply, a black Mustang entered the school parking lot. Her dad's words rushed through her mind. *If I ever catch you in that car again, so help me—.* But he hadn't given her much choice now, had he? She pushed his voice out of her head and slid into the backseat.

A buzz announced someone entered the door of Blake Realty.

"Sam, what a surprise!" Laura turned from the copy machine with a file in her hand. She bent down with open arms. "And Olivia. How are you, sweetie?"

Olivia accepted the invitation and wrapped her arms around Laura.

"Is this a bad time?" Sam surveyed the office. He waved to a receptionist looking in his direction. Another agent appeared to be filling out a contract with a young couple, probably buying their first home.

"Oh, no. This is a perfect time." Laura took Olivia's hand in hers and stood. "I was supposed to show a property, but the clients cancelled. What's up?"

"I want to talk business."

"Oh." Laura's eyes diverted to Olivia, and she cleared her throat. Sam couldn't read her reaction, but it wasn't what he had hoped. His whole plan depended on this. The tone of her voice was uneasy. "Okay. Let's go to my office."

He followed Laura and Olivia to the glass enclosed office illuminated by fluorescent lights hovering over a humming computer, files stacked on the desk, and an open file cabinet drawer, all attesting to Laura's busy day. In sharp contrast, the office next door was dark, its door closed. Sam felt strange entering Laura's office instead of the one next to it. The one that Maggie once filled with such energy.

Laura pulled paper from her printer and fished a box of crayons from her lower desk drawer. She handed the supplies to Olivia and invited her to sit in the big chair behind her desk. Laura took a seat in a client chair next to Sam. "What's up?"

He shifted in his seat, uncertain how to proceed. "About an hour ago, I thought I was coming here to see if you would buy the business—"

Laura shook her head. "There's no way, Sam. I thought you might consider selling, so Jason and I crunched the numbers, and well, I don't think we can swing it. In a couple of years maybe. But not right now. Financially, we just can't."

Sam laced his fingers and leaned back. "Well, that's not why I'm here. Actually, I have a slightly different proposal. I don't want to let the business go. Maggie worked so hard to develop all this, and she loved it. She loved working with the people, helping them sell, helping them buy. She loved the houses, the beautiful ones, the ones that needed a little TLC. The business end of it, and the personal end of it—matching the right buyer with the right home." Sam laughed. "She used to drive me crazy, talking about it all the time." His voice grew softer. "She loved it. All of it."

"Yes. Yes, she did." Laura smiled in spite of the tears that threatened to spill.

"I can't let that go. I feel like I'm giving up part of Maggie if I do."

"I understand. And I'll help you keep the business going anyway I can."

"I want a little more than that. I need you to run the business, but—" Sam turned in his chair to face her more directly. "I want you to be a partner."

Laura's hand went to her mouth.

Sam continued quickly, desperate to be heard before Laura declined. "Now, I know you said you can't buy the business right now, but can you buy in? I'm willing to do whatever it takes it to make this work for us both. What do you think?" Sam held his breath.

Laura reached for a tissue from the corner of her desk and dabbed her eyes. Sam waited for her to find her voice. Finally, she smiled. "Well, I have to talk to Jason, of course, but I think it's . . . possible. I mean, I can't say for certain without talking to him, but Sam, I think the answer is yes."

Sam slowly released the breath he held captive. "Yes?"

Laura nodded, shaking more tears loose. As he extended his hand and enclosed it around hers to seal the agreement, she leaned into him and pressed her forehead against his shoulder. Sam felt her body shake. He tried to retreat, but he couldn't find the familiar wall he took refuge behind, or fight the swell of emotion. Instead, the warmth of tears rolled down his face. "I know, Laura. I know." The words were barely audible, his voice broken with grief. "I miss her so much."

Then two small hands pushed between them, separating Sam and Laura. Olivia looked up at them.

"Don't cry, Laura. Daddy, don't cry." Olivia pulled them both to her and put an arm around each of them. "It will make Mommy sad."

Laura pulled her close. "You, Miss Olivia, are precious."

When Laura released her, Sam rumpled his daughter's hair. "She sure helps me keep it together. Don't you, Livi?"

"Yes, Daddy." She returned to her business at Laura's desk. "What would you do without me?"

Sam laughed as he reached for a tissue. He took a breath and gathered himself. The business partnership was only half the reason for his visit.

"Laura, you talk to Jason, and then why don't the three of us get together over dinner to discuss the details. Isn't Travis Fisher the attorney Maggie keeps on retainer? Would you feel comfortable with him drawing up the contract?"

"Sure." Laura's enthusiasm was evident in her smile. "I can't believe we're doing this."

"Well, if you can't believe this, you're really not going to believe what I have to say next." Sam shook his head. He couldn't believe it himself.

The smile on Laura's face was replaced by two creases between her eyebrows. Did she know? How could she? Would she tell him it was a big mistake? Doubt gnawed at him again, but he shook it away.

"Well, are you going to leave me in suspense?"

Was this it? The next right thing, like Roxy said? He was certain it was. Almost. Sam laughed out loud.

"I want to buy the Hitching house."

Maggie was convinced the day would never end. After Sam read her journal and left so quickly, she was certain he had decided to return to work, to bury his guilt in his job. Why else would he take his gun and badge? Then she started to worry. How much more could he take? He was grieving her death. He was struggling to parent the girls. He certainly wasn't thinking clearly when he left the house in the middle of the night while the girls slept. And now that he read the journal, now that he knew Maggie suspected he'd had an affair, was it too much? Had he reached a breaking point? Without the girls in the house, without Sam, Maggie was weak. She lay on the couch, watching the minutes pass too slowly.

Finally a car pulled into the drive. Hoping it was Sam, she willed herself to the living room window. Rachel emerged from the same car her father ordered her to never get into again. Seeing her daughter fueled a fire that ran through her veins. How could Rachel continue to defy her father so intentionally?

Then panic replaced her fury. If Rachel came home in that car, where was Sam? Why hadn't he picked her up? And where was Olivia? A picture of her child waiting at an abandoned playground flashed through Maggie's mind. No, that wouldn't happen. The school would have called home if no one had arrived for Olivia, and the phone had not rung all afternoon.

Rachel's key turned in the lock. She entered the house, slamming the door behind her, mumbling. Maggie moved closer to listen.

"Picking up Olivia. Ride the bus. Yeah, right. I took the bus, all right, Dad. Hope you're happy." She grabbed a cheese stick and a juice box from the refrigerator and stomped to her room.

Relief washed over Maggie. Sam had Olivia. They were fine. So she turned her attention to Rachel and followed her into her bedroom. Other than to eat dinner, she doubted Rachel would come out the rest of the evening.

Rachel powered up her laptop and dropped her backpack on top of her desk. She opened it and rummaged through the contents. Then she opened a side pouch and found what she must have been searching for, a half-empty bag of Skittles. She took off the rubber band that held the bag closed and poured the contents into her hand. Maggie watched her fish through the candy, expecting her to choose a specific color, a red one maybe, or purple. When Rachel found it, Maggie gasped. Another pill. Rachel popped it into her mouth and washed it down with juice. Maggie had watched a similar scene every day after school, each time as disappointed as the first time, pain stabbing clear through her. But this was different. This time Rachel hid the drug in a bag of candy. What was she thinking? What if Olivia found the candy and accidently took the pill?

"Think, Rachel. *Think.* This isn't just about you. You're making dangerous choices for more than just yourself here."

Rachel stood immobile. Emptiness floated between them. Then, with a sudden, violent motion, she swept the backpack off her desk. It slammed into the wall and landed upside down, gaping open to let the contents spill onto the floor. With a swift kick, she sent loose papers flying.

Maggie's frustration mounted. She knew, somehow, on some level, Rachel was aware of her presence. But why couldn't her words get through? She was certain, without a doubt, God returned her to her family for a reason. But she was failing. What was she doing wrong?

Rachel sat down at her laptop, inserted the earbuds from her cell phone, and navigated to a website to chat. Maggie hated that laptop. That's all Rachel did now. She ignored her homework, her family, her art. Nothing mattered except the pills and her life on the Internet. Maggie read over her shoulder as Rachel chatted with strangers about trivial stuff, school, parents, normal things Maggie would expect to overhear in a teenage conversation. But there was something about it she didn't like. Maybe it was Rachel's ability to connect with a stranger on a computer and her inability to connect with people who care about her in the real world, like her father or Kristen or the youth pastor whose calls she continued to refuse. It all made Maggie heavy.

Rachel's fingers danced across the keyboard and then began to slow. Her shoulders relaxed, and her head fell slightly forward. Maggie recognized the drug's effect on her daughter. At least now she wouldn't be so agitated. Maggie hated the thought as it surfaced, but it was true. Only in the hours that Rachel was under the influence could Maggie stand close to her, touch her, or lie beside her. During those moments she talked to Rachel, encouraging her to work at her easel or go to her darkroom, willing her the strength to cope, loving her as a child hiding behind anger and grief. Sometimes she sang their favorite lullaby, changing the original words to list, instead, Rachel's favorite things, just like Rachel insisted when she was little.

Certain Rachel was lost in the haze, Maggie stood behind the chair, wrapped her arms around her daughter, rested her lips on top of her head, and breathed in the scent of her shampoo. "No matter what, you're still my little girl. I love you, Rachel."

Laughter echoed from the kitchen. Sam and Olivia were home and Maggie's family was intact. Happy sounds slipped down the hallway, a welcomed surprise. It had been several days since laughter rang through the house. And after Sam's discovery and disappearance this afternoon, laughter certainly wasn't what she expected to hear.

"Rachel!" Olivia called out as she ran to her sister's bedroom. "Rachel! We got pizza!"

Rachel's head bobbed to the rhythm Maggie could hear through the earphones. Olivia grabbed her sister's sleeve to get her attention.

"Quit it!" Rachel snapped, but it didn't squelch Olivia's enthusiasm.

"Come on. We got pizza. It's a celebration!"

Rachel narrowed her eyes. "What's to celebrate?" Venom marked her words.

Olivia shrugged. "Daddy just said we're celebrating, so come on."

Sam celebrating?

Olivia pulled at her sister's arm, but Rachel shook off her grip, a little too aggressively Maggie thought.

"Leave me alone." Rachel turned her attention back to her music and the laptop.

Olivia's shoulders dropped in disappointment. Maggie's heart sank.

"Rachel Nicole!"

Sam's voice bellowed from the bedroom door. In three long strides he was at Rachel's desk. He slammed down the lid of the laptop and jerked the earphones from her ears. As Rachel looked up at her dad, Maggie recognized her attempt to mask the fear in her eyes with a plea of innocence.

"Did you hear your sister? Get yourself to the dining room table. Now!"

Rachel searched for an excuse. "I, uh, I'm not really hungry." Her eyes darted to Sam's face and away again.

"Now!" Sam stood like a soldier at attention, his arm extended, finger pointing toward the bedroom door. "And leave your attitude here. We're going to have a pleasant family dinner whether you want to or not." He waited for Rachel to get up from her desk and lead the way.

"That's more like it, Sam." She patted him on the shoulder, though he didn't know it. "Take charge."

In the middle of the dining room table was a carry-out pizza box, a stack of paper plates and napkins, and three cans of A&W root beer. Maggie took her usual seat while Sam served dinner. Olivia picked at the slice of pizza on her plate, but Rachel devoured hers. Sam chewed slowly, inspecting her. What was he thinking? It was several minutes before he broke the silence.

"I thought you weren't hungry." He raised an eyebrow as Rachel reached for a third piece.

Maggie detected the expression on Rachel's face, the declaration that she'd been caught. She shrugged. "Guess I was hungrier than I thought."

"Hmm." Sam continued to study her.

She began to squirm, apparently aware of her father's stare. "So, Olivia said we're celebrating. Celebrating what?"

Maggie didn't like her daughter's diversion tactic.

Olivia's face brightened, and she bounced in her chair. "Yeah, Daddy, what are we celebrating? Is there cake?"

Sam locked his gaze on Rachel and held the tension in the room a moment longer before relinquishing. Then he cleared his throat, and Maggie watched the revival of the man she knew was buried deep in the shell of what Sam had become.

"Sorry, Livi, there's no cake, but—"

Maggie could feel Sam's energy, his pause to capture the girls' attention.

"But what?" Olivia's eyes were wide with wonder. "What is it?"

"Well—" Sam looked from Olivia to Rachel and back to Olivia. Then he glanced at Maggie's chair. She longed for him to know she was there. "I retired today."

Maggie stiffened.

"What's that?" Olivia's forehead wrinkled.

Rachel stopped chewing and stared at him.

"It means I don't have to go to work anymore. I can be a dad and take care of you."

"But, don't we, like, have to have money?" Rachel turned her head and looked at him sideways.

"That's the nice thing about retirement. I still get paid, and I've done a little investing. We're going to be fine. I planned to work a lot longer." He nodded toward Rachel. "To at least get you through college. But things have changed. I think my job is too dangerous, too demanding, for a . . . single dad."

Enthusiasm drained from Sam's words, but only momentarily.

"I'm not actually retired yet. Retirement won't be official until I run out of sick days and comp time, which . . . well, never mind. It's too complicated. The bottom line is I don't have to go to work."

Maggie had difficulty gauging Sam's tone. His excitement hinted at genuine, but something conflicting lay beneath. And then his tone turned almost jubilant.

"But there's more." His eyes widened, adding mystery to his announcement.

More? Maggie was still reeling from the shock of Sam's retirement. When he talked about his future, retirement was never part of the conversation. Promotion was. He had lofty career goals, plans to rise through the ranks, long before he considered retirement. And she knew he was well on his way up. Her heart was burdened by the sacrifice he made, another loss suffered, because of her.

"What else, Daddy?" Olivia wrinkled her nose. "I hope it's better than tirement 'cause I don't get that."

Sam laughed. "Better than retirement, huh? Well, maybe it is." He sat back in his chair and grinned at his daughters. Maggie was perplexed by the excitement in his face, confused about what could be better than retirement, when retirement wasn't something that Lieutenant Samuel Blake would be excited about. Maggie worried as Sam prepared to deliver the news, clearly satisfied with himself.

"Rachel, Olivia . . . we are buying the Hitching house."

His words hung in empty air. Maggie's body went limp. Her head felt hollow as "Hitching house" bounced around inside.

"But we already have a house." Olivia's voice rang with more confusion, and Maggie felt sorry for her, certain Olivia must still be waiting for something to celebrate. "I don't want to live in another house."

"You're right, Livi. We do have a house, and we're not moving. I bought the Hitching house because—"

"Because you can't let things go, can you, Dad?" Rachel interjected, slamming her fist on the table to accentuate the indictment, increasing her volume as she continued. "Mom is gone. Dead. Not coming back. What part of that don't you get?"

"Hey." Sam rumbled a warning.

"No, Dad. You're in denial. You still let Olivia talk to Mom like she's here. This house is a shrine." She waved her arm through the air. "Everywhere I look I see her stuff. Aren't you supposed to get rid of a dead person's stuff, give it to Goodwill or something? I'm sick of the reminders." Her tone grew with accusation. "And now you've found another way to hang on to her, haven't you? How many times did Mom practically beg you to buy that house? But you always said no. Why now? And if you tell me you're gonna make it a bed and breakfast, I swear I'll puke!" By the time the last words came out, Rachel's voice had reached another octave. She pushed her chair back so hard it crashed into the wall behind her. "Well?"

"Well what, Rachel? Am I having a hard time letting go of your mom?" Sam's voice broke. "What do you want me to say? Of course, I am." Silence surrounded the table.

When Sam spoke again, his voice was confident. "But that's not why I'm buying the house. Really, I don't know if I can even explain why. I just know it's what I need to do. And it's what I should have done a long time ago, when your mom wanted to. But it's not about hanging on to your mom." Sam looked down and twisted the platinum band around his ring finger. His voice was soft. "Somehow it's about letting her go."

Rachel shook her head. "Well, good luck with that!" She turned and stormed away from the table.

Maggie placed her hand over Sam's, sensing his warmth, his strength. She didn't understand it either, why Sam had chosen this point in time to buy the Hitching house, but that didn't stop her tears. "Thank you, Sam. Thank you."

Olivia got down from her chair and put her hand on Sam's chest to push him back from the table. Sam made room for her and lifted her to his lap. She kissed his cheek and wrapped her arms tightly around his neck. Sam squeezed her back.

"Thank you, Daddy."

"For what, sweetie?"

"For making Mommy happy."

Olivia pulled away from the embrace and found his eyes. He stared back. For the second time that evening, Maggie wondered what he was thinking.

His voice was cautious, almost a whisper. "Is Mommy happy?"

A smile captured Olivia's face and her blond curls bounced as she answered with a single exaggerated nod.

Sam pulled Olivia back into his embrace. Maggie rose and stood beside them, her arms enveloping them both.

CHAPTER 16

"I want this one to go up high, but I can't reach. Can you do it for me, Aunt Erin?" Olivia stretched on tip-toe with a crystal snowflake ornament in her hand. "Right there by the blue light. That will make the snowflake sparkly!"

"Sure, honey, how's that?"

"Perfect!"

As her sister and aunt decorated the Scotch pine the family picked out at the tree farm that afternoon, Rachel removed lids from plastic storage containers, persistent in her search to find her mother's snow globes.

"They're not here." She made the announcement again, trying desperately to recruit her dad to join her search, but he was occupied with unraveling strands of outdoor lights.

"Have you checked every box?"

As her dad glanced her way, Rachel waved her arm toward the plastic lids and exposed containers surrounding her.

"Well, that's every box I could find in the basement. That's all of it."

"It can't be all of it." Rachel couldn't hide the

desperation in her voice. She had to find the snow globes. As she surveyed the living room, nothing was right. Aunt Erin put the old lights with the big colored bulbs on the tree, and her dad didn't even say anything about it. Her mom hated those lights. Only the clear blinky lights go on the tree. And the garland was gold and fake and ugly that her dad found in an old box, not the homemade popcorn and cranberry garland she and her mom and Olivia made every year. Her dad didn't know how to pop popcorn the old fashioned way he said. But it was tradition. *Their* tradition. How could they skip the garland? And now nobody cared about the snow globes, her mom's collection that grew by one every year as they searched after-Christmas clearance sales for the perfect bargain. What else would decorate the mantel, the coffee table, the end tables? Rachel needed to find the tiny, serene worlds captured in balls of glass that her mom would scatter around the room. Defeated, she sat down among the open containers and listened as Olivia told Aunt Erin about various ornaments.

"This one is a birthday cake for Baby Jesus I made in Sunday School." Olivia displayed a paper cutout hanging from a loop of yarn. "And this is a seashell we found on vacation. Mommy glued this string on it and made it an ornament."

"How pretty." Aunt Erin made a serious face. "This is a very beautiful tree you have decorated, Miss Olivia."

"Yeah, but it's not pretty like the fancy matchy-matchy trees in the stores. Mommy says our tree is a memory Christmas tree because our ornaments are memories, and we get to remember every year when we decorate it."

"Like this one." Aunt Erin held up a glass icicle. "This

was my mom's ornament, your grandma's. When I was a little girl, our tree had lots of these icicle ornaments."

"See? Isn't it fun remembering that?" Olivia hung the seashell on the tree.

Aunt Erin's lips pressed together. "Yeah, sweetie. It makes me a little sad because I miss my mom, and your mom, but I like remembering, too."

The room grew still. Rachel watched as Aunt Erin hung the glass icicle and admired it, her head tilted to the right, her arms crossed in front of her. Even though her aunt was her mom's sister, Rachel never thought they looked very much alike. But standing as she was, if her hair were a few shades darker. . . .

Rachel didn't know why. Maybe because it was Christmas. Maybe because she was tired of constantly fighting the pain. But instead of strangling the longing that stirred inside her, she allowed it open like a tiny bud beginning to blossom. She studied Aunt Erin's silhouette in the glow of the Christmas tree and imagined, instead, her mom standing before an art piece Rachel just finished, thoughtfully admiring it, telling Rachel how proud she was of her talent. For a moment, she remembered what it was like to have a mom. A breath later, the feeling was lost as if it never existed.

Sam watched Rachel quietly leave the room, debating whether to stop her or to follow her. He knew this was a difficult night for her, for all of them. He had spent the last two months as a full-time dad trying to master when to push Rachel and when to back off. Tonight he decided she might need some time alone.

"How's she doing?" Erin placed another ornament on the tree.

Earlier that afternoon Sam was irritated when an unexpected doorbell interrupted the football game on TV, but he couldn't express how relieved he was to see his sister-in-law on the other side of the door, loaded down with a suitcase and Christmas presents. He wouldn't have to get the girls, or himself, through the holiday alone.

"Rachel's doing as well as she can manage, I suppose. But better, I think, although I wonder how much is genuine and how much is just to appease me."

"What do you mean?"

"Well, her grades are coming back up, and although she still spends too much time alone in her room, at least when she's with us she doesn't seem so angry. She's doing enough to keep me off her case, but she doesn't really talk to me. And I'm not sure if she has friends anymore. The only real communicating she does is on that stupid laptop."

"You mean like chatting?"

Sam heard the concern in Erin's voice. "Yeah, that's what I mean. I know. It worries me. How can she tell total strangers what she can't tell me?"

"Sam, you can't—"

"I know what you're going to say." He stopped untangling a strand of lights and looked at her. "But I monitor what she's doing, who she's talking to. I'm a detective, don't forget."

"Does she know you're. . . ?" Erin's voice faded.

"What, spying on her? I don't think so, but quite frankly, I don't care if she does."

Erin cleared her throat. "Well, uh, do you think it's okay? I mean, what you're doing? I'm not a parent, but

I was a teenage girl. Isn't there some boundary you're crossing?"

Sam prepared to defend himself, although he'd wondered the same thing in the beginning. "First of all, Rachel often leaves the site open. When her computer hibernates, all I have to do is hit a key and everything appears. If she were so concerned about her privacy, she would do a better job protecting it. But more importantly, as a father, I have to know what my daughter is going through. With the way she keeps her feelings all inside, this website has been a lifeline for us both. She chats, and I get an insight into what she is thinking and feeling. Honestly, I don't know where either of us would be right now without it." Sam hesitated before asking, but he wanted to know. "Do you think it's wrong?"

During the few moments of silence before Erin's response, he was surprised at how much he wanted to hear her opinion, whether she agreed or not. Parenting alone was so difficult.

"Nope."

"No?" Somehow that wasn't the answer he expected.

"Your motives are pure, Sam. You're not trying to control her life or catch her doing something wrong. You're trying to protect her, and right now, with the way she has shut people out, this is the only option she has given you."

Sam was surprised as his throat tightened. Warmth filled his eyes, and he turned away so Erin wouldn't see. Hoping his voice would sound normal, he said, "Thank you."

"Hey, Dad, look."

Sam laid down the strand of lights he had been wrestling and hurried to relieve Rachel of the large container she carried into the living room.

"You found Mom's snow globes!" Olivia cheered.

"No. I mean, yes. But, Dad—"

A plea in Rachel's voice caught Sam. It was then that he noticed the path of fresh tears staining her cheeks. Rachel lifted a thick file that lay on top of the container.

"I found this."

There was only one other place Rachel could think to search for the snow globes, her mother's closet. If they weren't in the basement with the rest of the Christmas decorations, the closet was the only other logical place they could be. But she couldn't imagine opening the door that had been closed for months and walking into a miniature room where she would be surrounded by the very essence of her mom.

As she gripped the door knob, the coolness of the metal disappeared into the heat of her palm. She squeezed tightly, willing her hand to turn, her arm to push, her feet to walk—until she found herself inside. The faint scent of her mom's perfume still lingered on the clothes, ushering in memories: how grown up she felt as a little girl when her mom shared her expensive perfume on special occasions; the smell of the car when her mom picked her up after school; her scent as she kissed Rachel for the last time before she hurried out the door. Rachel braced herself for tears, but they didn't come. She ran her hands across the clothes hanging lifeless in front of her, picturing her mom in the tweed jacket or the purple blouse or her favorite summer dress. Still no tears. She was relieved.

Then she remembered her mission. The snow globes. Boxes on the shelves would be too small to hold them, so she searched the closet floor. In the back corner she spotted a container identical to the ones her dad brought up from the basement. As she pulled the container toward her, it tipped forward, dumping a stack of papers at her feet. Frustrated at the inconvenience, Rachel grabbed the scattered contents and shoved them back into their folder. It wasn't until she closed the cover that she realized what the folder contained. In her mother's handwriting were the words *Bed and Breakfast*. Rachel gently opened the folder and searched the pages inside—notes, pictures, fabric swatches, paint chips. In her hands she held her mother's dream. And then the tears came.

"What is this?" Sam took the folder from Rachel.

"What is it, Daddy?" Olivia echoed.

Sam glanced from Rachel to the folder. He traced the letters on the cover and quickly thumbed through the first few pages inside. "Is this?"

Rachel began to shake with sobs. Erin rushed to her and wrapped her arms around her.

Numbly Sam sat down and began sifting through the contents, oblivious to Olivia's repeating question. As he deciphered Maggie's handwriting, followed her arrows that pointed to pictures, touched the samples of fabric, Sam had the beginnings of a vision. When he looked up to answer Olivia's question, tears filled his eyes.

"These are Mommy's plans for the Hitching house, Livi."

Erin cleared her throat. "I'm sorry, but, I don't understand. The Hitching house? You mean that old place Maggie talked about?"

"Yep, that old place." Olivia nodded.

"Yeah." Sam said. "I bought it."

"What?" Erin's arms dropped to her side as stared at him. "Are you kidding?"

He laughed. How could he explain what he really didn't understand himself? "Well, if I'm gonna retire, I need something to keep me busy—besides the girls, that is. I sold part of the real estate business to finance it."

The expression on Erin's face begged for more information.

Certain he would create more questions than he would answer, Sam continued. "When the idea first hit me, it was kind of an impulse, but it seemed like the right thing to do." He shrugged. "But when I closed on it a few weeks ago, the reality of it sank in. The dream was Maggie's, not mine. Without her vision, I had no idea where to begin. I started thinking I'd made a big mistake."

"But now?" Rachel whispered.

Sam gripped the file, trying to read his daughter's face. Was she still accusing him of trying too hard to hang on to Maggie? "But now I have Mom's vision, literally." He reached for Rachel's hand and squeezed. When she squeezed back, Sam closed his eyes, relishing the connection she had not allowed him to feel in months.

Olivia poked his shoulder. "Daddy."

"Yeah, Sweetie?"

"Mommy says Merry Christmas."

The room was silent. Sam pulled Olivia onto his lap and kissed her cheek. He looked at Rachel, at Erin, and then at the glowing tree.

"Merry Christmas," he whispered.

Maggie hadn't been this sad in weeks, even as she sat on the sidelines, forced to accept the inner battles her family fought. But this night, as Christmas came to life inside her home, her separation from her family was too much. How she wished she could join Olivia as she rummaged through boxes of decorations, or pop popcorn so Rachel could make her garland, or hug her sister for the rare gift of leaving her office for the holidays. But most of all, at this moment, she wished she could make herself known to Sam.

She was so grateful for the connection she had with her youngest daughter, but often her attempts to prompt Olivia to communicate for her were frustrating. She had to remind herself her child didn't possess the capacity to understand or express complex adult emotions. Olivia couldn't tell Sam how proud Maggie was that he was trying so hard to be the father he wanted to be, or thank him for being patient when Olivia talked about her, or to her, or for her. She wanted to tell Sam she realized how difficult it was for him to know when to allow Rachel room to work through her grief and anger when years in law enforcement had developed his desire to control every situation.

And she wanted so badly to be a part of renovating the Hitching house, but she couldn't. Aside from him having her conglomeration of ideas in a tattered folder, he had to do it on his own. But more important than all of it, Maggie wanted desperately to warn Sam. He was right. Rachel was isolating herself from friends. When she replaced Kristen with that girl Cricket, Maggie was worried about the changes she saw in her daughter. But now, Rachel had replaced Cricket, and leaving that website open was only a ploy to keep Sam from snooping into her real online activity.

The ache in Maggie's chest ran deep. She listened as Olivia's sweet voice sang "Away in a Manger" and watched as Rachel arranged snow globes around the living room. Rachel unpacked another globe and walked to the mantel where Maggie stood.

"This is the one we got after Christmas last year." She shook it and placed it next to a stocking holder, pushing it back to make sure it rested securely on the mantel like Maggie had taught her.

Maggie watched the fake snow swirl and fall on the tiny ice skaters inside the glass. She used to be mesmerized by the little depictions of happiness preserved inside a world of beauty and serenity. But now, as she placed her hand on the glass globe, she felt alone, trapped inside her own little world. The ache inside her grew claws. She imagined heaving the glass globe on the stone hearth beneath her.

A loud crash startled her. Both girls screamed.

"What the—?" Sam turned suddenly in Maggie's direction.

Maggie looked down to discover what everyone else in the room already knew. The snow globe lay shattered in a puddle on the floor. How?

"I'm sorry!" Rachel began to cry as Erin rushed to pick up the pieces.

"It's okay, honey." Sam looked from her to the debris. "It was just an accident. You must not have put it all the way on the mantel."

"But—I did, Dad. I'm sure I did. I checked to make sure it wouldn't fall. I put it right here." Rachel reenacted placing the globe.

A puzzled look crossed his face as he walked toward her.

"Right there?" He pointed. "Are you sure?"

"Yes, I'm sure."

"Then how did—?"

Sam didn't finish the question. But Maggie knew what he was going to ask. How did the globe end up smashed on the other end of the hearth?

CHAPTER 17

"This place is going to be magnificent." Erin sat at the top of the staircase beside Sam holding Maggie's folder open on his lap. She pointed to the paint chip Maggie had marked *foyer*. "Look at this color, and she wants it in satin finish. See how the light is going to come through the front door and windows and reflect off the paint? She had such a good eye for seeing past the flaws, all the hard work, to find the potential."

Sam laughed. "I think that's the only reason she married me." He joked, but he wondered how far he was from being the husband Maggie envisioned when she said I do all those years ago. Did the work she put into their relationship produce the potential she had hoped for? Sam knew his flaws, his failings. Maggie deserved more. He looked at the house around him, at Maggie's dreams he held in his hands. Rebuilding a man wasn't like rebuilding a house. Besides, it was too late for Sam to be the man Maggie had deserved. Fixing up the Hitching house was the only way Sam knew how to be that man, if only she were still here.

"So, not to change the subject, but I didn't want to ask in front of the girls, not that it's any of my business." Erin tilted her head. "This retirement. Sam. Really?"

"Really."

"I mean, they say after you lose someone, you shouldn't make any significant decisions for a year. Within weeks you ended the career you love and bought the house you hate."

"I think hate is a little strong. I didn't *appreciate* the house before."

"Okay." Erin raised a shoulder. "But you're missing my point, which is your career. I know how you threw yourself into your work. How are you not going to go crazy without it?"

"I feel crazy every day without it." But would his explanation make sense to anyone but himself? "I don't know, Erin. Some things are more important. It took sacrificing almost everything for me to realize that. And right now, raising Rachel and Olivia is more important than my career. It was easier to give up one job and focus on the other—rather than do both poorly, which is what I was doing. Besides, I stay connected. I testified on a couple of my cases that went to trial. And my detectives call me in every so often to consult on investigations, although sometimes I wonder how well I trained them. They shouldn't need me to answer some of those questions."

Erin tapped her chin. "Sounds to me like someone is trying to keep you around."

Sam hadn't considered that, because staying around wasn't a consideration. "No, when the time I accrued runs out, retirement will be official."

"Oh? So you aren't officially retired yet?"

Sam detected a question hidden within Erin's question. "No. Why?"

"No reason. Just curious."

Erin stood and started down the staircase. Sam followed. He, too, had something he wanted to ask, something he was embarrassed to say out loud.

"Since you already think I'm crazy," Sam joked, trying to find a way into the subject, "can I ask a question that will convince you I really am losing it?"

Erin stopped at the bottom of the steps and turned to Sam. "Sure. Shoot."

"Olivia. Well, you know, she says things, things that can't be . . . real."

"You mean about her mom?"

"Yes. Like she, like Olivia thinks—"

"Her mom is still here."

"Yes." Sam was relieved Erin said it so he didn't have to.

"And?" Erin prompted.

"Well, it's crazy, right? I mean, it doesn't make sense that—that Maggie would be . . . still here."

Erin smiled. Sam's sudden defensiveness surprised him. Why should he feel defensive? He didn't believe it himself, right? Because it wasn't possible.

"Are you trying to tell me I've been sleeping in a haunted house the past week?" Erin teased.

Sam's temper flared and his face flushed with embarrassment. "No." He failed to mask his reaction.

"I'm sorry." Erin put her hand on his arm. "I'm being insensitive. Look, Sam. You know me. I'm an attorney. Everything has to be based on evidence. It's hard to gather evidence that you can't . . . see. As for Olivia, it's just her way of coping. She's five. She doesn't understand the finality of death."

Erin was right. Detectives base decisions on evidence, too. But Sam knew there was risk in that, because sometimes when a detective wants to see something badly enough, the evidence may seem to lead in that direction, even though it really doesn't. Objectivity is vital. So what was Sam's evidence? It wasn't *just* what Olivia said, it was when she said it. The timing of her delivery was beyond the scope of a child. And the snow globe. Was that evidence? He explained it away by insisting Rachel had not placed the snow globe exactly where she had thought, but his attempt to debunk the truth caused hurt to surface in her eyes. And then there was her scent. Maggie's. Or was it his imagination? Ever since the accident, sleep had not come easily to him. But the past few nights, when Sam laid his head on his pillow, the scent of her lavender lotion surrounded him, settled his mind, and sleep would find him.

"Sometimes I wish it were true." Sam whispered his confession. "I just wish I could talk to her."

"Then talk to her."

Sam's forehead creased. "Okay, so first you say Maggie isn't there, and now you say she is? I'm confused."

"No, I'm saying talk to her. If you have things to say, Sam, just say it. It helps to say things out loud. Don't you ever talk to yourself when you need to process? Right now it sounds like you need to work through some things, emotionally. So talk to her."

He thought about Maggie's journal. It was her way of processing, talking. Maybe Erin was right. Then he imagined himself sorting laundry or cooking dinner, holding one-sided conversations. He felt ridiculous thinking about it.

A knock drew Sam's attention to the front door. He

peered through the glass and recognized the intruder. "Oh great."

"Who is it?" Erin strained to see.

"Rob. The pastor from Maggie's church. What the heck is he doing here?" Sam exhaled as he walked to the door. He opened it and a look of relief crossed the pastor's face.

"Sam." Rob stepped inside with an outstretched hand.

Sam accepted the handshake. "Pastor Rob. You remember my sister-in-law, Erin."

"Yes, of course. Hello, Erin." The pastor returned his attention to Sam. "So Olivia was right? She told me a few Sundays ago that you bought this house. I thought I recognized your pick-up in the drive, so I decided to take a chance and see if I could catch you."

"Yep. All true." He could see the questions bouncing around Rob's mind, but Sam wasn't about to explain to him of all people why he was now the owner of this property. "What can I do for you?"

"Nothing. Nothing at all. I just wanted to check in, see how you and the girls are doing." Rob hesitated. "Holidays can be rough."

Sam's defenses eased, not because of Rob, though. "Yes, it's been rough. But not as rough as it would have been without Erin." Sam smiled at Erin as he realized it was the first time he had expressed appreciation for her spending Christmas with them. "She's been a good distraction for Olivia and Rachel." Sam didn't want to imagine the past few days without Maggie's sister nearby, the pit he would have been trying to pull himself and Rachel from, or the task of faking Christmas spirit for Olivia's sake. The holiday hadn't been all candy canes and gingerbread, but it had been bearable.

"So, you're a pastor." Erin pursed her lips and squinted. "I have a question for you. Do you believe in ghosts?"

"Erin!" Sam's cheek's flushed.

Erin made a quick, dismissive face at him. "I mean, here Sam has bought this old house that he plans to make into a B&B. But I told him, you never know what could be lurking in these empty rooms, and that could be bad for business. Do you think ghosts exist?"

Rob cupped his chin as if he were considering his answer. "Well, my initial response is no, I don't believe a person can manifest himself after death as a ghost. I believe the Bible is clear that believers immediately enter into the Lord's presence, like the story of Lazarus and the rich man."

The threat of disappointment stung Sam.

"I do believe the memory of someone, our sense or connection to them, can be very powerful. So, maybe we can have a *sense* of someone who has gone on. But the only way I can explain that biblically, and this is a loose explanation, is by considering Hebrews 11, often called the Faith Hall of Fame. Hebrews 11 lists heroes of the faith—Abraham, Isaac, Moses, and many others. Then the very next chapter, Hebrews 12:1, refers to us as being surrounded with a 'great cloud of witnesses,' meaning all the heroes of the faith. Some interpret the word witness to mean spectator. So, I suppose one could argue this makes a case for the possibility of someone still being here. The very *small* possibility."

"Well, there you go, Sam." Erin held out her hands. "This house could be haunted. Or not. That clears up everything."

Rob and Sam smiled at Erin's declaration, though Sam a bit nervously.

"There's one thing I know for sure," Rob held up a finger. "We have miniscule human minds that try to figure out God's incomprehensible mysteries. The intersection of the physical and spiritual worlds is one of those mysteries."

Sam glanced at Erin, but she was looking at Rob. So it's possible? He decided to dismiss Erin's betrayal.

"Thanks for stopping by Rob, for checking on the family." And he meant it. Sam offered his hand as the pastor turned toward the door.

"A B&B, huh?" Rob examined the foyer. "I think you could be on to something here. Good idea."

"It was Maggie's idea," Sam confessed. "Something she'd wanted to do for a long time. It just took me too long to get on board."

"It's never too late, Sam—to get on board." The pastor stepped onto the porch.

And there it was. The thing about Rob that set Sam off. "Quit trying to save my soul!" he wanted to scream. Instead, Sam gritted his teeth and closed the door.

"You really don't like him very much, do you?" Erin grinned. "He seems really nice, you know. Like he genuinely cares."

"The guy just rubs me the wrong way."

"It was thoughtful of him to check on you and the girls." Erin looked at her watch. "Hey, we've got to be going. I'm meeting someone in town."

"Oh?" Sam was surprised. "Anyone I know?"

"Maybe." Erin smiled.

Sam smiled back, but Erin left the mystery hanging in the air.

CHAPTER 18

Maggie missed her sister. Erin left that morning with a promise to return soon, but she knew Erin's job as assistant prosecutor was quicksand. As soon as she stepped into her office, she would be sucked under, along with any memory of her promise. Still, Maggie was blessed that Erin made time for the holidays, for her family. She was generous with her attention and affection, which Olivia monopolized. But Erin had good moments with Rachel, too. Fruitful moments. Through her, Maggie learned Rachel didn't choose to quit painting or drawing. She said it was like the artistic part of her had been filled with wet cement; she just couldn't create anymore. What about photography? Erin had asked. "I can't" was all Rachel said. Erin talked to Rachel about how much time she spent online and encouraged her to spend more time with friends, to go back to youth group. She asked about school, and about Maggie. Maggie appreciated the words Erin shared that she couldn't, as well as her approach—brief conversations in intervals throughout the week, a little at a time for Rachel to digest. Rachel didn't talk much, but at least she seemed to listen. Maybe the wall she had built around herself was beginning to weaken. Maggie wondered if it was because of the snow globe.

The shattered snow globe. After the incident, Maggie retreated to her bedroom to escape the confusion, maybe even fear, she heard in her family's voices, saw in their eyes— and to escape her own disbelief. She wasn't certain she had moved the snow globe, but she had no other explanation. Did she dare hope? A phrase kept repeating in her mind. She could still see it on Rachel's computer screen: *develop an ability to interact.* Could Paulie Milton and his theories on lingering spirits have been right? Maggie wanted to try again, to interact with the world around her. She stood at Sam's bedside and looked for something to move. Next to the frame on the nightstand, a pen rested on a legal pad where Sam had scribbled notes for the renovation. Maggie fixed her gaze on it. Hesitant, she started to reach for the pen, but quickly drew back. She was afraid. What if it didn't work? What if there was some other explanation for the snow globe? Maybe it was a fluke. Or maybe, like Sam said, Rachel didn't set it securely on the mantel. But what if it did work? What if she reached down, curled her fingers around the pen, and lifted it?

Chatter from the living room echoed down the hall and into the bedroom. Only moments before, that same chatter should have created a barrier to prevent Maggie from moving the snow globe, but it didn't. And now it should prevent her from moving the pen that lay in front of her. Would it? Carefully she laid her hand on the pen. She could feel the round barrel, the cool metal. She willed her fingers to close around it. And she lifted. Slowly the pen rose with her hand. Maggie laughed, amused, as she watched her hand continue to rise, controlling the physical object inside. She pressed it against her heart.

She didn't know why, or how, but she had broken through. Maybe it was the agony of being alienated from her children, her husband, her sister at Christmas. Or maybe the simple passing of time had given her an element of control over her existence. The reason didn't matter. As she returned the pen to the legal pad, she wondered what she would do with this new gift. She thought of the girls and remembered their faces when they saw the snow globe in pieces. She must be cautious. She didn't want to scare them, to be some ghost to them. Maybe, she decided, she shouldn't use her new ability. But still, she wanted it. It would be nice to feel a little more . . . alive.

Now Maggie enjoyed interacting in her home again, but only when her family was asleep. She sought out safe tasks nobody would notice, hanging the crumpled towels in the girls' bathroom so they would dry better, sweeping the kitchen floor. Sometimes she would pretend Sam was working late, the girls were in bed, and she was finishing the last few chores before calling it a night. In those moments, she could almost remember how it felt to be someone's wife, someone's mother.

Rachel tapped her keyboard to waken her laptop, typed in her password, and checked to see if Smiley15 was online. Yep. She began typing. She made sure to include some details about how good it was to talk to Aunt Erin, that she was studying for the big science test next week, and that she was considering going back to church—only some of which was true—but it would make her dad happy and keep him off her case when he creeped her laptop.

Then she opened another tab and prepared to start a new message, but she couldn't decide. Who did she want to be tonight? LocoLola, who never takes anything too seriously, or, Jezebel, who is emo and cutting with her words, or Dqueen—the D was for drama. She looked at the clock, an hour until bedtime. Maybe she had time to be all three. She logged in as Dqueen first.

As she waited for the page to open, she thought about her talks with Aunt Erin. She felt like a soda that had been shaken too hard, and one pull of the tab would cause her to spew. So she shared only surface stuff, enough to relieve some of the pressure, cautious not to make a mess. It was hard though, because Aunt Erin was an expert at cross examination, and Rachel really wanted to tell somebody. But how could she tell Aunt Erin the two things that would disappoint her the most? I used drugs. And, I'm the reason your sister died. But Aunt Erin would forgive her for the pills, right? Because she quit when her dad's prescription ran out. The pills didn't make it easier like Cricket said. It just made it weird. But the text she sent her mom—Aunt Erin would never forgive her for that. No one would.

She looked at the page that loaded on the screen, her fake profile for Dqueen. She didn't know what made the idea come to her, but she thought it ingenious. She couldn't change who she was in real life, but online, she could live any life she wanted, say anything she wanted. And she had since the beginning of November, confident her secrets were safe, confident her dad would never dig further than the screen she created just for him. Rachel's fingers skated across the keyboard as she began messaging one of her "friends." Suddenly they stopped.

"What the—"

Her screen was black.

Rachel hit the escape key multiple times. Still, no screen. Then she held down the power button. Instantly the screen blinked, and the computer turned on.

"Weird."

She returned to the website and began typing again.

The screen went black.

"Dad!" Rachel called over her shoulder. "Something's wrong with my laptop!"

Sam lay in bed listening to the familiar house sounds—the ice maker dropping ice, the furnace kicking on, the clock ticking in the hallway. It was too quiet. He missed the noise, the laughter, the games and movies, staying up too late and collapsing in bed, too tired to hear the sounds that now penetrated the emptiness. He worried about the girls. Erin brought joy back into their lives, but it left abruptly, as soon as the door closed behind her. Olivia clung to him all afternoon, whiney and dejected. Rachel returned to her usual sullen self. And Sam missed the elements a woman's presence added to a home. He missed Maggie.

The numbers on the clock glowed 10:05 p.m. Sam continued to wait in the stillness. For what? His imagination? A touch of insanity? Because it couldn't be real. Yet, there it was. It was faint at first, but the scent grew stronger as Sam turned toward Maggie's side of the bed. He inhaled deeply and imagined Maggie propped against her pillows, massaging lotion into her hands, her arms, her elbows. How many times had he watched her nightly ritual, never realizing how important it would be to him now?

"Maggie."

His voice tightened. He felt ridiculous, saying her name out loud. But that's what Erin said to do, wasn't it? Talk, process. Except Sam didn't want to process. He wanted to communicate, to connect. With what? An empty pillow? In spite of the absurdity, he spoke again.

"I don't know if you can hear me, but—I thought you might like to know tomorrow is the big day. The renovation officially begins. I have to tell you, I'm a little nervous. This is kind of a big deal—for you, for me—and I'm not sure I'm ready for this. But I gotta start sometime. I figure tomorrow is a good day."

Olivia cried out in her sleep, now a rarity, interrupting him. Erin's departure must have awakened feelings of loss Olivia had suppressed. He waited for a second cry to spring him to action, but it didn't come. So he continued.

"I have an idea, Maggie, and I think you'll like it. I have the file you know, all your notes for the B&B. Since you won't get to see the work in progress, I thought I could take pictures, and I could show you the changes, see if you approve." Sam smiled, knowing if she could hear him, she was smiling, too. He was surprised at how quickly awkwardness left the conversation. The sense of connection was real, but so was the weight settling in his chest, the tears forming in his eyes.

"Maggie, I'm so sorry. I loved you so much while you were here, but, if it's possible, I love you even more now. If I could go back and change everything, I would be the man you always knew I could be. But now it's too late."

Sam pulled one of Maggie's pillows to his chest and breathed deeply, imagining her in his arms, his face nestled in her hair. As he exhaled, his body relaxed, exhaustion moved in. His mind tried to wrestle it away, but within moments the fight was over. Sam rested, unaware his wife was beside him, her arm across his chest, her hand placed so she could feel the beat of his heart.

CHAPTER 19

Sam started his third lap around the old house, inspecting the peeling paint, the rotting window frames, the crumbling chimney. He had made as many trips around the inside of the house. He'd spent the last hour literally walking in circles. When he reached the back porch, he pushed open the screen door and let himself fall into the hammock. "What were you thinking?" He ran his hand through is hair. "You don't have the first clue what to do, where to start. Just because you swung a hammer and hung a little drywall as a kid doesn't mean you have the skills to remodel an entire house, especially this one."

He was on the rollercoaster again, plummeting from the height of possibility to the depth of impossibility. So he made a decision, to lie in the hammock and stare at the deceptive blue sky that looked like spring but felt like winter. The tree branches were grey and barren. He longed for tips of green to appear on the outstretched fingers of the branches, to soften the harshness and bud into full open leaves.

A car door closed, startling him. He pushed himself out of the hammock, walked to the side of the porch, and peered around the corner to see who had pulled into the drive. An unfamiliar truck was parked behind his pick-up. He ducked back, hoping he wouldn't be discovered. He didn't feel like talking to anyone. But then there was a knock at the front door, and after a few moments, the door creaked open. Sam's chin dropped to his chest.

"Hello? Anybody here?"

He sighed. He might as well greet the unwanted guest before the guy walked into the house and found him hiding on the back porch. Sam opened the back door that led into the kitchen. "Yeah, I'm in here." He stepped into the hall and in view of the intruder. Sam didn't recognize him, an older man. He looked harmless enough. "Can I help you?"

"Hi, there." The man stood half inside the door. "Would you mind if I come in?"

"Would you mind if I did?" Sam mumbled as he started down the hall, urging himself to be a reasonable host. "No. Sure. Come on in."

"My name's Gary." The man extended a hand.

"I'm Sam." He accepted the handshake, firm and calloused, a working man's grip.

"So, you bought this place? I saw the sold sign in the yard a while back."

"Yep, I did." Sam lowered his eyes, pretending to study the hardwood floor that begged to be refinished, certain the guy must have stopped by to meet the fool who bought the unsellable relic.

"I love this old house." Gary looked up the staircase, across the balconies that circled the perimeter of the foyer.

"Really?" Sam didn't hide his surprise.

Gary nodded. "The last time I passed, I saw it had

been sold. Today while running errands for the missus, I decided to drive by. I was glad to see your truck parked outside. Hope you don't mind a nosey old man stopping in to visit."

"No, not at all." Sam was surprised again. There was something about this guy that thwarted his tendency to distrust strangers, a side effect from too many years of dealing with criminals. "So, what do you do, Gary?"

"Currently I try to find things to stay busy. I'm a contractor. Well, a recently retired contractor. I'm still adjusting."

Sam blinked. "Are you kidding me?" Had he fallen asleep in the hammock and been caught in a dream? Gary seemed confused. "It's just that—um. How do I say this?" He shoved his hands into his pockets. "Would you be interested in a job?"

Gary chuckled. "What do you have in mind?"

"I sure could use some help with this place. I don't have the first notion how to start." Sam shook his head.

"That was a pretty bold move then, buying the old gal. What do you do?"

Sam half grinned. "I'm, what was it you said, adjusting? To retirement."

"Retirement? You don't look old enough to retire. You have to be twenty years younger than me. What are you retired from?"

"I'm a—was—a detective. I had enough years in. It was time."

"So, you decided to invest in real estate?" Gary's eyes narrowed.

"Oh, it's a long story, Gary. Maybe save it for another day." Sam smiled, acknowledging his diversion.

"Okay, another day." Gary winked and crossed his arms. "So, let's talk about this house. What are you thinking?"

"Well, the plan is to turn it into a bed and breakfast— my wife's idea. She was an interior design major in college. I have a fat folder full of detailed plans for the inside cosmetic work. A lot of that I can handle. However, the structural stuff, that's way out of my skillset. But, I want to do as much of the work as I can." Sam felt the need to explain, but was it to Gary or to himself? "I could hire it out. I could hire out all the work, for that matter, but I don't know. It just seems like something I need to do, the work I mean. I want to be a part of the process." He looked at Gary, expecting to see his puzzled expression again. Instead, Gary nodded his head as if Sam had revealed a great secret of the universe and he was contemplating the implications.

"Most of my career was residential construction." Gary rubbed his chin. "But I spent a good deal of time renovating, too. It's hard work, I'll tell you. It can be a real challenge compared to building a house from the ground up. But there's something different about a remodel, almost spiritual. See, you take this old structure—everything that's flawed, broken, useless—and you make it new again."

Sam turned around and surveyed the staircase, the front parlor, the hall leading to the galley kitchen, imagining the old house coming back to life. Spiritual. Somehow that made sense.

"The old has gone; the new has come." Gary grinned. "Kind of like a man's life, except—now, that's a hard job."

"What do you mean?" Sam's arms crossed in front of him.

"These days I tend to get a bit philosophical, so please forgive a rambling old man, but seems to me that when a man is flawed, broken, sometimes the rebuild can be pretty complex. As big as this job is going to be—" Gary motioned toward the house. "Compared to a man remaking himself, this is simple. A gallon of paint can cover a multitude of flaws, but it takes something mightier to cover a man's sin."

An image flashed in Sam's mind. From the deepest crevice where he had forced it, locked it away, it surfaced. Atlanta. Waking up in the hotel room. The absence of the familiar, of Maggie's leg entwined with his, her arm across his chest. Reaching out to pull her to him. An empty space. Opening his eyes to see her sleeping on the other side of the king bed. Red hair. The realization. *She's not Maggie.* Sam remembered how instantly, in that precise moment, the blinders were removed. He saw himself for who he was and what he had done. How had his judgment been so muddled? How could his decision have been so justifiable, so acceptable one moment, and then—so repulsive the next? He remembered getting out of bed quietly, returning to his own room to shower and pack his things, and flying home a day early to salvage his marriage. Gary was right. Remaking himself hasn't been easy. He'd spent the last two years trying, and now . . .

"Are you preaching?" Sam attempted a joke to cover his guilt, certain his voice had betrayed him.

Gary laughed. "Maybe. But not to you. To me. We've all sinned, but we're blessed that's not how the story ends."

Sam's stomach knotted. It was just his luck. A Bible thumper. He didn't invite an explanation since he was pretty certain he knew where the story was going. Where did this guy come from? Pastor Rob? It was too good to be true, that someone with the experience and skills he needed would simply show up. But, Sam had to admit, there was something about him, something that didn't hack him off. Not like Rob, the poor fella. The pastor tried so hard. For a moment, he felt kind of sorry for him. But only for a moment. Sam studied Gary. What choice did he have?

"So, back to the house." Sam nodded toward the area behind him. "Should we take a tour? We can see what this is going to involve and talk about fitting you into the budget."

Gary pulled off his cap and scratched his head. "I'm not doing this for the money. I'll be glad to have something to keep busy. I'm always working on a project, and right now I'm out of projects." He replaced his cap.

"But we need to discuss fair compensation."

"Really, Sam. I'm not doing this for the money, and if you try to pay me, I won't do it." Gary held his gaze. "Understood?"

Sam studied his eyes. Was this guy real? He scanned his carpenter jeans, his work boots, the years of hard work evidenced by his hands. For free, Sam decided, Gary could quote scripture all day long, as long as he could help turn the Hitching house into Maggie's dream. "Not really, but if you insist—"

"I do." Gary's face was stern. "This is just something I feel like I need to do. And I've learned when I get this feeling, I shouldn't ignore it."

Sam held up his hands in surrender. "I don't know what to say—but thanks. Really. I'm not sure I would have found the courage to actually pick up a hammer or a paint brush. I was intimidated to say the least." He chuckled. "I might have stayed in the hammock all day if you hadn't shown up."

Sam's cell phone interrupted. He looked at the number and excused himself. "Detective Wade, what can I do for you? Okay. Did you talk with the prosecutor? Yeah, I can come in later this afternoon. See you in a few." Sam hung up.

"I don't mean to eavesdrop, but that doesn't sound like retirement." Gary nodded toward the cell phone.

"Actually, right now I'm using up time I've got banked. I still go in every once in a while when my detectives need me. Retirement will be official when I'm out of days."

"And tell me again, why did you retire?"

"I didn't tell you before." Sam grinned. Gary was digging.

"Oh, you didn't, did you?" Gary leaned his head back and squinted, waiting.

"Well—" Sam debated how much to reveal. He decided to keep it simple. "I've got two daughters, five and fourteen, and I'm recently a single dad. It's just easier this way." He welcomed the approval, maybe respect, in Gary's eyes.

"I understand."

Sam was grateful he didn't push for more.

"Now, before you go back to detecting, how about you show me what you've got in mind for this old place."

CHAPTER 20

Rachel loathed going back to school after Christmas break. It was if the school year had two first days. She detested first days and losing her freedom to the regimented school bells that divided her life into fifty-minute segments, so teachers could hold her captive in their crowded classrooms and uncomfortable desks. But today had been especially difficult. Rachel missed her aunt. She knew Aunt Erin had wanted her to talk more than she did, and Rachel wanted to say more than she'd said. Even so, a place inside her chest wasn't as heavy, didn't take up so much room, allowing her lungs to fill a little fuller with oxygen, even though her breaths remained shallow.

But now that Aunt Erin was gone, her absence only heightened Rachel missing her mother. Because this morning, her mom would have *oohed* and *aahed* over Rachel's new outfit, one they would have picked out together on their traditional after-Christmas clearance shopping spree. *There's just something about new clothes that makes a day better*, she'd have said. It was her mom's way of making the end of Christmas break less dreadful. And once they pulled into the school parking lot, her mom would have grabbed her hand and prayed for a good day.

But there'd been no shopping spree this year. There were no new clothes. And Rachel doubted God even heard prayers. Still, she missed her mom's touch, her comforting words, and her assurance that Rachel could endure the next seven hours.

Once the day began, it wasn't as if anything happened that made it worse than any other day. Except maybe lunch with Cricket. Cricket dropped her tray on the table and demanded to know why Rachel was sitting so close to the "Emos" and not in their usual place. Instead of telling her she'd picked the spot hoping Cricket wouldn't come over, since she was so vocal about her aversion to "freaks in black who can't handle their emotions, wa-wa," Rachel simply shrugged. But she suspected a fine line separated Cricket from the kids she claimed sickened her.

"I texted you like a gazillion times over break. Why didn't you text me back?" Cricket had asked. Aunt Erin was an easy excuse, family stuff, her dad wanted them all together. Then Cricket reminded Rachel why they had become friends.

"I was worried, you know. This being your first Christmas without your mom and all. You could have at least let me know you were okay."

Cricket always knew. She was the only one. But just as quickly as Rachel remembered why she'd been drawn to her, Cricket reinforced Rachel's decision to pull away.

She leaned in and lowered her voice. "Because if you weren't, you know, okay, I had some really good stuff for you. New stuff my brother got. It was like—wow."

The rest of the day crawled. After school her dad

picked her up as usual, but his incessant chatter was unusual. He talked about the Hitching house and some guy who miraculously showed up and how much easier it was going to be to turn the house into her mom's dream with his help. A pause prefaced the caution Rachel heard sneak into his voice. "Maybe you'd like to help sometime." She'd turned away and stared out the window. The Hitching house was his penance, not hers. She wouldn't step foot in that place, and he couldn't make her. She'd rather gouge her eyes out with a plastic spork from the school cafeteria. As his chatter continued, the drive home seemed like a million miles long.

But, just as every day since her mother died, Rachel had survived this one, too. Now she lay in bed, reluctant to sleep, even though it was nearly midnight, because sleep meant morning would arrive too soon. But her eyelids had grown heavy, so she rolled on to her side to turn off the lamp on her nightstand. Instead of reaching for the switch, she picked up a tiny plastic figurine she had propped against the base of the lamp—two ice skaters wrapped in winter coats and scarves, hand-in-hand, each with one leg extended behind. Rachel imagined the skaters sliding around a blue acrylic pond as a tinny "I'll Be Home for Christmas" played from her mother's snow globe. After the crash that destroyed their idyllic world, Rachel salvaged the couple, uncertain why she could not bear to put them in the trash with the rest of the broken mess.

Then she pulled open the nightstand drawer and fished for something she had tucked in the corner. Her fingers found the cool, smooth object. She lay back on the bed and rubbed her thumb against the curvature of a thick piece of glass from the globe. Her thumb rested perfectly in the roundness, which she had discovered while picking up the broken pieces the other night. Rubbing it soothed her, like the worry stone Aunt Erin had shown her that she sometimes rubbed during court trials.

As Rachel's thumb slid over the glass, she pushed harder, feeling the thickness of the piece in her hand. She winced. She had pushed her thumb too far, and the edge of the glass sliced it. At first she saw only the opened skin, but a second later a line of red appeared. She watched the blood form into a heavy drop and roll down her thumb, pooling in her palm. Fascinated with the runnel, she was only vaguely aware of the sting. When the blood threatened to drip from her hand, she reached for a tissue, wiped her palm, and wrapped her thumb.

She held the glass in front of her and studied the defined edge. She pressed her finger bluntly against it, careful not to slip, until the edge sunk in, firmly but not deep enough to break the skin. She released the glass and examined the indention it left. Then she pressed her finger against it again. It was enticing, empowering, to manipulate the glass, to control the pain—how much, how deep.

Rachel sat up. She unwrapped the tissue to see her thumb had stopped bleeding. Her eyes moved to the soft skin of her forearm. She rubbed her finger across delicately, just below the bend of her elbow. The firmness of her fingernail replaced her fingertip, and she dragged it up and down, etching a path in her skin. Then she picked up the glass and placed it on her arm, wondering how it would look, how it would feel, to sink the edge into her flesh. She wouldn't do that of course, she told herself. Yet, she studied her arm, locating veins close to the surface, so she could be careful not to cut too deep. *If* she were going to cut, which she wasn't.

And she didn't mean to, at first. She had only pushed the edge of the glass deep enough to turn her skin pink. Then she traced the path again. And again. Until tiny red dots surfaced. Then she cut another line parallel to the first. And another. She had positioned the glass to begin once more, but a knock surprised her. She quickly laid back and pulled the covers up to her shoulders just as her dad opened the door, hair tousled from sleep.

"I woke up and saw your light. It's late, Rach. You should be asleep."

"I know. I'm trying." She hoped her dad was too sleepy to hear the guilt in her voice.

He walked into her room. "Well, I find it easier to sleep in the dark." He reached for the lamp but stopped. "What's that?"

The blood-stained tissue was on her nightstand. Her mind spun, searching for an explanation. "I, uh, had a nosebleed."

"Oh." Sam looked at her face. "Everything okay now?"

"Yeah, sure. Everything's okay."

Her dad kissed the top of her head and turned off the lamp. Once he had closed the door behind him, Rachel pulled her arms from under the covers and ran her finger over the moist lines on her skin. She had an odd feeling, strange but familiar, almost like the feeling that slowly washed through her when she took the pills, except her brain didn't feel like a swollen sponge submerged in water.

She thought about the next morning, the dreaded routine, the stupid teachers, the phony people. The clothes she had picked out lay across the back of her desk chair, her favorite jeans and a grey t-shirt Aunt Erin had given her with a black graphic of a vintage camera like Rachel's.

Even though the t-shirt reminded her of her camera, it also reminded her of her aunt, and she appreciated that Aunt Erin had tried her best to help. Suddenly Rachel realized that outfit wouldn't work. She did a mental inventory of her closet. She would wear her t-shirt from the Smokey Mountains instead. It had long sleeves.

Maggie recalled a pleasant late fall morning that had broken a cold streak, likely the last warm day before winter would bluster in to reign. Rachel, then four, had begged to go to the park for one last chance to master the monkey bars before the season's end. She remembered a little boy chasing Rachel, playfully at first, but then he began to shove her when he would catch her. Maggie called Rachel over, and when the little boy followed, she asked him to please play nicely. But the little boy narrowed his eyes, and the next shove sent Rachel to the ground. Before she could get up, he shoved her again, this time sending her face first into the metal ladder on the slide. As Maggie rushed to Rachel, the little boy laughed. Maggie surveyed the adults scattered throughout the playground, expecting a parent to reprimand the little boy. But when he sprinted toward a row of houses nearby, she realized he had been at the park alone. Blood rushed from Rachel's chin, and an anger so deep, so despicable, rose within Maggie as she imagined pushing the boy to the ground with all the force a protective mother could muster.

Now, as Rachel slept, the moonlight glowed through a narrow opening in the curtain, and Maggie could see the scar on her chin that took eight stitches to close. She

recognized the anger that settled in her chest, the same
fury that had washed over her that day in the park as she
watched someone else's child harm her daughter. But this
time, as she watched her daughter's blood surface from a
self-inflicted tear in her flesh, Maggie's anger was cloaked
in shame. What kind of mother would allow her daughter
to behave that way?

CHAPTER 21

Sam spent two days trailing Gary through the attic, the crawl space, and every inch of the property as he inspected the foundation, the roof, the plumbing, the wiring, the insulation. He left nothing untouched. Sam was astounded by how much he had learned already, and they hadn't even begun to work. Now they sat at a make-shift table of plywood laid across two saw horses with a thermos of coffee and pages of notes Gary had scrawled after each inspection.

"Well, we have some challenges." Gary tapped an ink pen against his notepad. "But overall, we're in pretty good shape."

Sam exhaled. "That's good to hear. So what's the game plan?"

"Foundation is solid; the updates the previous owner did, the HVAC and the wiring, look good. Our biggest challenge will be the plumbing. You have lead pipes that are a hundred years old and corroded. Replacing the exposed pipes in the crawl space will be pretty straight forward, but replacing the interior plumbing means getting inside the walls. Plus your plans here add two additional guest bathrooms upstairs." Gary laid his hand on Maggie's folder sitting on the table between them.

Sam cringed. "So, how difficult is it going to be?"

"It can get a little complicated, but I've done complicated a thousand times. We can do this."

He was relieved by Gary's confidence. They hadn't demoed one board or driven one nail, but already he trusted Gary's expertise.

"Plumbing is our starting point. We'll replace it first. Otherwise, we risk water damage to any work we'd do before the plumbing."

"Makes sense." Sam rested his elbows on the plywood.

"So I suggest roughing in the upstairs bathrooms, and then remodeling the kitchen and main-level bath. We'll work inside while it's cold and through the spring rains. Then when the weather cooperates, we'll start on the exterior."

"Sounds like a plan." Sam was back on the rollercoaster, riding up the hill of possibilities. He thumbed the edge of Maggie's folder, notes in her handwriting scrawled across the cover, her dream inside. For the first time, he believed—not hoped—he might actually be able to do this.

"You know, Sam, I have to confess. I'm a little jealous."

Sam cocked his head, curious for an explanation.

"I was this close to making an offer on this place." Gary gestured with his thumb and forefinger.

"Really? What stopped you?"

Gary lowered his chin and pressed his lips together as if searching for an answer. "I guess it wasn't mean to be. After we looked at the place back in the fall, Susie and I were certain this was supposed to be ours. I called the real estate agent to make an offer, but she didn't return my call. Then the very next morning over coffee, Suze shook her head and said, 'We can't buy that house' and I said, 'I know.' Just as sure as we knew we were supposed to buy this place, suddenly we knew we weren't. Sounds crazy, doesn't it? But I never could get the old house out of my head."

As Sam listened, Gary's voice sounded farther and farther away. His heart drummed in his chest and pressure filled his head. A single question circled and circled, searching for a place to land.

"Sam, are you okay? You don't look so good, buddy."

"I—uh—yeah." Sam cleared his throat, took a deep breath, and tried to slow the pounding in his chest. It can't be. It can't. But he had to know. "Gary, do you remember when it was, when you called the agent?"

"Sure. It was right before we moved here, last September, to live closer to the grandchildren. We met the agent here—Megan or Margot—something like that, a lovely lady. We could see she really admired this property, and we couldn't wait to tell her we wanted it. We weren't fifteen minutes from here when we decided to call her, and, well, you know the rest of the story."

The rest of the story? Sam's thoughts whirled as he tried to puzzle together the possibility. Her last text to him: *Cross your fingers. On my way home,* came at 8:00 p.m. He read the accident report, practically memorized it, trying to understand what could have distracted Maggie, why Maggie had crossed the centerline. Estimated time of the accident, 8:16 the report had said. The evidence, his instinct, both led to the same conclusion. Sam forced himself to control the tremor in his voice. "So, this may seem like an odd question but—do you remember about what time you made that call?"

"Time?" Gary repeated as if to clarify the question. His brow lowered and he looked puzzled. "Well, let's see. It was close to dark when we left, and we had made it back to town, so I'd say about 8:15, 8:20."

Sam hesitated. He didn't know how far to push, but he had to know. He reached for the file on the table and pulled it to him. As he stared at it, he swallowed and forced the words to come out. "Maggie. Was the agent's name Maggie?"

"Why, yes, Maggie. I believe that's right. Sweet girl. Do you know her?" Gary beamed.

Sam met Gary's eyes. He tried, but he couldn't return the smile. The man across from him, the man whose generosity had given Sam a new hope, was the reason he sat at this make-shift table, in this empty house, holding Maggie's file, instead of holding Maggie. He didn't know his broken heart could crumble even more. He was unsure what to say next, how much he would say, should say. He proceeded with caution, his voice a distant echo. "She was my wife."

Gary's smile melted. Sam watched the man across from him search his face for more information, but he didn't offer more.

"Was?"

"There was an accident—" A wave of emotion surfaced and choked back his words.

"Sam, I am so sorry." Gary reached across the table and gripped Sam's arm.

Sam swallowed, forced his lungs to take in air, cleared his throat. "It was a head-on . . . last . . . fall." He paused for Gary's reaction, uncertain what he expected. Was he waiting for realization, for Gary to make sense of the

information the two of them had pieced together, for guilt
to consume him and allow Sam to finally place blame for
Maggie's death? Or did he hope Gary wouldn't understand,
that he would continue to live in oblivion, letting Sam alone
carry the weight of the truth?

Gary moved his hand from Sam's arm and placed it
firmly on the folder. "This." He patted. "This is Maggie's.
This is the house we are renovating . . . for your wife."

Sam nodded.

Gary sat back in his chair, limp.

Quiet hung between them. Sam's chest swelled with
emotion, but it was emotion he couldn't name. He never
expected this moment to occur, but if he had, he would
have anticipated fury . . . hatred . . . revenge to dominate
his heart, his words. Instead, he felt what? A sense of
peace maybe, for details that made Maggie's last moments
clearer? Disbelief, that the one thing Maggie wanted, a
buyer for this house, was the one thing that caused her
death? Sadness that the kindest man Sam had ever met
had no idea of the pain he'd caused?

Or did he? Sam studied Gary's eyes, his face, his body
language, and was strangely relieved. He exhaled and wiped
his sleeve across his mouth, certain Gary hadn't figured out
the rest of the story.

CHAPTER 22

Maggie was waiting in Rachel's room when her daughter walked in, dropped her backpack next to her desk, and laid her cell phone on the nightstand.

"Coming," Rachel called as she left to join Sam and Olivia.

Maggie stood inside the bedroom doorway and listened. Chatter drifted down the hall from the kitchen where she imagined the family seated around the island, grabbing dinner from Chinese take-out boxes. She must work quickly.

It wouldn't be the first time Maggie risked an action that could reveal her presence. In the last few weeks her resolve to limit her abilities had waned to dangerous degrees. When Olivia awoke in the night, searching anxiously for Lambie who had fallen off the bed, Maggie gently squeezed the stuffed toy and placed it on the pillow while Olivia tossed the covers at the foot of her bed. And when Sam left their picture on the table beside her chair one evening, Maggie returned it to the nightstand while he was in the shower, fearing—and hoping—he would notice.

But he didn't. At times it had been so tempting, felt so vital, to be known by her family that only by sheer will power, which Maggie was certain could not be her own, was she able to control the desire. And then she would scold herself, knowing her motive was selfish. How could it be anything but terrifying for two girls to believe their mother was a ghost in their home? And how could Sam move through the grieving process if he knew his wife was not gone? The only one with something to gain was Maggie, and she couldn't justify the damage her selfishness could cause. So she would renew her resolve and remain strong . . . until the next temptation surfaced.

But this time Maggie was certain her motive was genuine. She had wrestled with it, analyzed it, dissected it twenty different ways. This wasn't about her. It was about Rachel and how her inability to cope continued to escalate to more frightening behaviors.

Satisfied her family was occupied, she grabbed Rachel's cell phone from the nightstand. Her fingers sprinted across the keys as she began to compose a text, recalling the message she once typed on the laptop and then attempted on paper.

Rachel, I'm here. I haven't left you. I know you still need me. I'm trying to help you, but I can't. You have to stop hurting yourself. Talk to your dad. He loves you. I love you. You don't have to go through this alone. I'm here. Your family is here. Please, Rachel. You are breaking my heart.

As Maggie desperately punched keys, the screen on the cell phone flashed. Not again. She panicked. But when the screen flashed back on, the text was still there. Maggie's fingers raced. And then she noticed it, the battery icon in the top corner rapidly draining, the percentage next to it decreasing: 15, 10, 5, 0. The phone went black.

"Hang on, Dad."

Rachel's voice entered the room seconds before she did. Maggie shoved the cell phone toward the nightstand. Rachel walked in just in time to see the phone fall from the edge and tumble to the carpet below. She stopped. Slowly she walked to the phone and stared at it. Then she looked at the nightstand where the phone should have been. Finally, she bent down, picked it up, and tapped the black screen. She pushed the button to power up the phone and waited. When the screen appeared, she seemed satisfied, unsuspecting, and left the room.

Maggie should have been relieved Rachel hadn't stepped in a second sooner, but she wasn't. She was exasperated. She was certain this time it would work. This time she would get a message to her daughter. This time she would save Rachel.

CHAPTER 23

Rachel wrapped her wet hair in a towel, tied her robe tighter around her waist, and opened the bathroom door. Olivia's giggles drifted down the hall from her dad's bedroom. She listened to the carefree sounds of her little sister, wishing she could give Olivia the nine years that separated them. Then maybe she, too, could disappear into the oblivion of a child. She wanted to giggle again, to laugh, to feel it, really feel it. To not feel this—this heaviness invading her, replacing the pain that stabbed her inside with every breath, every move, every thought of her mom. It will take time, people told her. She didn't understand then. She thought they meant it would take time for her to forget, but she didn't want to forget. Now she realized they meant it would take time for the pain to ease, but no one told her it would transform into a weight that is physical and ever present. Time. She counted in her head. Six months. It seemed like only yesterday—and it seemed like a lifetime ago.

"What are you guys doing?" Rachel stood in the doorway while her dad and Olivia laid on the bed looking at an iPad. "Isn't it past her bedtime? It's a school night."

"We're gonna show Mommy some pictures. Aren't we, Daddy?"

"Um, uh-huh."

Rachel caught a sheepish glance from her dad.

"Pictures of what? Why do you have Mom's iPad?"

"Daddy used it to take pictures of the house. We're going to show Mommy how Daddy fixed it."

"Dad, seriously?" Rachel shoulders dropped. She was so tired of this.

"Oh, don't be a drag. Come over here and look at these pictures with us." Sam patted the space beside him.

Rachel remained in the doorway a moment, fighting her curiosity. Then she sauntered toward the bed, careful not to let her interest betray her. Her dad moved over, and as she sat beside him, she sensed his excitement.

"Okay, let's get to the beginning." He quickly scrolled through the pictures. "But first, Rachel, I want you to remember what the house was like the last time you saw it. Now we've only been working about eight weeks, so there's still a lot to do, but just wait 'til you see what your old dad has accomplished. Ready?" His smile was so big, Rachel almost couldn't resist smiling back.

"Here are the bathrooms we put in upstairs. Remember the bedroom that was here? We divided it in two, ran some plumbing, and voila."

"It's only a bunch of pipes and wood now, right?" Olivia leaned forward to see Rachel. "But Daddy will make it more better, won't you?"

"Yep. Your mom wanted claw foot tubs, tile, and custom vanities. The paint she chose for the bathrooms is 'Lavender Dust.' They will be the prettiest bathrooms you've ever seen. What do you think?"

Although the work was still rough, Rachel could fill in the blanks from the layout she had seen in her mom's notes. "Nice." She nodded, and she meant it.

Her dad scrolled to the next picture. "Here's where we've spent most of our time."

Rachel hardly recognized the kitchen. The remodel looked almost complete—new windows, paint, cabinets—except the spaces left for appliances, like gaping holes in a first grader's smile. "Wow. You really did this?"

"What? Don't you know your dad has some serious carpentry skills?" Sam grinned, but his fake confidence didn't fool her.

"Uh, that Gary guy you talk about has the skills. All you have are Mom's designs—and maybe a hammer." Rachel rolled her eyes, surprised at how important her approval seemed to her dad. He pushed his elbow into her side, and she caught herself just before tumbling off the bed. "Dad!"

He feigned innocence and continued scrolling from one picture to the next. Rachel had leafed through her mom's plans a million times, trying to envision the house as her mom had. Now, she could see it coming into view, her mom's signature reviving the rooms.

"Well, what do you think?" He lowered the iPad.

"I think you are making a good house, Daddy." Olivia patted his stomach.

Rachel's awe was slowly replaced by sadness. She didn't want to say what she thought, to let honesty give words to the ache. But her dad was waiting for her approval, so she forced a whisper through the tightness in her throat. "I wish Mom could see it."

Her dad's arm wrapped around her, and instead of

resisting, she allowed him to pull her close. "Me, too." His words were warm on her hair.

"But she can." Olivia sat up and scolded them both. "She sees the pictures."

It didn't matter how much time passed, rage still surged through Rachel each time her sister talked as if their mom were present. But she wasn't prepared for her dad's response.

"Does she, Oliva? Does Mom see the pictures?"

Rachel's jaw clenched. Her dad glanced at her, but ignored her reaction.

"Yeah, they make her happy."

"Is she . . . here . . . with us . . . now?"

Rachel could not believe the words actually came out of his mouth. "Dad, are you kidding me? No, Mom isn't here 'with us'! What's wrong with you?"

Her eyes locked with his, only inches away. What did she see? Disappointment? Embarrassment? Demanding an explanation, she held her stare steady. But he relented. His gaze found a picture on the iPad. When he finally spoke, it seemed like he refuted the accusation more to himself than to her.

"I just miss her so much. And sometimes, sometimes I think maybe she is here, somehow. Or maybe I need her so much that it only feels like she's here. I know it sounds unbelievable, Rachel. Just hearing myself say it out loud is crazy. But . . . what if? What if Mom somehow, someway, is here? Or maybe she isn't here, but maybe she gets to look down on us sometimes. Or maybe none of that is possible at all. But if it is, even if Olivia is even a tiny bit right, I don't want to miss it because I convinced myself otherwise."

Rachel's heartbeat quickened. The pounding in her ears was thick and deafening. Never had she allowed herself to think "what if." Always, she had refused to consider the possibility. Because . . . if her mom were here, if she did communicate with Olivia, and now maybe her dad, why couldn't Rachel feel her, too? But she knew the answer, and the answer made the pounding quicker, louder. Because it was her fault. She was the reason her mom was gone.

But that wasn't all. Her next thought stopped the pounding all together, leaving a terrible notion floating lonely through the silence inside her head. What if Olivia had been right all along? What if her mom could see, did see, everything Rachel had done, how ugly she had become inside? Her heart wilted. No wonder her mom wouldn't come to her. She probably didn't know her own daughter anymore. Why would her mom still love her? After everything Rachel had done. After what she'd done to herself, how could her mother still love her?

Her dad's voice broke the silence and launched a diversion. "You know, you girls haven't seen the house since we started working on it. Would you like to take a ride Saturday and check it out?"

Olivia bounced on the bed and clapped her hands. Rachel had to consider. She swore she would never step foot inside that house. Walking into the dream her mom never got to realize was just another reminder of one more thing Rachel had taken away from her.

"I'll tell you what." Sam scrolled through the pictures again. "Look here. This is a plot of ground I worked up yesterday. You can see it from the kitchen window over the sink. Your mom designed a butterfly garden for this spot, nice and sunny with butterfly bushes and colorful flowers. How would you girls like to plant the garden Saturday? It can be your project, something you can do for Mom."

"Yeah!" Olivia shouted, bouncing higher and clapping louder.

Rachel inspected the dirt rectangle in the picture and debated. Technically she would be outside the house, which wasn't inside, which didn't go against the promise she had made herself. "Okay."

If her dad tried to hide his surprise, he didn't do a very good job. He raised an eyebrow, but she didn't offer more. She calculated. If her mom were here, and if she knew everything, now she would know she agreed to help with the butterfly garden. Maybe her mom would see she wasn't all bad, and—maybe—her mom could start to love her again.

Maggie curled up in her chair and waited while Sam tucked the girls in, too late for a school night, but the moments she witnessed were worth a little lost sleep. For the first time since the accident, she saw glimpses of healing . . . a family, instead of broken individuals existing in the same space. This was good—but, she missed being a part of it. Except maybe, in a way, she was part of her family tonight, if Sam really believed what he said. And the pictures! Maggie was delighted and amazed. It's one thing to design a room, but seeing a room designed is quite another. Sam followed her plans exactly. The kitchen was a stunning combination of vintage and modern, and she couldn't wait to see the finished bathrooms.

As Maggie listened to the sounds of the girls' bedtime routine, she glanced toward the table beside her where her journal lay. Fingerprints had disturbed the sheer layer of dust on the leather. A few nights ago Sam sat in Maggie's chair, picked up the journal, and opened it to the first page. He was intense, brows furrowed, reading and rereading. The next night he read more, as if investigating, searching for evidence. Evidence of what? Maggie felt like he was studying her soul.

"Night, girls," Sam called as he started down the hall to their bedroom. She waited for him to settle in. She'd learned his signs. If he stacked the pillows and reclined against them, he would talk to her, share his day with her. If he crawled under the covers, the day had exhausted him, and she would hope tomorrow would preserve a little of Sam for her. Tonight, he pulled back the covers. Before turning off the bedside lamp, he touched their picture. "Night, Mags." Then it was dark.

Maggie moved into position beside him, intertwined her leg with his, and laid her arm across his chest, her hand on his heartbeat. Tonight she would stay until Sam was deep asleep, and then she would make her rounds to check on Rachel, and to watch vigilant over Olivia to keep bad dreams away. She felt Sam breathe in deeply.

"Are you here?" he whispered.

"I'm here."

Every cell in every muscle of Sam's body begged for rest, but he couldn't settle his mind. Thoughts circled like the tea cups Olivia begged to ride over and over at Disneyland, leaving him dizzy and nauseated. When he closed his eyes, a video of the accident played nonstop. He imagined the eighteen wheeler, the dusk of evening that deceives one's vision, the cell phone ringing, her car crossing into the other lane. And each time, he imagined being a passenger, grabbing the steering wheel, pulling Maggie back to safety.

And Gary. How could he be the man on the other end of the call, the reason his wife had been distracted from the road? He didn't deserve to be that man. In the weeks Sam spent getting to know him, he learned the two things that made up the core of who Gary was—selflessness and transparency. At first Sam couldn't understand how a man could literally give away his expertise and labor. And while Sam still didn't understand it completely, he understood it better, because on some mornings if Gary was late, he had repaired an elderly woman's air conditioner or set up forms for a new concrete patio for a neighbor. If he ended his day early, it was to give someone a ride to a doctor's appointment or to inspect a house a young couple wanted to buy. Doing for others, expecting nothing in return—accepting nothing—it's just who the man was.

There was no guesswork, no mystery, no need for caution around Gary. Sam's best description of his new friend was "What you see is what you get," but with Gary, it wasn't cliché. He was the origin of the expression. And for Sam, that took some getting used to. In law enforcement, most people he dealt with were not as they tried to appear. Skepticism was a weapon as important as the 9mm Glock he had secured in his holster every day. But there was something about Gary that challenged Sam's instinct and disarmed him. It made Sam vulnerable, but with Gary, there was no need for defense. Sam felt safe.

Then there was the guilt. The guilt of knowing a dirty secret, which would devastate this good man, encased Sam like a cocoon. When they were working, tearing down a wall or building a new one, measuring and cutting, sweating and aching, Sam restrained the guilt. But without distraction, before the work began, or at the close of the day, it would creep up from his chest and threaten to hijack his words and reveal the truth. Especially at lunch, when they sat at the sawhorse table and Gary would ask the same question every single day: "Can I pray for you, Sam?" He didn't ask if he could bless the food or say grace. Instead, he wedged a sword right into Sam's chest. But the prayers. At first, it was awkward, being talked about in third person to a God who had surely written Sam off by now. But he couldn't tell Gary no. Within days, though, he found himself anticipating Gary's prayers, the soothing agent they had become, and hoped maybe someone was listening.

And tonight he wondered that, too. Was someone listening? He had convinced himself, true or not, that Maggie was. But, was God? Even if he wanted to pray, he didn't know what to say besides the rote phrases he had heard on the intermittent occasions he had gone to church: Dear God, thank you for this day. Thank you for all your blessings. Blah, blah, blah. Empty words. Then Sam thought about Gary's prayers, honest words that came so naturally. And he remembered the prayers in Maggie's journal. And Olivia. *Just talk to God like he's your friend sitting right in front of you,* she had said.

He opened his eyes to the darkness. The clock cast a dim light on the picture beside his bed. He felt self-conscious. But hadn't he felt the same way when he first talked to Maggie? How different could it be, talking to Maggie and talking to . . . Him, either of which may or may not be present? Sam rolled on his back and stared at the ceiling. *Forget about what you should say,* he told himself. *What do you want to say?*

Sam considered the girls—a long way from perfect, but improving maybe? Definitely prayer worthy. The bed and breakfast, no complaints. Everything was according to plan—Maggie's plan. Except Sam had been so preoccupied with the remodel that he gave little thought about what would come next. Did he really want to own a B&B? Would he consider selling it? Could he sell Maggie's dream? And what about his retirement? He should have finalized the paperwork a week ago. With his comp time and vacation days depleted, if pension didn't start soon, he would have to draw funds from savings. But Sam had realized something: it was easy to think about turning in his badge permanently when it wasn't permanent yet. He didn't regret the time he spent away from the job. And he wouldn't trade the time he got to be just Sam, a dad, and not Lieutenant Blake, not a detective. But was he ready to put his signature on the official paperwork? What choice did he have? And what about himself? How was he, really? Since the remodel began, he hadn't stopped long enough to know. But maybe that was the secret—stay busy, don't think, don't feel—a temporary solution until he found a permanent one. He definitely had a lot to pray about.

"Here goes." He laced his fingers together and laid his hands on his chest. "God." He look up toward the ceiling. "I'm trying to figure it all out. But, like Gary prayed, please make my path clear."

CHAPTER 24

Rachel was surprised. She didn't realize how much she would enjoy working the dirt with her hands. When her dad had tried to hand her gardening gloves, she decided not to hold him accountable for his lack of fashion sense. "Do I look like I'm fifty? I'm not wearing those granny gloves." He shrugged and tossed the gloves on the ground beside the array of plants they bought from the greenhouse that morning. As Rachel ran her fingers through the loose soil, she knew going gloveless was the right decision. She liked the substance in her hands, the warmth from the sun, the moisture from the morning dew, a perfect combination to give life to the butterfly garden sketched in color pencil that her dad handed her two hours ago and said, "You're in charge." As she studied the diagram, she admired her mom's untapped artistic ability and knew exactly where her own artistic skills had come from.

But she didn't want to think about art. It had become too difficult many months ago. An obstacle always got in her way. At first it was the clawing emotion that shredded her creativity, leaving her frustrated when she sat before a canvas. Then, it was her fear of the person she was becoming under Cricket's influence, so she avoided the art room. Now, it was mostly the tremors, the fine vibrations that ran through her fingers each time she held a pencil, a paintbrush, chalk. She would relax her hands and loosen her grip, trying to make the tremors stop. When that failed, she would tighten her grip, try to control her fingers. It was useless. She couldn't bring herself to explain all that to Mrs. Swane when she had stopped Rachel in the hall and asked where she had been. She gave an excuse she knew was transparent: "I've been busy." When Mrs. Swane put a hand on her arm and squeezed, Rachel tried not to cringe as the teacher pressed on the cuts beneath her sleeve, which now reached almost to her wrist. She reminded Rachel the art room door was open to her whenever she was ready. Rachel mentally chalked up another mark in the loss column— Mrs. Swane, one more person she'd disappointed.

But now as she admired her progress on the butterfly garden, she decided the garden was a work of art in itself. It started as an empty plot of dirt, but the composition had taken form. Texture, color, line, dimension merged together to create a whole. So what if it wasn't her original design? It was her hard work, and it felt good.

A vibration in her back pocket distracted her critique. She swiped her hands across her jeans to brush off loose dirt before digging for her cell phone. She wondered who would be texting her at 10:15 on a Saturday morning—or who would be texting her at any time, on any day, for that matter. Both Kristen and Cricket had stopped long ago. She hoped it wasn't Pastor Rob, or the youth pastor. It was about time for their monthly check-in, their conspicuous inconspicuous attempt to remind her Jesus still loved her.

She retrieved her phone. An unfamiliar number displayed on the screen along with a text: *Hey u looked cute at school yesterday.*

Rachel read the text again before deciding it had been sent to her by mistake. She texted back: *u sent this to the wrong person.* She hit send, put her phone back in her pocket, and kneeled down to dig a hole for the next plant. The phone vibrated again.

No i didnt ur rachel

She read both texts again. Should she be freaked out or flattered? She wasn't the kind of girl boys noticed. She accepted that in fifth grade when Valentine's Day abruptly became a very serious holiday. Couples paired off a week in advance, and during the class party, she was the only girl without a box of candy or a heart necklace or a bouquet on her desk.

Maybe the text wasn't creepy. Maybe it was just someone being nice. Or maybe a boy really did like her. Suddenly she wished she could show it to Kristen. She knew exactly what would happen. Kristen would grab her phone and begin texting back as if she were Rachel, and she would be mortified and grateful at the same time, grabbing for the phone and giggling as Kristen kept it out of reach. Her smile blossomed as she imagined the scenario, but it didn't last. She missed her best friend. She rarely saw her at school since Kristen transferred to a different science class at the beginning of the semester, which was a relief. She no longer had to make an effort to avoid her ex-best friend every day. But, suddenly, Rachel felt the colossal void Kristen's friendship had once filled. She'd messed it up, she knew that, and now she didn't deserve Kristen.

Ra . . . chel u still there?

Now that was kind of creepy. But she grinned and did what Kristen would do. She texted back: *who is this*

secret admirer

im not texting back til i no who u r

"This is shaping up great, Rach."

Rachel spun around to face her dad, flustered, and shoved her cell back into her jeans pocket. "You scared me. I didn't hear you walk up."

"Yeah, you were pretty intent. Who were you texting?" Her dad had that look, his suspicious one with a hint of a smile.

Twenty shades of red raced through her cheeks and warmed her face. This was awful. She felt like she had been caught. But at what? What was she doing wrong? It was just a text. Kids text every day. Every minute for that matter. She tried to act normal, but her voice came out too high. "A friend."

Her dad squinted playfully and smiled bigger. "A friend, huh?"

Rachel turned away, hoping to avoid more questions. When she realized she was looking toward the flowers she had planted, she found her diversion. "So, you like it? I'm almost finished; those are the only ones left." She pointed to a flat of bright purple flowers.

Her dad put his arm around her and pulled her into a side hug. "Mom would love it. Now all we need are the butterflies."

Rachel let herself lean into his embrace. "Maybe when I'm finished, you can take a picture of it with the iPad."

"Yeah?"

Rachel sensed a question in his voice. Surely he didn't think she wanted to show the picture to—

She answered slowly, emphasizing each word to clarify. "Yeah . . . so we can remember what it looks like now and see how much it grows this summer."

"Oh, yeah, right." He cleared his throat.

The cell phone in her back pocket buzzed again

"You better get that. Might be important." He winked, gave her another squeeze, and turned toward the house.

"Nah." Rachel tried to sound nonchalant and forced herself to wait until her dad was out of sight before she read the text.

CHAPTER 25

Maggie learned about Rachel's mystery boy the same way she learned most things about her daughter nowadays—by reading over her shoulder. At first she wasn't sure how she felt when Rachel started messaging a boy on her laptop. She was sad to miss this rite of passage, her daughter's first boyfriend. Even if the budding computer romance did not result in puppy love, it still reminded Maggie of all the other firsts she would miss. But then she noticed Rachel humming. Rachel playing tea time with Olivia. Rachel minus the tone that often colored her words. Maybe a boy could be a good thing. From his messages, Maggie learned he was an honors freshman, the kind of kid nobody notices, he said, Rachel included. He preferred to talk on the computer for now rather than risk Rachel meeting him and not liking him. Rachel assured him that wasn't a risk, because he was so respectful and funny and understanding. At that point, Maggie decided a boyfriend might catapult Rachel back into life. And she definitely needed someone who understood her, as this boy seemed to. Rachel had begun to open up to him, and by his responses, Maggie sensed he had experienced loss in his life, too, although he offered no specific details to substantiate that.

But that was two weeks ago. Now Maggie knew exactly how she felt about this mystery boy. She was terrified. Somehow their conversations had taken a shift, and Rachel was too naïve to notice. He knew too much about Rachel, and not just things he would know about her from school. But she was too preoccupied, constantly trying to coerce him to meet—before school on the breezeway, at lunch in the library, and if not in person, then by webcam. Each time he refused—until he finally offered his own suggestion. To meet after school. After school didn't work, Rachel responded. Her dad picked her up. Not at school, he clarified. After she got home. At the park by her house.

Rachel continued to insist they meet at school, which gave Maggie only a small degree of relief. They debated, and it was through the debate that Maggie was certain no fifteen-year-old boy was on the other end of the conversation. She had to stop Rachel, but how?

Sam had not monitored Rachel's online activity in weeks. He left in the morning with Rachel and Olivia, worked all afternoon, picked up the girls after school, and then filled her role and his the rest of the evening. Besides, Rachel used her real account to message this boy, not one of her fake ones. And instead of leaving easy access for Sam to see her online activity, as she had done previously to deceive him, she logged out when she finished. Unless Sam decided to look at the site specifically, he would never know the danger Maggie feared was stalking their daughter.

And now Maggie's horror escalated. He won the debate. Rachel typed on the screen: *ok when?*

Thursday 8:15 say u r sick go to bed early and sneak out i'll try

The word *sweet* appeared on the screen. Maggie felt sick. She placed her finger on the power button and pressed down. The screen went black.

"Uh, not again!" Rachel pounded the keyboard. "Dad, my stupid laptop died again!"

Sam dropped off the girls at school. He had to make a decision. Should he go to the house and work even though Gary wouldn't be there? Gary had some place to go he had said, and reminded Sam all the structural work was complete. Whatever task Sam wanted to tackle for the day he was capable of, because, as Gary assured him smiling, he'd had such a good mentor the past four months. He wasn't as confident in his new skills as Gary, but there was always a wall to be painted, and he was plenty competent enough to do that on his own. Or should he go to the station and sign those darn retirement papers? Neither option was appealing. The recliner, an old movie, maybe a nap—that was appealing. He turned the pick-up toward home.

Sam walked into the kitchen, tossed his keys on the island, and noticed the pile of clothes in the laundry room. If he settled into his recliner, the pile would still be there tomorrow, so he started sorting. He put the first load in the washer, adjusted a knob, and pushed some buttons. He waited for the water to begin filling, but instead he heard a beep and saw the red cancel light flash. The washer shut off. He repeated the start-up operation, waited for the water to begin filling, and ... the beep. The washer shut off again.

"You have got to be kidding me." He stared at the machine and decided not to tackle it. It was probably the computer system, and a repairman would be better suited for that job. He opened a drawer in the kitchen island and searched for a business card. He dialed, waited through five rings for an answering machine, and left a message.

He poured another cup of coffee and started toward his recliner. A faint noise stopped him. The noise grew louder. Music—and it was coming from Rachel's room. He had just left her at school. Who could be in her room? Instinct took over. He set his coffee gently on an end table and moved quickly, quietly toward the hallway. Rachel's door was open, as it should be. He listened for movement, but he could hear nothing over the blaring music. He walked stealthily toward the room, paused outside her door, and listened again. Then he pivoted to enter, scanning every corner. Nothing. Still on guard, he checked the closet, under the bed. Nothing. Only the music coming from the laptop.

He punched a few keys and the music stopped. A log-in screen appeared. He recognized the website, the one Rachel messaged on. She hadn't shut down her computer, again, but that didn't explain the loud music. Then he remembered Rachel complaining about her laptop acting strangely. The laptop. The washer. He didn't feel like dealing with this.

Suddenly the blinking cursor on the screen moved to the log-in box. One by one, letters appeared. Rachel's user name. "What the   "

The cursor moved to the next box. Dots indicated her password was being entered. A virus. Rachel must have downloaded a virus, and it was automatically logging her in. Surely it was possible for a virus to take over a computer, wasn't it?

He continued to watch the cursor move across the webpage and click to open a discussion. It had been a while since he creeped Rachel's online activity, as she called it, so he pulled out her desk chair, sat down, and read the most recent message in the conversation.

Panic clawed at his spine and crawled up the back of his neck. Rachel sneaking out to meet a boy in the park? He placed his fingers on the mousepad and took control of the cursor, clicking from message to message. He didn't have to read much to realize all the signs were there. He calculated. It was Tuesday. They were meeting in two days. He grabbed his cell phone.

"Wade, this is Sam. Where's Nikki Shaw? Get her and get to my house now. Yes, it's an emergency. No lights or siren. Just get her here." Sam hung up, struggling between the two parts of him that wanted to take over, a father penetrated by fear or a detective with an adrenaline rush and a case to solve. He had no choice but to let the latter win.

Maggie had no words to describe the relief that flooded over her when Sam hung up, unplugged Rachel's laptop, and moved it to the dining room table where he waited until the detectives knocked on the door.

She also had no words to describe how she felt when Sam asked for Nikki Shaw specifically. Was it suspicion? Was she jealous? Why should she be? Sam had made his choice. He'd come home to her. But now, Maggie was no longer an option. So when Nikki Shaw walked into her home, Maggie inspected her like the betrayed wife she had been. The flowing red hair, the trim waist, the confident stride. She was a threat.

Sam directed Shaw to the website. She scrolled through the messages and confirmed his suspicion. "This is no kid. Let me trace the IP address and find out where this is coming from."

"You called the right detective." Wade assured Sam as Shaw started digging.

"She's the expert." Sam knew that because he'd made her the expert by sending her to the best cybercrime conferences in the country, including Atlanta. He ran his hand through his hair.

"She'll find this guy, Lieutenant.'"

"Who would do this? Why Rachel?" Sam paced as Shaw manipulated the laptop to exhume information.

"Creeps are all over these websites." Her eyes were locked on the screen. "They message lots of kids until they find one they think is vulnerable."

Shame rushed through Sam. When had he allowed his daughter to become vulnerable? It was his job to protect his family. Had he become so oblivious that he'd let Rachel become a victim?

"I got it." Detective Shaw scribbled on a notepad and looked up at Sam. "It's local. We have to get to a judge and get a warrant for the ISP, and we have to do it now. We're on the clock."

"Call Judge Hubbs." Sam directed the order to Wade. "He'll push this through."

"I'm on it." Detective Wade punched numbers on his cell phone as he walked toward the door.

Sam's pulse quickened as Wade stepped outside, leaving him alone in the room with Shaw. He tried to ignore it, but the atmosphere changed. When he glanced at Shaw, she quickly looked away, appearing to study her notes. The silence was thick. Did she feel it, too? He couldn't leave it this way. He had a chance and he couldn't walk away again—like he walked out of the hotel room— and continue to pretend nothing ever happened.

"Detective Shaw, I'm sorry—"

"No bother, Lieutenant. It's been a slow couple of days."

"No, I don't mean this. I mean—"

When he hesitated, Shaw looked up from her notes and stared straight ahead. He waited for her to respond, but she remained silent.

"I was wrong. What I did to you. I never explained or apologized. I hurt you. I hurt my wife, my family. It was selfish and I will never forgive myself. I loved my wife. I still love my wife." Sam paused to judge her reaction, but none was visible. "It may be too late to apologize to her . . . but I can apologize to you."

Her face remained stoic. Sam felt a sense of urgency. He needed to finish this, before he lost his nerve, before Wade returned.

"Please, will you forgive—"

"Yeah, sure, Lieutenant." They were the right words, but her tone was flippant.

"Nikki." Sam let her name hang between them.

Finally, she looked at him, unguarded, and he saw the hurt that had been masked by anger since the day she returned from Atlanta, alone.

"I'm so sorry. Can you forgive me?"

As she continued to stare at him, he wished he could read the thoughts racing behind the emerald eyes he once could not get enough of, the eyes that now penetrated into the deepest crevice in his soul where he had hidden his darkest secret.

"Lieutenant—"

"Nikki. Please don't—" He closed his eyes and held up his hands. When he opened them again, she had turned away.

She wiped a smudge on the laptop screen, took a deep breath and dropped her hands in her lap. "Sam. It happened. I'm not sorry it happened, but it was wrong." She paused. "We were both wrong."

Sam bowed his head. Something inside of him wrestled free and released. The words had not come easily for Nikki, but before he could respond, Wade walked in.

"Judge Hubbs is waiting for us, Shaw. Lieutenant, we'll be back as soon as we have the exact location and a predator to arrest."

"Put your daughter's laptop back in her room." Nikki transformed back into a detective and hurried to the door. "And don't act like anything is up. We can't risk her tipping this guy off or saying something to make him suspicious. And keep an eye on her. I know the plan is for Thursday, but he can change that in a second. I have her login and password, and I changed the settings, so I'll get notifications on my phone when they chat. I'll monitor their communication."

The door shut behind them, and Sam stood alone in the aftermath of a tsunami. How in the world did Shaw expect him to return the laptop and act normal? Right now he wanted nothing more than to pick up his girls from school and barricade them inside his home for the rest of their lives. How could he allow her to continue to communicate with a—

Sam paced, running his hand through his hair, looking from the laptop to her bedroom, willing himself to pick up the machine and obey Shaw's instructions. He felt like he was handing his daughter the world's most venomous serpent. But, that was the father in him. Sam clenched his jaw and summoned the detective he knew he was, knew he had to be, to protect his daughter.

Maggie watched Sam mutate into a man she didn't recognize—and didn't want to know. She felt like she had entered a holy sanctuary, uninvited and unwelcome, as she eavesdropped on the conversation between her husband and the other woman. However vague, Sam acknowledging his sin was an intimate moment between the two of them, which Maggie was forced to witness. It was also foreign for her to see him plead, to genuinely admit his fault, to ask forgiveness. Maybe, she decided, that absolved Sam's transgression.

But that was not important now. She focused on Sam as he paced, fear visible in his expression. She didn't understand everything about the ISP, the judge, or the warrant, but she knew she'd been right to take control of the laptop—to play the music and type out the password and force Sam to see the threat that had invaded their home. She also knew the terror that trembled through her was justified.

CHAPTER 26

Rachel sat on a bench in the courtyard near the school entrance, pretending to read *To Kill a Mockingbird* for English class. At first she felt obvious, like a bullfrog in a koi pond. But soon she realized she was invisible. Kids ambled by in groups, loaded down with backpacks, laughing and elbowing, or in pairs, heads together, sharing secrets or answers to last night's homework. Occasionally, a couple walked by, hand in hand, floating in a little world created for just the two of them. Her heart fluttered. Would that be her soon?

She scolded herself for getting distracted. She had to stop watching the crowd and instead seek out an individual. He would be alone perhaps, like her, and look smart, with glasses. And his hair probably wasn't styled like the popular boys. But if others would really look at him—and not through him—they would see his dark brown eyes and a huge smile and realize he's cute. At least, that's how she imagined him.

She gazed into blankness, picturing the boy she was searching for, instead of actually searching. She would never pick him out of the flow of traffic if she didn't focus. She had to watch closely, for a sign perhaps. Maybe, just maybe when he saw her, he would summon the courage to identify himself—a shy wave of the hand or a wink. Maybe he would say her name silently, and she would recognize it as his mouth formed the syllables. Or maybe it would be a glance, quiet, all knowing, shared between the two of them caught in the middle of this sea of students hurrying to first period.

Hurrying? Rachel pulled herself out of her imaginary world once again. She must have missed the bell, and if he had walked by, if he had tried to give her a sign, she'd missed that, too.

Detectives gathered around the dining room table for the second day in a row. Maggie had been forced to silently, helplessly, witness many difficult moments in the past several months, but none were so agonizing as listening to the detectives, to her husband, gamble with her daughter's life.

"It's a decision only you can make, Lieutenant." Detective Shaw glanced from Sam to the other detective and back to Sam. "But if it were my daughter, I know what I would do. I would go with the plan that gave me the optimal chance to bust this guy and put him away for a very long time. I wouldn't risk leaving room for a technicality or reasonable doubt to let a jury go soft on him."

"It's unorthodox." Sam's jaw was set. "We get a stand-in or we wait for the guy to show up. We've got his messages, he makes an appearance at the location he selected, and we make a good arrest."

Detective Wade remained a silent spectator beside Maggie.

"A good arrest maybe. But there's risk. What if he recognizes the stand-in isn't Rachel? He won't make contact, and then he'll drop off the grid and we'll never find him—well, not until he victimizes some other innocent young girl."

"If he doesn't make contact, you have an address. We'll go pick him up." Sam sat back in his chair, laced his fingers through his hair, and squeezed his hands into fists. Was he giving in?

"Then why don't we do that now?"

Maggie recognized the challenge Shaw threw down. Sam released a disgusted sigh and thrust his hands in the air. He was about to admit defeat.

"Because the address is a boarding house." Shaw spoke slowly, reminding him of the complication. "If we go, we don't know which boarder we are after. If we spook him, he's gone."

Sam rested his elbows on the table and buried his face in his hands. "I know. I just wish there was a better way."

Wade broke his silence. "I know it's not ideal, Lieutenant, but we need to get this guy. If it were anyone else's kid, I'd never agree to this, and Shaw would have never suggested it. But Rachel is going to be safe." Wade pushed a legal pad toward Sam and pointed to a diagram of the park. "The guy wants Rachel to wait on this bench by the parking lot. Their meeting time is near dark, so he is counting on the park being empty, no witnesses. SWAT will be in this tree line. These restrooms here. Shaw and I will be behind them. We'll have full view and can get to Rachel in seconds. Unmarked cars will be near both park entrances."

"As soon as he makes contact, we go in." Shaw jabbed the table with her finger, emphasizing her words.

Maggie watched Sam consider the options. She was going to lose. He would not choose the safest plan, which was to keep Rachel out of it all together. He was going with the surest plan. How could he?

Sam pointed to the diagram. "I will be here. This dumpster gives me the closest access to Rachel."

"Lieutenant, I don't think it's a good idea for you—"

"Wade, she is my daughter." Sam's back stiffened. "It is my job to protect her. If I am going to put her in harm's way, then harm will have to go through me."

Maggie thought Nikki Shaw looked too satisfied. Clearly she didn't have a daughter of her own. Sam appeared resolved, but his pale complexion betrayed him. And Maggie herself experienced a heightened sense of terror, one she knew would only get worse in the next thirty-six hours, but still, she couldn't imagine how.

CHAPTER 27

Sam eyed the clock on the mantel. The minute hand seemed frozen, as if it hadn't moved from the minute before, although an hour had passed since dinner—the long, awkward, agonizing dinner. Sam had studied Rachel, wondering how she could pretend to be so calm when he was about to internally combust. But Rachel was simply meeting a boy. Another kid from school she had no reason to fear. He, on the other hand, was simultaneously risking and saving his daughter's life. The pizza he chewed tasted like a sponge, and the bullet-proof vest beneath his loose sweatshirt added its own challenge. Sam shifted to adjust his vest. How had he worn it all day every day for twenty-two years? But he knew how. Every day is a good day when you make it home from the job, he would say. The vest was his insurance policy, and a promise to Maggie.

They'd eaten in silence, just the two of them. After the plan had been devised and the detectives had left the day before, the next decision Sam made was to call Erin. He figured it would be a miracle if she was able to leave the office, but he had no choice. He needed her to take care of Olivia, and he would need Erin in the aftermath, even in the best case scenario. Fortunately, she was satisfied with Sam's vague explanation and promise for more details later. She agreed to arrive in time to pick up Olivia from school and take her to a hotel. Sam would tell Rachel that Olivia had been invited to a sleepover, which technically wasn't a lie. But during dinner, he missed the distraction of Olivia's chatter. He needed something, anything, to keep him from grabbing Rachel and shaking her, or holding her too tightly. Everything he wanted to shout caught in his throat, strangling him as he forced the words back down and tried to eat.

After Rachel cleared the table and put the leftover pizza in the refrigerator, she retreated to her bedroom, where Sam supposed she was messaging. He was nauseous. A predator might as well be crawling through his daughter's window while he sat only a room away. What could they be talking about? Maybe Rachel would change her mind, or the creep would back out. The idea was tempting, but this needed to happen. They needed to put this guy away. Tonight.

Are you monitoring? He texted Shaw.

On it.

Sam stared at the Cardinal's game on TV, but all he saw were different scenarios playing out in his mind. They had to take this guy down.

Just as Rachel noticed the time on her laptop changed to 7:45, *ready?* popped up on the screen. Her heart beat so hard she thought she could see her t-shirt pulsate. Her legs were wet noodles when she stood and walked to her bedroom door where she could see her dad watching the game. She rehearsed the lines in her head, willing her voice to sound normal when she had to say them out loud. She looked at the time on her cell. Five minutes had passed already. She had to do this.

Rachel approached her dad's recliner, in sight but out of his direct view. "Dad?"

"Yeah."

"Um, I don't feel so well. I think I'm going to go to bed early." Too fast, she said it too fast.

"Hmm. Are you sick?" He didn't take his eyes off the game.

"No. I don't know. Maybe the pizza isn't settling too well. I think I need some rest."

"Okay."

As Rachel leaned down to kiss his cheek, it occurred to her that her dad seemed . . . odd. In fact, he'd been acting weird all evening.

"Dad, are you okay?"

He broke his trance and turned his head sharply toward her. "Yes. Why?"

"I don't know. You seem . . . different."

"Oh." He cleared his throat and shifted in his chair. "I guess I don't feel so well, either. Think it might be the pizza, too."

Rachel nodded. "Okay, well, 'night."

Step one. Check. It was almost too easy, but Rachel didn't feel like she had expected to feel: bold, excited. Instead, she felt guilty. She'd just lied, boldface, to her dad. But, she promised herself the first chance she had, she would introduce this boy to him after school. No more secrets.

As soon as Rachel closed her bedroom door and turned off her light, Sam snuck through the front door and got into the unmarked car waiting at the end of the block. It would take her about ten minutes to walk to the park. Sam had to get there before her.

"An officer in plain clothes will be trailing your daughter to make sure she gets to the park safely." The sergeant updated Sam as he put the car into drive and accelerated. "The detectives and SWAT are in position. I'm going to drop you near the north entrance, opposite from where your daughter and the suspect will likely enter the park."

"Are there any civilians?"

"No. The last jogger left about a half hour ago. It's empty." The officer pulled to the side of the road and pointed. "Cut straight through there. Just inside the wood line you'll pick up a path that comes out right behind the dumpster. That should put you within thirty yards of your daughter."

"Thanks." Sam opened the door.

"We got this guy, Lieutenant. Don't worry."

"I'm trying not to." Sam closed the door, turned toward the trees, and started the most difficult three-minute race of his life.

She should have grabbed a hoodie before she slipped out the backdoor. As the sun sank in the sky, it took its warmth with it, and the walk to the park left goosebumps on her arms. Or maybe it wasn't the cold. Maybe it was the ominous feeling she had walking alone as the sky quickly turned grey and the faint moon grew brighter. The farther she got from home, the quicker she walked, often glancing back to make sure no one was following. Maybe this wasn't such a good idea after all.

But maybe it was. So far the plan worked perfectly, just like he said it would. Rachel looked at her cell. In only ten minutes, she would meet him face to face, the boy who liked her, who thought she had a beautiful smile, who knew things about her no one else understood because he cared enough to listen.

She walked through the park entrance and saw the green metal bench near the edge of the parking lot exactly as he described. She wondered where he was, if he could see her now. She tried to walk normally, but suddenly she was conscious of every movement she made. She felt like a marionette whose limbs were controlled by invisible strings as she tried to casually put one foot in front of the other. When she reached the bench, she was relieved to sit down.

As instructed, Rachel texted the number he gave her right before she left. *Here.* A few seconds later her phone buzzed. She read the text, confused. It was a change of plans. He had borrowed his cousin's car, so they could go for ice cream. But, she didn't want to get into a car. And he was only a freshman. He wouldn't have his license yet. Before she could reply, her phone buzzed again. She didn't read the text. This didn't feel right. Something didn't feel right. She quickly looked around. She was in an empty park, it was almost dark, and she was alone.

The ominous feeling returned. She was vulnerable, exposed. She wanted to run, but not into the growing darkness. She changed her mind. She didn't want to meet this boy here. They should meet after school, in the daylight, with other people around. She tried to think of something she could text to him to get out of this, but her brain was paralyzed. Suddenly, she wanted her dad to come get her. But how would she explain? He would be so mad. And she would be such a disappointment—again.

Her cell buzzed to remind her an unread text waited. She looked at the screen: *be there in a few.*

"No," Rachel said out loud. "I'm not doing this." She punched a number into her cell phone. "Come on, ring. Hurry!"

Sam's phone vibrated in his pocket. Not now! He kept his eyes glued on Rachel in spite of the approaching darkness, which made it difficult to see her clearly. It buzzed again. What if it was Shaw or Wade? He didn't want to risk anyone seeing a glow from his cell, but he couldn't chance it. If something came up, if plans had changed, he needed to know. Then he saw the number on his screen.

"Rachel!" he whispered into the phone.

"Daddy! I'm at the park. Please come get me. I—"

"Rachel, listen to me. Listen. I know everything. I'm here, at the edge of the parking lot, to your left. See the dumpster? I'm behind it."

"Daddy, I'm so scared! I think I really messed up bad." She started crying.

"You have to listen to me, Rachel. You have to help us get this guy. Hang up or he'll see you on the phone and leave and we won't catch him."

"Daddy, I can't!"

"Rachel, you have to. I'm right here." Sam didn't want to risk it, but he briefly stepped out from behind the dumpster, so she could see him. "You see the bathrooms behind you? Shaw and Wade are there. Police are in the woods all around you. Now, hang up the phone and go through with his plan. I will not let anything happen to you. I promise."

"Daddy, please—" Rachel begged and the fear in her voice pierced him.

It was a familiar struggle. Dad. Detective. Dad. Detective.

"Hang up the phone. Act normal. Do not, *do not*, do anything to scare him away." And then Sam spoke the most difficult words of his career. "I'm hanging up now, Rachel." As Sam returned his phone to his pocket and watched Rachel stare at hers, he felt like Judas turning over his daughter to her captor. But it was too late to change plans now. Headlights turned into the park to confirm it.

"You can do this, Rachel." He whispered into the dusk, hoping his daughter could sense the courage he willed to her.

As the headlights approached, her head turned frantically left, then right. She was caught between fight or flight, and the next instant would determine her decision. "Please, God," he spoke into the darkness.,"be her strength. Protect her."

The car approached the dumpster. As the headlights passed, Sam's eyes adjusted, allowing him to assess the situation. The driver's window was tinted, but he could see the outline of the occupant, definitely an adult. The headlights illuminated Rachel. She froze. Sam readied himself, weapon drawn. As the car slowed to a stop, red brake lights lit up the back of the car. And that's when Sam knew. The BMW insignia. Tennessee plates. It was the car that had parked in front of his house the night he interviewed Crystal Starr, the now deceased Crystal Starr. A dark line of armed men slowly advanced out of the tree line, but Sam didn't wait for the signal. He took off in a dead run toward the driver's door, trusting Shaw and Wade to whisk Rachel away as planned.

The driver, turned in his seat, talking to Rachel through the passenger window, was unsuspecting when Sam yanked open the door and grabbed him by the collar. Sam pulled the guy out, shoved him against the car, and pressed the weight of his body into him. He twisted the collar tighter, pressed his weapon next to the suspect's face, and willed himself to keep his finger off the trigger. "I should kill you right now," Sam hissed between clenched teeth.

The pounding of boots surrounded the car. "We got it from here, Lieutenant." Sam gave the collar a final twist and shoved himself off the guy, certain he wasn't going anywhere with the arsenal aimed at him. Sam holstered his weapon, pulled handcuffs out of his waistband, and secured the culprit. As he spun the suspect to hand him off to SWAT, he saw his face for the first time. Manny Jackson. He stared into eyes of molten malice.

"Lieutenant Samuel Blake." A sneer slowly crept across his face. "There must be some mistake."

Sam breathed deeply, filling his lungs for the first time in hours. "Yes, there is. And you made it."

Then Sam scanned the parking lot, searching for Shaw or Wade. He needed to see his daughter.

"Over here, Lieutenant."

He turned in the direction of the voice. When his eyes locked with Rachel's, she dropped the blanket around her shoulders and sprinted toward him. He caught her in an embrace and pulled her close, wrapping his arms around her tightly, completely. "Thank you, Jesus," he whispered into her hair.

Maggie lay curled in Rachel's bed, helpless, a pillow hugged to her chest as terror trembled through her. "Though Rachel walks through the valley of the shadow of death, I will fear no evil, for You are with her, Lord." Over and over she prayed, imagining her child surrounded by multitudes of angels with swords drawn. It was the only way she could contain her panic. "Though Rachel walks through the valley of the shadow—"

The front door opened. A surge of strength flowed through her, and she raced to the living room. Sam carried Rachel inside as an officer stood on the porch holding the door.

"If you need anything, Lieutenant, give me a call."

"We're good, Sergeant. Thanks. Thanks for everything."

"You bet." The officer closed the door behind him.

Sam dropped to the couch, cradling Rachel as if she were a toddler. She clung to him, her arms wrapped around his neck, her face buried in his chest. Maggie could hear her soft gasps, uncontrollable, the remainder of the sobs Maggie imagined had surfaced once Rachel realized the horror she had walked into.

"Dad-dy." Her voice was broken as she tried to force out words. "I-I-I'm so-rry."

Sam closed his eyes as if fighting for control. Maggie dreaded what was coming, the fear and fury he had pent up for the last two days. But now wasn't the time. He was too angry, Rachel was too fragile, and Maggie feared the potential damage.

But it wasn't fury Sam released. He pulled Rachel tightly to him, even closer, as first one sob and then a torrent broke free.

"Daddy!" Rachel pulled back to look at him.

Maggie knew how disturbing it must be for her daughter to see her dad cry so violently. She had only witnessed it once before, that night in the shower, the night she had returned.

"What have I done?" Sam gasped, trying to gain control. "Why did I think I could do this on my own? I failed you, Rachel. It's all my fault."

Maggie watched the roles reverse as Rachel tried to console her father. "No, Daddy, it's not your fault. You did everything to try to make things better. It's . . . it's just this whole thing, losing Mom, it's bigger than us. It's just too much." She wiped at the tears on his face.

"But it shouldn't have been. I made so many mistakes. I'm the only one to blame."

Rachel sat up and slid off his lap to sit beside him. She was silent for a moment. Then she took her cell phone from her back pocket, tapped the screen, and stared at it. Maggie was confused. How, in this moment, could her daughter text?

Rachel took a deep breath and looked at her dad. "You're not to blame. I am." She handed her phone to Sam.

"What is this?"

Her eyes filled with tears. "A text to Mom. My last text to Mom."

"Love you, Mom. Home soon?" Sam read out loud.

Rachel nodded, releasing her tears in streams down her cheeks. "It's my fault. Mom died because of me."

Maggie was baffled. How could Rachel think such a thing?

"Rachel." Sam turned to face her. "Honey, it's not your fault. There is nothing in this world, nothing you could ever do, that could make you responsible for your mother's death."

"But I am." She pressed her hand to her chest. "I heard the detectives that night. They said it was like Mom got distracted. That's why she crossed into the other lane suddenly. That maybe she reached for something, like her cell phone. Dad, I texted her." Rachel's voice cracked. "I'm the reason she reached for her phone."

"Oh, Rachel."

Maggie watched Sam get off the couch and kneel in front of their daughter. He placed the cell phone beside her and took both her hands into his. "Listen to me. You are not the reason Mom crossed the centerline. You are not—"

"But how do you know?" Rachel's voice held the slightest hint of hope.

"Because." Sam held up her phone to show her the text. "What time does it say this text was delivered?"

"8:36."

"Yes." Sam turned her chin to make her look in his eyes. "And the police report said the accident happened between 8:16 and 8:20. See? You sent the text *after* the accident. Rachel, honey, you are not the reason Mom died." His tears pooled again. "This is what you've believed all this time?"

Rachel searched his face as if trying to read the truth in it, then leaned into her dad. He pulled her to him as her body racked with sobs, sobs born from the grief Maggie now realized Rachel had buried beneath a mountain of guilt that had nearly suffocated her. So many questions were answered in a few brief moments.

When her sobs quieted, Rachel leaned back. Sam remained in front of her, and Maggie watched as he enveloped Rachel's small hands in his. Suddenly Sam's expression changed. His brows furrowed, and he pushed up Rachel's sleeve. Quickly, she pushed it back down, gripping her cuff with her fingers. Shame covered her face.

"Rachel." Sam whispered. "Rach—" He searched her face for an explanation.

Maggie's hand covered her mouth as Rachel allowed her dad to gently tug the cuff from her grip and slowly raise her sleeve again, revealing the scars she had carved into her arms. Sam's eyes filled with tears. The harsh voice Maggie expected was instead tender and pained.

"Honey, what happened?"

Rachel's gaze locked on the scars. She shrugged.

"Did you do this?"

She inhaled deeply and nodded. Sam gripped her wrists and gently rubbed his thumbs over the pink marks on her skin.

"Why?" He whispered as he brought Rachel's hands to his mouth and held them there. "Why?"

Finally Rachel found her voice. "I don't know." She pulled her hands from him. "It's just been so hard." She raised her sleeves and looked at the healing scars. "I've been trying to stop." Maggie was relieved there was no evidence of fresh cuts.

"Rachel, I'm so sorr—"

"No, Dad. It's not your fault. I've been awful. To you.

To Olivia. Kristen. Nothing mattered, not grades, not church. And I've made some . . . bad choices—"

"You know what, Rachel? I've made some bad choices, too. But sometimes you do what you think you have to do. And if it's the wrong thing, well, you learn from it. Yes?"

Rachel leaned forward and pressed her forehead against his. "I'm so sorry for everything, Dad."

"I'm sorry, too. But we have to promise each other something. No more secrets. No more silence. We need each other. We have to help us get through the bad stuff, together. Okay?"

Rachel nodded. "I love you, Daddy."

"Love you, too, baby."

Then Maggie knew. It was Sam, not her, who needed to save Rachel. The past months of agony, of watching helplessly as her family suffered, were necessary. They had to go through it, to find each other. Without her. Amazed, she witnessed her daughter coming through the other side of crisis—and her husband leading the way.

CHAPTER 28

Sam rested in the hammock, weary from the previous night but somehow lighter than he had been in months. From the back porch he could see the girls exploring the property, enjoying their unscheduled day off from school. He had decided to let Rachel sleep in and called Erin to suggest a picnic brunch at the Hitching house where he would fill her in on the details of the past two days.

He glanced at Erin sitting in a lawn chair across from him, trying to read her disposition. Was she preparing to give him the riot act, which Maggie would probably do, and which he probably deserved? Or would she share his perspective, her criminal court experience allowing her to understand his motive? She sipped her lemonade, and when she finally spoke, Sam realized it was neither.

"Do you miss it?"

Sam tilted his head. "Miss what?"

As she raised her glass to her lips again, her focus moved to the girls playing in the backyard.

"Miss what?" Eyebrows raised, Sam shifted to one

shoulder and stared at her, but she continued to ignore him. He tossed an apple core her direction.

"Hey." Erin grinned as if she knew a secret. "You know. The challenge of the investigation. The thrill of the arrest."

Sam inhaled, shook his head, and settled back into the hammock. "It doesn't matter if I miss it. I can't do that job and be this dad."

"But, you admit you miss it?" She continued to sip her drink and watch the girls.

Sam contemplated. If he took Rachel out of the equation, if he only considered last night's plan, the perfect execution, and the arrest, then yes, he could admit the satisfaction was unequalled. That's what had fueled his drive as a detective.

"You should go back."

"Erin, that's crazy. There's no way I can go back. I can't do this alone—not without Maggie."

"Maybe you don't have to do it alone." Erin leaned forward, elbows on her knees, hands clutching her glass.

Sam struggled against the hammock and sat on the edge of it, so he could look directly at her. He didn't need this. Instead, he needed her to understand that any thoughts of returning to detective work he may have entertained were now nothing but fantasy. It was time to sign the retirement papers. He was certain of that. But before he could explain, Erin spoke again.

"What would you say if I told you I'm moving to Cape Spring in a few weeks?"

Sam laughed. "And leave your assistant PA job in Louisville? Look, we've gone through a rough spell, but for the first time, I feel like we're going to pull out of this. Don't make a rash decision."

"Actually it's not a rash decision. This has been in the works since Christmas. Of course, I came to spend the holiday with my nieces, but I also had an interview set up with your prosecuting attorney. I had some cases I wanted to see through to the finish, so he gave me a few months. I won my final case in Louisville last week." She raised her glass to toast the occasion.

Sam stared at her, waiting for his brain to catch up with her words. So many questions whirled through his head as he tried to process what she suggested—and where it was leading. "Wait." He narrowed his eyes, thinking out loud. "So you're moving here? In a few weeks? And you'll be working for the prosecutor's office?"

Erin laughed. "Yes, Sam. Is that so hard to believe?"

"Actually, it is." He couldn't imagine his sister-in-law, who they were lucky to see more than twice a year, interrupting her career, taking a step down like that.

"No, it's not, really. Maggie was the best big sister a girl could have. She was always the giver, taking care of everyone first, herself last. Me? I've always been the taker, focused on college, then my career. It was all about me. Now it's time for me to think of someone else. My sister, my nieces, you. I can never replace Maggie, but Rachel and Olivia need me right now. And if I'm here to help with the girls, that means you, Lieutenant Samuel Blake, can go back to the work you love."

Too much was coming at him too fast. He tried to envision the plan, to determine what could work, to uncover hidden flaws. He fought the idea as it rose from his heart to his head, what he wanted to do competing with what he'd finally accepted he should do.

"There is no reason for you to give up your career. You make a difference, Sam. You catch the bad guys. And now, I'll get to put the bad guys away for you." She smiled. "We'll coordinate our schedules the best we can. It may not be perfect, but we'll make it work."

"I—I don't know, Erin." He squeezed one hand, then the other. He rubbed his thumb across his wedding ring.

"I thought you would be surprised, excited even—"

Sam hated the disappointment he heard in her voice, but she didn't understand. After everything he and the girls had been through, after the battle he fought within himself to walk away from his badge, he was petrified to allow her grandiose plan become his own. What would he risk if he did? But what would he risk if he didn't? He needed to talk to somebody. Not Erin, she was convinced she had it all figured out. Maybe the chief? No, the chief would think his sister-in-law was a veritable genius. He needed to talk to someone without an agenda. Gary. Sam reached for his cell phone but stopped. This was a face-to-face conversation. He searched his memory. Where did Gary live? Meadow Heights townhouses? The last unit on the south end? Gary mentioned his wife wanted to plant azaleas. Maybe he could find the right place.

Sam stood. "I am surprised, to say the least. And I want to be excited, but, well, you've been thinking about this a long time obviously. And I had finally accepted that wearing my badge again was outside the realm of possibilities. I appreciate what you're saying, what you're doing for the girls, for me. But you have to give me a few minutes here. I need to process all this."

Erin nodded. "I guess this must have come of out of left field for you. I didn't think about that. I've been waiting so long to tell you, and I didn't want to say anything until I knew for sure."

"Do you mind if I take a drive? Will you and the girls be okay? I'll be back in an hour or so." He dug his keys out of his front pocket.

"We'll be fine. I'll steal your hammock there, and the girls are having fun. Go process."

Sam stopped in front of the townhouse that fit the description he remembered: south end, azaleas. But he didn't see Gary's pickup. Maybe it was the wrong unit. Or maybe Gary was out doing his good deeds. He had texted Gary that it would be a few days before he could work on the house again, so he likely found another project in the meantime. Sam decided it was worth a knock on the door. If Gary's wife was home, she would probably know where Sam could find him. When the door opened, he was greeted by a woman he was sure was Mrs. Hill. She had a familiar kindness in her eyes.

"Hi, I'm Sam. You must be Gary's wife, Susie."

"Yes." She tilted her head and smiled. "I'm Susie. Who are you again?"

"Sam. Sam Blake. I'm the guy your husband has been helping with a renovation." Her smile faded, replaced by knitted brows and confusion. "He's surely told you about it, the old house, how he rescued me from disaster because I got myself into a mess I didn't have the skill to get out of." Sam grinned, imagining the stories Gary must have told about him. But Gary's wife just stared at him, puzzled. He decided to get to the point. "Is Gary here?"

Sam could not read her reaction, but she was certainly reacting, somehow, to something. Her mouth twitched as she tried to force it into a curve. She started to speak, then paused. After a moment, she tried again. "That sounds like Gary, but you must be thinking of someone else."

"Gary Hill," Sam said.

"Yes, Gary Hill." Her fingers pressed against her lips. "Wait a minute. Wait right here." She stepped inside and returned with a picture frame. "This is my husband." She pointed to the man standing next to her in the photograph. "He's not the Gary Hill you're looking for."

Sam looked at the picture. "Yeah, that's him. He's the one."

She pulled the frame to her chest, shaking her head. "It can't be." Sadness shaded her voice. "You must be mistaken."

"I'm certain it's him." Sam was losing patience. "I've spent five days a week working with him for the last four months. I'm not mistaken."

Color rushed from her cheeks. She reached out and gripped Sam's arm to brace herself. "That's impossible. My Gary passed away in his sleep. On the second of January."

It was Sam's turn to be confused. He glanced at the picture again. Yes, he was certain. That was Gary Hill. January second? The first day he started to work on the house, the day Gary unexpectedly showed up. Sam looked from the picture of Gary to his wife. What should he say? What could he say? Would she believe him? Did he believe himself?

"Suze?" he said softly.

"Suze." Tears filled her eyes. "My Gary called me that."

"I know."

They stared at each other, but neither spoke. Sam was in awe of the possibility of something he couldn't explain, but it was the only conclusion the evidence led to. How could it be? Mrs. Hill finally broke the silence.

"Please come in and tell me again about the house you've been working on." She opened the door wider.

Sam stepped inside. She offered him a chair in the living room and sat across from him. He proceeded to tell her the story, that the bed and breakfast was his wife's dream, how he was in over his head, about the morning Gary offered his help. After listening to himself, he wondered if he'd gone insane. Was everything that happened just some crazy dream? He studied the woman sitting across from him. She was real, living, breathing. He inspected his hands, rough and scarred from months of remodeling. All that work had been real. "This, this isn't possible, is it?"

Her eyes locked on his as she shook her head slowly. "I don't know." Her voice softened. "But if it is, does that mean my Gary is . . . like an *angel*?"

Sam looked blankly at Mrs. Hill, uncertain what any of it meant. He was grateful she continued without expecting a reply.

"You know, I often dream about Gary. In fact, sometimes it seems he's right here with me. Last night I dreamed he said he had a gift for me, a surprise. Maggie's Bed and Breakfast, but that didn't make sense."

Sam sat back, stunned. His pulse pounded at his temples. "I didn't tell you my wife's name."

"No, I don't believe you did." She was clearly unaware of the impact of her words.

"Maggie," Sam said. "My wife was Maggie. That's going to be the name of the B&B."

Mrs. Hill put her hand to her mouth. Tears swelled in her eyes. "What does this mean?"

"I'm not sure. But why do you think your husband would tell you it's his gift to you?"

A far away look surfaced in Mrs. Hill's face. "We'd always talked of running a bed and breakfast after he retired. In fact, we almost bought one when we moved here."

"The Hitching house." Sam nodded. "I know. Gary told me. That's Maggie's B&B."

Again, silence settled between them. Finally, Mrs. Hill leaned forward and placed her hand on Sam's knee. "Will you take me there?"

Neither one spoke during the fifteen-minute drive to the property. Sam replayed conversations, the tricks of the trade Gary taught him, the projects they had completed. It didn't make sense. By the time he pulled into the drive, he was convinced there had to be some other explanation.

"This is it," Mrs. Hill nodded. "The house we were going to buy."

As Sam imagined Maggie welcoming the Hills to the Hitching house that September evening, he realized Mrs. Hill was unaware of the backstory, of how intertwined the lives of four strangers had become.

"And there's the sign." She pointed toward the front yard that joined the road. "The one Gary showed me in my dream."

"What sign?" Sam turned his head. He threw open the door and strode to the beige sign standing in the yard. Dark plum lettering declared "Maggie's B&B." Sam inspected the fresh dirt around the bottom of the post.

"Hey there." Erin rounded the corner of the house. "I thought I heard you pull up. Looks nice, doesn't it?"

"Where did this sign come from?" Sam stood like a statue beside it, unable to move.

"Some guy named Gary brought it. Said he'd been working with you to fix up the place. You just missed him." Erin peered down the road as if Gary's truck might still be visible in the distance. "He said to tell you that you've got it from here."

"Gary's my husband." Mrs. Hill smiled at Erin then looked at Sam through her tears. "You know, I think something like this happened before. I wanted to plant azaleas this spring. One day I came home from the grocery store, and there they were. I never found out who planted them."

Sam pressed a fist to his lips. There had to be a reasonable explanation. He recalled his last conversation with Gary. All the structural work was finished, Gary had said. He was confident Sam could do the rest on his own. Was that his way of saying goodbye? Sam examined the sign again. No, this—the sign—was his way of saying goodbye. To him. To Susie.

"What's going on here?" Erin glanced from him to Mrs. Hill. "Is everything okay?"

"Yeah." A cautious grin spread across his face. "I think everything is going to be okay." Then he turned toward Mrs. Hill and took both of her hands into his. "Mrs. Hill, Suze, when it opens, would you like to manage Maggie's B&B for me?"

Her eyes opened wide with surprise. She pulled her hands from his and pressed them to her heart. "Well, I think you already know the answer to that." Her tears spilled over.

Sam pulled her into an embrace and blinked back tears of his own. The moment held so much loss—his wife, his new friend and mentor, her husband. But at the same time, the moment offered celebration, new beginnings.

"Okay . . ." Erin interrupted again, smiling awkwardly, "will someone please tell me what's going on?"

Before Sam could answer, Olivia's shouts from the backyard startled him. "Daddy, Daddy! Hurry!"

The urgency he heard sent Sam sprinting across the front yard, his adrenaline surging as he prepared to face the crisis signaled by the shrillness of Olivia's voice. As he rounded the corner of the back porch, both girls came into view, and he came to an abrupt halt.

"Look!" Olivia squealed and clapped. "Butterflies!"

"They're so beautiful, Dad." Rachel's voice was barely above a whisper.

As Sam moved closer to the girls, he could not believe the scene before him. The butterfly garden—Maggie's butterfly garden—was saturated with brilliant color. So many delicate wings danced from flower to flower, it was almost impossible to discern the butterflies from the foliage. Erin and Mrs. Hill stepped up beside him.

"I've never seen anything like it." Mrs. Hill's voice was soft with awe.

Olivia moved closer.

"Don't, Olivia," Rachel warned. "You'll scare them away."

But Olivia persisted and placed her hand beside a cluster of butterflies and waited. First one, then two, and then another and another lit on her palm until it looked as if she were holding a bouquet. "Look, Daddy." Sam was captivated by the delight sparkling in his daughter's eyes.

Rachel bit her bottom lip. "I wish I had my camera."

Erin glanced at Sam. He filled his lungs with crisp

spring air, welcoming the familiar words his daughter hadn't spoken in so long. "I wish you did, too, sis. But maybe you can take some pictures with your phone."

"Yeah, it's not the same, but it will have to do." Rachel pulled her cell phone from her pocket and began to frame pictures in its screen.

Erin put her arm around Olivia. "I think you have the most beautiful butterfly garden in the history of butterfly gardens."

"Like the Garden of Eden." Mrs. Hill reached forward and a butterfly lighted on her hand.

Sam marveled as his girls were absorbed in their private paradise, a moment of perfection. With no sorrow, no worry, no danger for him to protect them from. And in that moment, he realized he could no longer be their sole protector. No gun, no bulletproof vest could fully protect him or his family, and he was a fool to have ever thought otherwise. What was it Gary had said? Put on the full armor of God? He didn't understand at first, but maybe it was beginning to make sense.

"Mrs. Hill," Sam interrupted the hush. "Would you excuse me? I need to leave. Would it be okay if Erin drove you home?"

"Of course." Mrs. Hill patted his arm. "I hope to see you again soon."

"Yes, soon." Sam winked. "We have a lot of planning to do."

"Where are you going?" Olivia was still mesmerized by the butterflies gathered on her hand.

Sam grinned at Erin. "I have a meeting with the chief."

CHAPTER 29

Rachel's phone buzzed. She read the text and replied *darkroom*. She and Kristen had been texting nonstop all day, but Kristen would understand her reply meant she would be off grid for a while.

Rachel could smell the remnant of chemicals as she closed the darkroom door behind her. The space was close, secure, quiet. Her sanctuary. She reacquainted herself with the equipment, gently touching each piece as if to wake it from a long slumber—the developing trays, the timer, the enlarger. She shook a few bottles to see how much chemical each contained. Then she plugged in the red light and turned off the overhead switch. As she stood in the red glow, she tested herself to see if she remembered the process. Mentally she performed each step—place the film in the developing tank; wash with developer, then stop bath, then fixer. She imagined removing the newly developed negative, holding it up to the light, and searching the miniature images for a potential masterpiece. She recalled the satisfaction that arrived when one image stood out among the rest—the lighting or the angle or the moment frozen by the lens—

the quality that made this one *the* one. Rachel envisioned placing the negative into the enlarger, framing it for focus, setting the timer, and hitting the switch to burn the image onto photo paper. Yes, she remembered.

And being in her darkroom, her refuge, helped Rachel remember who she was. Not the Rachel who had become a stranger to herself and everyone around her, but Rachel the artist, the friend, the good daughter, the girl who loved her family, who missed her mother. Then she allowed herself to remember the last time she was in the darkroom, her last evening with her mom. She replayed the events like a rerun in her mind—making dinner, planning a photo shoot of an old barn, finishing a roll of film so she could reload for the next day—

The roll of film! *Come on, Mom, strike a pose*, she had teased as her mom stirred a pot of spaghetti and laughed. Rachel willed herself to remember what she had done with the film. She had to find it. Retracing her steps in her mind, she closed her hand around the imaginary film canister. She'd walked downstairs to the darkroom. What did she do with it? She scanned the work area. The timer. She had set it beside the timer. She examined the counter, and there it was, exactly where she had left it, still waiting for her. Rachel held the canister like a priceless gem, her last moments with her mom. Then skill took over. She grabbed the developing tank and started the process, in search of a masterpiece.

It was early evening, but Sam had already showered and surrendered the day. He lay in bed with the remote in his hand and the game on TV, forcing himself to think about nothing, literally. For the moment, he wanted the most pressing event in his life to be the 3-2 count and the runner on third. As the pitcher began his windup, Rachel entered the room.

"What you doing, Dad?"

Sam patted a spot on the bed beside him. "Awww, come on." His hand swatted the air as he coached the pitcher. "For twenty million bucks you can't throw a strike?"

Rachel scooted in next to him. "Chill, Dad. The Cardinals are winning by five runs."

Sam nudged his elbow into her side, pretending to push her off the edge. As she flailed to catch her balance, something in her hand caught Sam's attention. He grabbed it playfully.

"Dad!" Rachel reached to snatch it back, but he was too quick.

"What do we have here?" He smirked as he held it out of her reach. But when his eyes settled on the paper in his hands, his mischievous demeanor faded. He studied the image. His pulse quickened, yet a calmness washed over him. "This is good. He nodded slowly. "Really good."

Rachel picked at a thread on the hem of her t-shirt, her lips pressed together in a slight smile.

"I haven't seen this one before." He bent forward trying to see her face, but she remained preoccupied with the loose thread.

She bit her lip and peeked at him. "I just developed it."

"You did?" The surprise was so sudden that Sam failed to mask it. So Rachel had returned to her darkroom. A weight shifted inside him, allowing his lungs to expand more freely. He smiled at her and then admired the photo again. "When did you take this? She looks so . . . happy."

When Rachel didn't respond right away, Sam turned toward her. Tears pooled in her eyes, glistening in the glow from the TV.

"It's okay, Dad. I'm okay." She wiped her eyes and took a deep breath. "Remember that night, when Mom cooked dinner before leaving to show the house? I was at the end of a roll of film and wanted to reload new film, so I snapped a few pictures of her." She took the picture from Sam. "She was happy, wasn't she?"

An abrupt bounce on the bed interrupted the conversation. A second bounce landed Olivia straddling Sam's chest. She leaned down, and touched her nose to his. "Hi, Daddy." Sam's fingers found her ribs and skillfully counted each one until her squeals reached an octave human ears could not endure.

While gasping for air between giggles, Olivia pointed to the picture in Rachel's hands. "Hey, what's that?"

Rachel turned the picture toward Olivia. Sam admired it again. The delight in Maggie's smile, the soft laugh lines around her eyes, the precise moment Rachel captured with the lens. He was pulled into the photograph.

"Oh, look how pretty Mommy is." Olivia's giggles stopped as her fingers touched the image of her mother's face. "Daddy, will Mommy be an angel in Heaven?"

Sam, cautious not to upset Rachel, glanced at her for approval. She shrugged.

"I don't know, Olivia." Sam cupped both of her hands in his. "I'm not sure what Heaven is like."

"Oh, I do, Daddy. And it's so beautiful, like the most beautifullest you can think. Mommy told me."

Sam didn't reply. Instead, he closed his eyes and filled his lungs, allowing the moment to settle his soul.

"Daddy," Oliva whispered, "Mommy loves us."

With his eyes still closed, he whispered back. "We love her, too."

"Dad?"

The question in Rachel's voice compelled Sam to look at her.

"Is she here?"

The doubt she had clung to, the hurt, had been replaced. Did he see hope? Gently, Sam nodded, studying Rachel's face, still guarded for a possible retaliation. But she didn't strike.

"How do you know?"

"Close your eyes, Rachel." He waited. "Now breathe in. Breathe deep." Sam lay still and counted her breaths. Finally, on the third one, she looked at him.

"It's like—" Slowly she smiled. "How she smelled when she tucked me in at night."

And for the first time since Maggie's death, Sam was certain in this moment his family was whole. But the moment didn't last.

"Daddy," Olivia whispered, "Mommy should go to Heaven."

Sam recognized by now that Olivia's words delivered Maggie's message. He put his arms around his girls and pulled them both close. A familiar fear, panic, threatened to surface, but he fought for control. He pressed his face close to Rachel's and kissed the side of her cheek. Then he leaned into Olivia and whispered into her blonde curls. "Is it okay for Mommy to go?" Olivia nodded and snuggled closer.

Sam's throat tried to strangle any words that attempted to escape, but he forced them out anyway. "Thank you, Mags, for waiting."

Maggie stood beside her bed where her family lay entangled, secure. She brushed the back of her hand against Olivia's tender cheek. So precious. Then she ran her fingers through Rachel's hair, and for the first time since her return, her daughter received her affection. As Maggie gazed at Sam, she wondered if she had ever loved him as much as she did in this moment. She leaned down and rested her lips on his forehead. As she breathed him in, she closed her eyes and a familiar sensation slowly passed through her, leaving her weightless. In the distance, she could hear the melodic symphony created by the rain shower of diamonds in the lavender place. Maggie sensed that when she opened her eyes, she would no longer be in her bedroom with Olivia and Rachel and Sam. But was she ready? She reached for Olivia one last time. She ran her fingers down Rachel's cheek. With her lips still pressed against Sam, she whispered, "I will always love you."

Slowly, Maggie opened her eyes and watched the lavender horizon rise up and surround her. In the distance a figure approached. She waved and smiled when he started to run, his blonde messy hair falling into his eyes. When the little boy reached her, he was out of breath, laughing. He rested, bent over with his hands on his knees, looking up at Maggie.

"Hi. I'm Nate. You prayed for me."

Maggie's smile grew. "Yes, Nate, I did."

He caught his breath and stood up. "I've been waiting for you." He reached for Maggie's hand and tugged.

"Come on. He can't wait to meet you!"

CHAPTER 30

Sam sat in Maggie's chair, uncomfortable, maybe from the tie he hadn't worn in months, or maybe from the expression he imagined on Pastor Rob's face when Sam darkened the doorway this morning. The one, he could do something about. He loosened the knot and decided no tie. The other? Rob and church were a package deal, so Sam decided he'd have to give the guy a chance.

He held Maggie's journal and brushed his fingers across the inscription: "If nothing ever changed. . . ." How much had changed in seven months—Maggie, his job, Rachel, the B&B. But most of all, Sam. He couldn't name it, but somehow he was a better version of himself, closer to the man he wanted to be for Maggie. Yet he found little satisfaction in that, only regret. He was too late. He flipped the pages of the journal he had become so familiar with. He had read every page, every word, and he knew Maggie better now than ever. He loved her now, like he should have loved her before, and although he would never get to tell her, Sam hoped she knew.

He wondered if Maggie knew he was sitting there,

waiting for the girls to get ready, regretting all the excuses he gave for not going to church with her.

"Funny how things work out, Mags." Sam's voice was quiet. "You look back and wonder how you missed it."

You look back and wonder how you missed it. The words sounded familiar, significant somehow. Was it a line from a movie? Lyrics to an old song? He couldn't place them, then—

The bartender. What was her name? Rita? Trixie? Roxy. That was it. Sam remembered the day he walked into her bar. It seemed like decades ago. God is at work, Roxy told him, but Sam wouldn't see it if he didn't know what to look for. Now Sam heard her voice as if she were standing in his room. *But one day you'll look back. . . .*

One thing he could not deny: life's recent events had been strategically manipulated like chess pieces in threat of checkmate, and Sam wasn't the one controlling the board. Looking back, he could see that now. He marveled at the conversation he and Roxy could have. Maybe, Sam decided, he needed a tall glass of raspberry ice tea.

Sam rubbed his hand across the cover of the journal. Its words had become his lifeline, his connection to Maggie. How he longed to feel her again. He thumbed through the pages, but all he sensed now was the weight of the journal in his hands. As he closed the back cover, a page caught his attention. He thought he had read them all; he was certain he had. How had he missed that one, isolated at the end of the journal? He opened the back cover and found the date. Yesterday? The handwriting was too familiar. Sam was baffled, stunned, elated. His eyes wanted to rush across the words, absorb them desperately, so he could cling to every trace of Maggie he could grasp. But his heart was reluctant.

Last night when he accepted that the—grace period—was ending, the emptiness rushed in suddenly, too soon. But here, in this final journal entry, Maggie had created one last instant for them to share. He wanted to preserve this moment, this fraction of Maggie that still existed in future tense.

Sam, my love.

He caressed the letters with his fingertips and imagined Maggie writing, speaking, the words. He remembered his late night monologues, lying alone, unsure if his voice delivered any meaning. How many times he yearned for Maggie to say something, just one word, so he would know his words were not abandoned in the empty air. And now, she had. He could resist no longer.

I broke our promise, the one we made our last night together when I confessed my biggest fear was losing one of the girls. We promised to keep our girls safe and healthy and happy—together. But I left you alone. I'm so sorry. Now, my biggest fear is not being able to raise Rachel and Olivia. I don't get to finish being their mom. But I know they will be okay. Because they have you. Thank you for learning to love them the way two wounded girls need their daddy to love them. Thank you for loving me— through my journal, through sharing your thoughts and regrets and fears, and through becoming who you are. I don't want to leave, but it's time, and now I can because you are the husband and father who, in our brokenness, makes our family complete. Tell the girls each night when you tuck them in, they are, and will always be, my world. And remind yourself every day how completely I love you—and always will. I promise. Mags

Sam pressed his palm to the page, protecting the words as if they would evaporate. "I promise, too, Mags."

Rachel stepped into the doorway. Olivia pushed her way past and posed for Sam.

"Am I a princess, Daddy?"

Sam admired Olivia's ponytails and dimpled cheeks. Then he studied Rachel. She had her mother's brown hair, the same green eyes. The touch of make-up she wore reminded him she wasn't his little girl anymore.

"You are both beautiful."

Olivia curtseyed and then twirled in place.

Rachel clapped for her little sister and smiled at Sam. "Are you ready?"

Sam closed the journal and laid it in its place, lightly touching the butterfly imprinted on the cover.

"Yes." He returned her smile. "I'm ready."

THE END

Dear Friend,

Of the millions of books you could have chosen, you picked mine. Thank you for reading *Waiting for Butterflies* and for giving life to the words within its pages, because without you—the reader—my story would remain bound between book covers, meaningless.

I hope Maggie and her family have touched you in some way and that, even though you have reached THE END, the story stays with you for a while. If so, it would be my pleasure to invite you back to Cape Spring when my "works in progress" are published.

If you would like to continue with me on my writing journey, please visit my website and sign up for my newsletter. For a more personal connection, find me on Facebook, Twitter, Pinterest, and Goodreads or follow my blog, The MOM Journey. Even better, email me. I would love to hear from you! Or if you're in a book club or reading group, let's Skype.

When I started writing this book, the idea that it would find its way into a reader's hands was a far-away dream. But now, here you are, holding my book, making my dream a reality. Thank you.

May all your butterflies be blessings!

Karen
karensargentbooks.com
karensargentbooks.com/blog
karen@karensargentbooks.com

DISCUSSION QUESTIONS
For Book Clubs & Reading Groups

1. What is the meaning of the title *Waiting for Butterflies*? Who or what is a butterfly in the story? Is there more than one butterfly?

2. In Chapters 1-3 the Blake family seems almost perfect. What evidence hints at flaws in the family? How do the flaws contribute to the downward spiral Sam and Rachel experience after Maggie's death?

3. Olivia's character is not as developed as Maggie, Sam, or Rachel. How is her character important to the story? Is she necessary?

4. Maggie's state of existence as a "lingering spirit" is an obstacle as she helplessly witnesses Rachel's dangerous choices. How does a mother who is physically present experience similar obstacles?

5. What is your reaction to the bartender Roxy? Can she do the work of Jesus as she claims? Why or why not?

6. What is your reaction to Gary? Were you surprised? Was his character believable? If not, what made it hard for you to believe?

7. After Rachel is rescued, Maggie realizes it is Sam, not her, that had to rescue Rachel. Why is this necessary for Maggie? For Sam? For Rachel?

8. In what ways is Sam redeemed? How does he change throughout the story? How does the Hitching house symbolize Sam's redemption?

9. In Chapter 1, Sam promises Maggie they will keep the girls "safe and healthy and happy—together." Is the promise fulfilled?

ACKNOWLEDGMENTS

If only the depth of my gratitude could be expressed in words . . .

Rusty Sargent and Anna-Marie Beard, you heard the first whispers of my dream to write a book. You believed I could, and then you made me believe it, too.

And when I did, my first readers challenged my storyline, questioned my characters, and cried in the right places. Anna-Marie Beard, Thea Hitchings, Susie Hill, Michelle Swane, Vicki Brunk, Toni Erpenbach, Maggie Wallace, and Don Barzowski, thank you for being part of my story.

Thank you, Bryan Mills, for helping me navigate the biblical controversy in my book, and Gary Hill for guiding the renovation of the Hitching house.

To Amphorae Publishing Group & Walrus Publishing: Donna Essner and Lisa Miller, thank you for loving *Waiting for Butterflies* enough to take a chance on a debut author and put my book into print. Kristina Blank Makansi, your editing expertise made *Butterflies* a better story and me a better writer. You are angels for answering my questions, welcoming my opinions, tolerating my pickiness, and approving the cover.

The cover! Heidi Wharton, your photographer's eye made it possible. Ashley and Ricky Turnbough, your Briar made it precious. Kinsley Stocum, you made it a masterpiece. Thanks to each of you for creating a work of heart.

When I am busy writing, sometimes I forget I'm a wife and a mom . . . but that's easy to do when no one complains. Rusty, Kelli, and Randi—someday I'm going to cook again, wash dishes again, and binge watch TV with you. Thank you for giving me the gift of time, so I could write.

Motherhood is a significant theme in *Butterflies*. I learned about being a mom by first being a daughter. Thank you, Mom.

My grandparents, Gaston and Carmel Lucchese, taught me something about work ethic and accomplishment. Nobody would be more proud of this book than them, except maybe my Aunt Barb, who was here for the beginning.

And finally, to all my students throughout the past two decades who allowed me to teach them to read great literature and to express themselves in writing—teaching you taught me how to write a book.

ABOUT THE AUTHOR

Karen Sargent creates characters whose imperfect faith collides with real-life conflicts, taking readers on a journey through grace and redemption to discover enduring hope. A romantic element is woven within each story. In addition to writing inspirational novels, she blogs at The MOM Journey. Her writing has been featured in Guidepost's *Angels on Earth* magazine and on ForEveryMom.com and ModernSimplicity.org. When she is not writing, she teaches high school and college English. A graduate of Southeast Missouri State University, she resides in the beautiful Arcadia Valley with her husband and two daughters. Visit her at karensargentbooks.com.